"Peach cobbler killed Donnie Boatwright!"

Donnie finished his cobbler and set the empty bowl on the table.

"Mighty good, Phyllis, mighty good," he said, but then he gave a little shake of his head and put a hand on the table to steady himself.

"Donnie, are you all right?" Phyllis asked.

"Yeah, yeah, just a little dizzy. Must be the heat." He lifted his water bottle and drank what was left. "I'll be all right in a—"

But then he stopped abruptly, his eyes rolling up in their sockets. He lurched back a step, staggered into a half turn, stiffened, and pitched forward onto his face, toppling like a felled tree. Donnie hit the ground hard, without any attempt to catch himself. Screams came from the crowd. Phyllis just stood there behind the table, shocked into motionlessness by the sudden collapse, but Mike's emergency training took over and sent him hurrying to Donnie's side. He rolled the old man onto his back, and Phyllis recoiled in horror as she saw Donnie's glassy eyes staring sightlessly up at the red, white, and blue canopy over the table.

In the middle of all the sudden commotion and chaos, she heard Carolyn exclaim as plain as day, "Oh, my God! Phyllis's peach cobbler killed Donnie Boatwright!"

A PEACH OF A MURDER

A Fresh-Baked Mystery

Livia J. Washburn

A SIGNET BOOK

SIGNET
Published by New American Library, a division of
Penguin Group (USA) Inc., 375 Hudson Street,
New York, New York 10014, USA
Penguin Group (Canada), 90 Eglinton Avenue East, Suite 700, Toronto,
Ontario M4P 2Y3, Canada (a division of Pearson Penguin Canada Inc.)
Penguin Books Ltd., 80 Strand, London WC2R 0RL, England
Penguin Ireland, 25 St. Stephen's Green, Dublin 2,
Ireland (a division of Penguin Books Ltd.)
Penguin Group (Australia), 250 Camberwell Road, Camberwell, Victoria 3124,
Australia (a division of Pearson Australia Group Pty. Ltd.)
Penguin Books India Pvt. Ltd., 11 Community Centre, Panchsheel Park,
New Delhi - 110 017, India
Penguin Group (NZ), cnr Airborne and Rosedale Roads, Albany,
Auckland 1310, New Zealand (a division of Pearson New Zealand Ltd.)
Penguin Books (South Africa) (Pty.) Ltd., 24 Sturdee Avenue,
Rosebank, Johannesburg 2196, South Africa

Penguin Books Ltd., Registered Offices:
80 Strand, London WC2R 0RL, England

First published by Signet, an imprint of New American Library,
a division of Penguin Group (USA) Inc.

First Printing, October 2006
10 9 8 7 6 5 4 3 2 1

This novel is dedicated to all the teachers who have touched my life, starting with my mother, Naomi Washburn, my teacher in life, and both my daughters' first-grade teacher.

To Iris Hamilton for teaching a fourteen-year-old how to cook better.

To Marsha Hardin, Rita Heatley, Thomas and Sharon Hicks, Chelsa Holder, Jan Johnson, Marsha Lindenmeier, LouAnn McLaughlin, Jamie McNeil, Mary Nelson, Larry Prather, Kathy Raine, Joan Schmitter, David Slininger, Lisa Tadlock, Linda Tindall, Sherman and Sue Wall, Fred and Talana Weir, and Andy Zapata, just to name a few, for going above and beyond the job of teaching.

To my agent, Kimberly Lionetti, for guiding me to this story.

And, last, to my husband, James Reasoner, my one and only.

Chapter 1

The smell of peaches filled the air, sweet but with a particular bite all its own. Warm sunshine flooded the orchard. Later, the sun would be hot, oppressively so, but now, in the early morning, basking in its glow was like luxuriating in a warm bath. The peach smell could have come from a scented candle, but was instead the real thing, which made it even better, Phyllis Newsom thought.

Balanced on a wooden ladder, wearing blue jeans and one of her late husband's shirts, with the sleeves rolled up to the elbows, she reached up carefully into the tree and took hold of a particularly nice-looking peach. With just a little tug, the fruit came loose from its stem. Phyllis turned and handed it down to Mattie Harris, who was helping her fill the bushel basket that sat on the ground.

Mattie was a sight. Somewhere between eighty-five and ninety, which made her approximately twenty years older than Phyllis, Mattie was still as spry and nimble as a bird. She wore a dress covered with a bright flower print that was even more brilliant in the sunlight, and a straw hat with a huge brim that shaded her face. Like Phyllis, she wore gloves to protect her hands, which could get pretty scratched up from the tree branches while picking, not to mention itchy from the peach fuzz.

"I remember when this orchard was just a sorghum field," Mattie said, tilting her head back so that she could look up

at Phyllis on the ladder. "That was before Newt Bishop got
the bright idea of growing peaches. Land's sakes, everybody
else in Parker County was doing it already, but Newt was always slow to catch on. I remember a time . . ."

Phyllis knew it was rude, but she tuned out Mattie's rem-
iniscences and searched the tree for the next peach she
wanted to pick. Mattie remembered all about the Depression
and World War II and working at the bomber plant over at
Fort Worth. She had an endless supply of stories about those
days. Phyllis had been born just before the war started, but
she didn't remember it, of course. She had been too young.
As a history teacher—a retired history teacher now—she
had a vested interest in the past, and most of the time she
really enjoyed listening to Mattie's stories. This morning,
though, she was thinking about the upcoming Parker County
Peach Festival and trying to come up with a recipe for the
cooking contest.

Everybody knew that Parker County peaches were the
best peaches in Texas—and, therefore, the best in the world—
and every summer the peach festival was the biggest thing in
the county seat, Weatherford. The State Fair in Dallas was
bigger, of course, and the Stock Show rodeo in Fort Worth
was bigger than the Sheriff's Posse Rodeo, held in conjunction with the peach festival, but those events lacked the
small-town charm of the celebration in Weatherford.

Half of the courthouse square in downtown was blocked
off and surrounded by portable fences, as were some of the
side streets off the square, and into that area were packed
dozens of booths showing off the best arts and crafts and
food that the county had to offer. Two stages were set up, for
musical entertainment at various times during the day.
Whenever a live band wasn't playing, recorded music blared
from large speakers. There was a kids' area, filled with
games and rides, puppet shows and face-painting booths. A
little bit of something for everybody, and during the day of
the festival, it was almost possible to forget that Weatherford

was part of a much bigger, not-so-nice world. There was nothing like eating cotton candy and homemade ice cream, listening to a high school band and strolling through a display of homemade quilts to make it seem as if time had stood still, as if Weatherford had indeed somehow gone back to a slower, more gentle era.

The high point of the festival, at least for Phyllis, was the cooking contest. Everything revolved around peaches, of course. Peach cobbler, peach pie, peach ice cream, peach preserves . . . If there was any way to work peaches into a recipe, somebody was bound to try it. And at the climax of the festival, a winner would be named by a panel of judges. There was a blue ribbon, of course, just a little thing made by the local trophy shop that read BEST PEACH RECIPE—PARKER COUNTY PEACH FESTIVAL, with the year printed on it.

Phyllis wanted that ribbon. She told herself it wasn't because Carolyn Wilbarger had won it the past two years while Phyllis's recipes had finished fifth and second, respectively. She just wanted to be recognized for the good work she'd done.

But if that involved beating Carolyn, then so much the better.

Phyllis picked another peach and turned to hand it down to Mattie. As she did so, she saw a burly figure strolling toward them along the row of peach trees. Phyllis had often heard someone described as being "about as wide as he is tall," but Newt Bishop came as close to actually fitting that description as anyone she had ever seen. Despite the fact that it was summer, Newt wore a greasy, stained pair of overalls and a long-sleeved white shirt. An old-fashioned fedora was on his head. Phyllis had never seen him in any other clothes. She knew he even wore them to church, when he went to church.

Newt stopped and turned his round, sunburned, jowly face up toward Phyllis. "You findin' some good ones, Miz Newsom?" he asked in a thick, rumbling voice.

"Yes, thank you, Mr. Bishop. It looks like you have a good crop this year."

"Ought to. Worked hard enough on it. You ladies need 'nother basket?"

Phyllis thought about it for a second. The peach festival was still a couple of weeks away, which meant she had time to experiment. She was thinking about trying a peach cobbler, but she wanted to give it some added spice. She wondered how it would taste with a little jalapeño pepper, but even if that worked out, it might take several tries before everything was just perfect. That might take all of one bushel, and it would be nice to freeze some this year. Store-bought frozen peaches were good, but home-prepared Parker County peaches were better.

"Yes, I believe I will get another bushel," she told the farmer.

"I'll have the boy bring a basket down from the barn." Newt tugged on the brim of his fedora. "Ladies."

He moved on, probably bound for the part of the orchard where Carolyn was picking her peaches with the help of Eve Turner. Newt was always trying to sell just a little bit more. He would probably tell Carolyn that Phyllis was buying a second bushel of peaches, in hopes that Carolyn would feel that she had to have another basketful, too.

He grew some really fine peaches, though.

Phyllis looked down at Mattie. "Didn't you have Newt's boy in your class once?"

"Darryl," Mattie said with a nod. "Yes, he was a very sweet little boy. I never saw Newt at school, though, except at Open House. Parents didn't have as much to do with the schools then as they do now, especially the fathers."

"Yes, I know. I haven't been retired all that long."

"But you taught junior high," Mattie pointed out. "When I substitute in the elementary schools these days, there are sheets stuck up all over the classroom for the parents to sign up for this and sign up for that, to go on this field trip and provide refreshments for that class party, to volunteer for this and that. In *my* day, that classroom was my domain, you could say, and I'd just as soon the parents kept their noses out and let me get on about my job. From eight thirty in the morning to three thirty in the afternoon, those were my kids. They didn't belong to the parents during that time."

Phyllis was old enough to understand Mattie's attitude, even though she knew perfectly well it wouldn't fly in today's modern classroom. She had come out here to pick peaches, not to discuss changing theories in education. She reached for another plump fruit hanging from the branch just above her head.

The slamming of a car door made her look toward the Bishop farmhouse and the barn, about three hundred yards away. She saw that a pickup had pulled up in front of the barn. A man stood next to it, talking to Newt Bishop, who had circled through the orchard and returned to the barn by now. Phyllis recognized Newt by his clothes and his barrel-like shape. She had no idea who the other man was, only that he was younger, taller, and leaner.

And perhaps angry, to judge by the way he waved his arms around as he talked to Newt. It was none of Phyllis's business, of course.

A boy about ten years old came trotting through the orchard, carrying a couple of bushel baskets woven out of wicker. He stopped and set one on the ground next to Mattie's feet. "My granddad said you ladies needed another basket," he announced.

"That's right," Phyllis said from the ladder.

Mattie looked down at the boy. "Lord have mercy! Darryl?"

He grinned. "No, ma'am. Darryl's my daddy. I'm Justin. I'm workin' here this summer, helpin' out my granddad."

"Well, that's mighty nice of you. Do you like it?"

The smile abruptly disappeared from Justin Bishop's face. He shrugged. "I guess so. It's work. I'm tryin' to earn enough money to buy me a copy of *Scorpion Clone Blaster Four: Armageddon Fever.*"

Mattie patted him on the head. "Son, I don't have the foggiest notion what you're talking about."

"It's a game, this really cool video game, about these giant scorpion clones from Mars, and you gotta blast 'em before they can sting you and suck your guts out—"

"Boy!" Newt called from the end of the row. "You get that basket on down to Miz Wilbarger and Miz Turner, you hear?"

"Yeah, Granddad, I hear," Justin called back. "I gotta go," he said to Phyllis and Mattie, then trotted off carrying the other basket.

"Those video games," Mattie said with a shudder. "I never heard of such."

Newt wandered back toward the barn and went inside. His visitor, whomever he'd been, was gone now, Phyllis saw. The pickup had driven off, leaving a slowly settling haze of dust over the dirt road that led from the farmhouse to the highway.

Mattie said, "I need to go visit the little girls' room. You be all right here by yourself for a little while, Phyllis?"

"Go right ahead," Phyllis told her. "I'll be fine."

That meant she would have to climb up and down the ladder more often, Phyllis thought, but the exercise wouldn't hurt her. It was a beautiful day, and she got caught up in trying to pick out the best peaches, considering each one carefully before she plucked it off the tree. Her attention strayed to the farmhouse and the barn only occasionally, just enough for her to notice that several more vehicles came and went while she was busy. Probably some of her competition coming to buy peaches from Newt Bishop, she thought. Judging by the way the last one left in such a hurry, peeling out in the gravel in front of the barn, they were eager to get to their stove and start cooking.

Justin Bishop, having delivered the bushel basket to Carolyn and Eve, ran up and down the orchard rows with the boundless energy of the young. Phyllis sometimes wished she still had that much energy, but at the same time she figured if she did, it might kill her. Mattie came back from the farmhouse and started taking the peaches that Phyllis handed down to her, placing them carefully in the wicker basket so they wouldn't bruise. A couple of jets flew overhead, probably bound for the Joint Reserve Base on the west side of Fort Worth, some twenty miles away. Even higher in the sky, big passenger planes droned along, taking off and landing from the Dallas–Fort Worth airport. Out here in the middle of the orchard, however, it was easy to forget there even were such things as jet planes and video games and cell phones and satellite TV. Out here there was only warm sunshine and leafy trees and the sweet smell of peaches. . . .

Somewhere, somebody started screaming.

Phyllis stiffened as she listened. It sounded like Justin screaming, but Phyllis couldn't tell if he was hurt or scared. At the foot of the ladder, Mattie exclaimed, "Land's sakes, what's that?"

Phyllis descended quickly to the ground. "I think it's coming from the barn."

She started along the row of trees, breaking into a trot as the screaming continued. Mattie followed, trying to keep up, but Phyllis was younger, taller, and had longer legs. She jogged a couple of times a week, too, in an attempt to stay in decent shape.

As she neared the barn, Phyllis could tell for sure that the screams came from inside the old, cavernous structure. The doors were open, and as she ran inside, going from bright sunshine into shadow, she was blinded for a second as her eyes tried to adjust. "Justin!" she called. "Justin, what's wrong?"

"Granddad!" the boy cried. "Granddad!"

Phyllis could see a little better now. Justin stood beside a large, heavy thirty-year-old car that was more like a tank than an automobile. Newt Bishop had been driving that big car ever since it was brand-new, at least when he went into town. Like everybody else, he had a pickup for work around the farm.

As Phyllis's eyesight sharpened even more, she spotted an old-fashioned bumper jack lying on its side at the front of the car. Stepping in that direction, she peered around the vast hood with its upthrust ornament at the prow. Her hand went to her mouth in horror as she saw the overall-clad legs sticking out from under the car.

Newt Bishop was a large man. Almost as wide as he was tall, Phyllis thought again. And as she forced herself to bend over and look under the car, she knew what she was going to see: the same thing that had made Justin scream and now cry in sniffles and ragged sobs. The bulging eyes, wide and glassy. The trickle of blood from the corner of the mouth. The arms fallen loosely to the side when the attempt to hold up the awful weight had failed.

When that big old car had slipped off the jack and fallen, it had crushed the life itself out of Newt Bishop.

Chapter 2

Phyllis dipped a spoon into the little bowl of cobbler, tasted the peach filling with its flaky crust, and made a face. So much for using jalapeños. That was truly awful. With a sigh, she said, "Those who fail to learn from the past are doomed to repeat it."

Mattie let out a laugh and said, "Or at least if they failed, they had to repeat your class, isn't that what you mean?"

"It's a good thing you weren't an English teacher, dear," Eve put in as she passed breezily through the kitchen of the big old house the three retired teachers shared, along with Carolyn Wilbarger. "Really, that's a terrible cliché, and I'm not sure but what you've misquoted it."

From the door between the kitchen and the breezeway that led to the garage, Carolyn said, "If Phyllis really wanted to learn from the past, she'd stop entering cooking contests against me. She ought to know by now that she's not going to win."

Carolyn had a grocery sack in her arms as she walked in. She always insisted on paper, not plastic, commenting loudly that paper was so much better for the environment. That was true, of course, Phyllis thought, but the plastic bags were easier to carry, and besides, you could reuse them as garbage bags. She had read somewhere, too, that if you cut the plastic bags into narrow strips, you could actually crochet with them and use them to make extremely strong,

flexible tote bags. She intended to give that a try sometime . . . but not until after the peach festival.

"I'm right here, Carolyn," she said. "Don't talk about me
as if I'm not present."

Carolyn sniffed as she set the grocery sack on the
counter. No doubt the sack was just full of ingredients for
whatever recipe she was going to make this year. "Well, I
didn't mean any offense. I just meant that I hate to see you
trying so hard when there's really no point in it."

I am a grown woman, Phyllis told herself. Long past a
grown woman, as a matter of fact. I will *not* walk over there
and kick her in the shin. No matter how much I want to right
now.

"I mean, maybe you should just take it easy this year and
enjoy the peach festival," Carolyn went on, "instead of
spending hours in the kitchen trying to come up with something new."

"I see," Phyllis said coolly. "In other words, everyone
should drop out of the contest and just let you win."

"Of course not! I was just saying—"

"We all know what you were saying, dear," Eve put in,
smiling and pleasant as always, no matter what sort of dig she
was about to get in. "You just don't like competition. I can understand that. When I'm interested in a gentleman, say, I don't
like competition, either." She touched her brown hair and
added, "Not that there's any real competition out there."

That was just like Eve, relating every discussion to romance, no matter what it was really about.

"Back during the war there weren't many men around,"
Mattie said. "They'd all gone off to fight. So if there was an
eligible man who was the least bit respectable, why, I'll
swan, he just about had the pick of any girl he wanted. I remember when I went to work out at the plant . . ."

Phyllis wondered what else she could use to provide the
spice in her spicy peach cobbler recipe. She still liked the
idea and thought it had promise, but jalapeño was out.

". . . Donnie Boatwright," Mattie was saying. "Of course, Donnie and I stopped dating not long after that."

"Did he go off to the war?" Eve asked.

"No, Donnie was 4-F. Had a bad knee. Didn't stop him from dancing, though. I remember he took me to Casino Beach one night—" Mattie stopped short and gave a little shake of her head. "What was I talking about? Oh, shoot, it doesn't matter. Phyllis, what are you making for the contest this year?"

Phyllis frowned, for a couple of reasons. She didn't want to divulge any secrets while Carolyn was standing right there, no doubt listening like a hawk. Did hawks listen? No, hawks watched like, well, hawks. She was listening, anyway, probably hoping to gain a little advantage. For another thing, Phyllis didn't like the way Mattie had suddenly lost her train of thought. It was true that Phyllis herself was of an age when she was more easily distracted, but Mattie was well over eighty, and it had been happening more and more often lately.

Phyllis felt a little cold inside when she thought that the day might come when she couldn't remember the things she wanted to. When she couldn't remember her late husband, Kenny, and all the wonderful times they'd had. Might not even be able to remember her own son, Mike . . .

Speak of the devil (not that Mike was the least bit devilish—he was actually a very sweet boy and always had been) the screen door at the front of the house creaked open, and Mike's voice called, "Mom? You home?"

Quickly, Phyllis dumped the bowl of jalapeño peach cobbler in the garbage disposal and hit the switch. She hated being suspicious and distrustful, but she didn't want Carolyn sneaking a bite to get an idea what she was up to in her preparations for the contest. Then Phyllis picked up a dishcloth, wiped her hands, and went down the hall to the living room, where Mike stood just inside the door waiting for her, his cream-colored Stetson in his hand.

He put a stern frown on his face as he said, "Mom, what have I told you about at least keeping the screen door hooked?"

"Yes, I know," she said, not liking the fact that he was talking to her like she was the child and he was the parent. But at least he was doing it out of concern for her, and out of professional habit, she supposed, since he was a deputy sheriff and dealt with crime and lawbreakers all the time. She looked past him, through the screen door, and saw the Parker County Sheriff's Department cruiser parked at the curb in front of the house, in the shade of the massive oak and hickory and pecan trees that lined the street.

Eve followed Phyllis into the living room and said, "Hello, Michael! My, don't you look handsome in your uniform, dear."

"Thank you, Miz Turner," Mike said politely. Phyllis and Kenny had raised him to be respectful. Mattie and Carolyn came into the room, and he gave them all a general nod. "Good morning, ladies."

Phyllis went over to him and hugged him. It had been several days since she'd seen him. His work kept him busy, and so did his pretty young wife and their baby. "How are Sarah and Bobby?"

"They're fine, Mom." He couldn't help but smile as he went on, "Sarah says Bobby's getting ready to take his first step. Any day now, more than likely. I sure hope I'm there to see it when it happens."

"So do I," Phyllis said. "Do you want to sit down? Did you just come by for a visit? I'll get you a glass of iced tea."

"Uh, no, that's fine, Mom, thanks anyway. I'm afraid I'm here on official business."

"Doesn't that sound exciting?" Eve said. "What sort of official business could the sheriff's department possibly have with a bunch of retired schoolteachers?"

"Well, I need to talk to my mother, actually, but the rest

of you ladies are welcome to stay. Nothing secret about any of it."

"Get to the point, Mike," Phyllis prodded gently.

"It's about Newt Bishop."

Phyllis stiffened. Several days had passed since that terrible morning in the Bishop barn, but what she had seen there still haunted her. She had seen death before—she had buried a much-loved husband, and she had seen illness claim many friends and relatives—but until that morning she had never stared right into the face of violent, unexpected death. She hadn't liked Newt Bishop, had in fact barely been able to tolerate the man, but still she would never have wished such an end on him.

"The, uh, official cause of death," Mike went on, "is being listed as unknown."

Carolyn snorted. "That's crazy," she said. "That old car of his slipped off the jack while he was working on it and fell on him. Crushed him like a bug."

Phyllis tried not to wince. Carolyn could be plain-spoken to a fault sometimes. In this case, however, she was pretty much right.

Mike fiddled with the hat in his hands. When he did that, he looked just like a little boy again, Phyllis thought. But he wasn't a little boy, he was a grown man, and he had a grown man's serious expression on his face as he said, "Well, it's true that the car could've just slipped off that old bumper jack, and Mr. Bishop didn't have it blocked up or anything. But somebody could've flipped the lever on that jack, too, and started it down."

"Why in the world would anybody want to do that while Newt Bishop was under the car?" Phyllis asked, and then she lifted a hand to her mouth and said softly, "Oh, my goodness," as one possible answer occurred to her.

Mike nodded solemnly. "That's right, Mom. The sheriff thinks that somebody might've meant for him to get caught under there."

"Nonsense," Carolyn said. "As big as he was, such a thing would be bound to . . ." She stopped and frowned.

"To kill him," Eve finished. "That would make it murder, wouldn't it, dear?" She didn't sound particularly upset by the prospect, but it took a lot to upset Eve.

"You ladies were the only ones out in the orchard that day," Mike went on. "Did any of you see anybody hanging around the barn while Mr. Bishop was in there working on his car?"

Phyllis didn't have to ponder the question. The events of that morning were still clear in her mind. "A man in a pickup drove up and talked to Newt for a few minutes," she said.

She heard an eager tone in Mike's voice as he asked, "Do you know who he was?"

Phyllis was almost sorry she had to shake her head and say, "I have no idea. I didn't see him that well. It's quite a distance from the barn down to where we were in the orchard."

"And Eve and I were even farther away," Carolyn put in. "I didn't even see this pickup Phyllis is talking about."

"It was there," Phyllis said, thinking that it sounded as if Carolyn were doubting her eyesight.

"What kind of pickup was it?" Mike asked.

"I don't know," Phyllis had to say.

"That was before Mr. Bishop went into the barn?"

"That's right." Something occurred to Phyllis, and she added, "It looked like the man was arguing with Newt. He was waving his arms around like he was worked up about something."

Mike frowned. "You didn't mention anything about this when you talked to the deputies who first came out there to the farm, Mom."

"Well, why in the world would I?" she demanded. "I thought that old car had just slipped off the jack and fallen on him. It was an accident, for all I knew."

Mike turned his hat over in his hands as he thought.

"Yeah, that makes sense, I guess. Can you describe the man, and the vehicle he was driving?"

Phyllis took a deep breath. "The pickup was dark blue. It wasn't an old, old one, but other than that I couldn't say. Since the man who came up in it was standing right next to Newt, I could tell that he was taller and thinner, and I got the impression he was younger, too, but I couldn't say that for sure. The man in the car . . ." She shook her head. "I couldn't say. I really didn't pay much attention to him. The car was dark. Gray, maybe brown. Not big, but not small, either. That's all I know about it."

"Wait a minute," Mike said. "What car?"

Phyllis frowned. "I didn't say anything about that? Later, after Newt had gone into the barn, several cars came and went. People were buying peaches from him, I'm sure. But I noticed that the last one left in a big hurry. That's the one I was talking about. I just recalled it now, while I was talking about what happened earlier."

"You don't remember any part of the license numbers on any of the vehicles?"

"I didn't *see* the license numbers. I was too far away, remember?"

"Yeah, that's right. But at least that's more than we knew before." Mike looked at Mattie, Carolyn, and Eve. "Did any of you other ladies see anything . . ?"

"Not me," Mattie said. "Your mama had a better view than I did, since she was up on the ladder and I was down on the ground."

"But you went up to the house, Mattie," Phyllis recalled. "Were you already back by the time the man in the car came up?"

"Must've been, because I sure don't remember seeing him."

Mike asked, "Why did you go to the house, Miz Harris?"

Mattie sniffed and said, "That's a mighty delicate question, young man."

"Oh," Mike said quickly, blushing. "I'm sorry." But he got a dogged look on his face as he went on, "You went into the house itself, then?"

"That's right. Newt knew me—knew all four of us, for that matter. When folks came to pick peaches in his orchard, he didn't mind them using the, ah, facilities."

"But you didn't see anybody else?"

"No, sir, I didn't."

Phyllis said, "Mike, do you think the man in the car . . . you think he could have . . . ?"

"It's possible," he said. "You said he wasn't there long, but it wouldn't have taken but a few seconds to start that jack lowering. I tested it myself. Knock the lever down and give the jack handle a good push, and it would come down quick on its own after that. Mr. Bishop really should have blocked up that car before he ever got under it."

"How in the world will you go about finding the killer?" Carolyn asked.

"Start looking to see who had a grudge against Mr. Bishop, I guess. I haven't been involved in all that many murder investigations, but they're usually pretty simple. You find out who was mad at the victim, and chances are they did it."

"But isn't it still possible that it could have been an accident?" Phyllis asked. "The man in the car could have gone into the barn, seen Newt under the car, and gone for help."

"We didn't get any 911 calls until the one from you, Mom. Still, you're right, it could have been an accident, just like it looked. Nobody's ruling that out. We just want to make sure it wasn't deliberate."

"Of course," Phyllis murmured.

"Well, I'd better be going. I'll write up everything y'all told me and turn it over to the investigating officers. The sheriff just sent me over here because he didn't want you any more upset than necessary, Mom."

"That was nice of him." Phyllis hugged Mike again, and then frowned. "You be careful. I don't like the idea of you poking into a murder. If somebody deliberately killed Newt Bishop, they might try to hurt you next."

"I don't think so," Mike said with a smile. "Chances are, if it was deliberate, the killer's so shook up and scared, he won't even think about trying to hurt anybody else. He'll just lie as low as possible."

"Well, I hope so. . . . I mean, I hope you catch him."

Mike said good-bye to the other three women, hugged his mother again, and then left. Phyllis stood at the screen door and watched him drive away in the cruiser. The idea that her little boy was mixed up with killers and criminals and suchlike disturbed her. It always had, ever since Mike had decided he wanted to go into law enforcement. Phyllis and Kenny had always assumed that he would grow up to be a teacher or a coach or even a principal. Children had to go their own way, though. You couldn't force them into anything, not if you expected them to be happy about it.

"A murder," Eve said. "What do you know about that?"

Phyllis didn't say anything. She stood at the screen, looking down the street, but Mike had already turned a corner and was gone.

Chapter 3

The central air-conditioning unit hummed quietly and effi-
ciently, but on a summer afternoon even it was hard put to
keep up with the heat coming out of the kitchen. Phyllis had
another small cobbler in the oven.

When this big old house had first been built more than
eighty years earlier, there had been no air-conditioning; it
was cooled in the summer by ceiling fans. Phyllis and
Kenny had bought it in the sixties and had installed a big
swamp cooler on both the first and second floors. By the late
seventies, the swamp coolers had been replaced by several
window air conditioners, and during the nineties they'd had
a central heating and air-conditioning unit put in. Sometimes
Phyllis thought that too much technology might not be a
good thing. She still wasn't too sure about the Internet, although the computer in the den was hooked up to it. But as
far as she was concerned, everybody in Texas owed a huge
debt to the man who had invented air-conditioning, as well
as everybody who had come up with every improvement in
it since then.

After Kenny passed away, Phyllis had come very close to
selling the old house, thinking that not only was it too big
for her to take care of properly, but also that she could never
be happy in a place that held so many reminders of her late
husband. She had come to realize, though, that the house

also held even more happy memories. She didn't think Kenny would have wanted her to leave if she didn't have to.

There was plenty of room for boarders. There were two bedrooms downstairs, along with the living room, kitchen, and den, and three more bedrooms upstairs. When she and Kenny bought the place, they intended to fill all of those bedrooms with children. Mike had been the only one to come along, though. So Phyllis had a sewing room and Kenny had a room for his trains, and unlike some families they had always had plenty of storage space. . . .

When Phyllis had put the word out among her friends that she would be willing to rent out the extra rooms, she'd had no shortage of people interested in boarding there. Until recently, there had been a fourth boarder—a retired social studies teacher named Susan Mallory—but she had moved to Houston to live with her daughter and son-in-law. That left an empty bedroom upstairs, but Phyllis knew it wouldn't stay that way for long. In fact, she had already had a serious inquiry about it.

Opening her home to her friends and fellow retired teachers was one of the best decisions she had ever made, Phyllis reflected. Carolyn was widowed, like her, and Eve was divorced . . . or "between marriages," as she put it. She had been between marriages four times. Fair or not, it was somewhat scandalous even in this day and age for a schoolteacher to have been married and divorced four times. That was Eve, though. And no one had doubted her ability as a high school English teacher. She always had more students pass the advanced placement test than any of the other teachers did.

But glad or not for the company, at times Phyllis almost regretted that she had let Carolyn move in. The woman could be infuriating. All day, ever since Mike's visit that morning, Carolyn had been ensconced in the kitchen, claiming that she needed privacy to work on her recipe. Phyllis had yielded reluctantly—it was *her* kitchen, after all—but ultimately her sense of fair play had won out. After a while, the delicious smells emanating from the kitchen had driven her away from the house. How could she hope to compete with whatever Carolyn was cooking up?

Unwilling to surrender so easily, Phyllis had gone to the store and spent quite a while going through all the various spices, searching for something that would liven up her peach cobbler and give her the edge she needed with the judges.

Cinnamon? No, that was too commonplace. Cayenne pepper? No, that would be worse than the jalapeños, Phyllis had thought with a little shudder. White pepper might be interesting, but it would probably overpower the peaches.

Finally, she had picked up a small jar of candied ginger and regarded it thoughtfully. Ginger was spicy and had a definite kick to it. It was also supposed to be good for a person's digestion. The question was whether or not it would blend suitably with the taste of the peaches.

The only way to find out was to try it. Phyllis had bought the little bottle of candied ginger, even though it was a bit pricey, and taken it home. When she got there, she found that Carolyn was finally through in the kitchen, at least for now. The smells that lingered in the air were taunting, though.

Phyllis put a metal bowl in the freezer and filled a large pot with water, setting it on the front burner. The old gas stove had become cranky and required a match to light the burner. Thankfully, the oven could be turned on without a match. She set the oven for 375 degrees. She turned an old radio on gentle jazz that played while she went about assembling the ingredients. When she had everything laid out, she took the chilled bowl out of the freezer. With a fork she mixed the flour and salt in the chilled bowl, and then cut the shortening into the flour. When the mixture resembled the texture of tiny split peas, she added ice water and combined it with the fork. Quickly gathering the dough into a ball, she flattened it into a four-inch-wide disk, and then wrapped it in plastic before putting it into the refrigerator.

While the dough was chilling, she quickly blanched the peaches in the boiling water. Peeling, pitting, and slicing the peaches was easy after that. She then minced the candied ginger as fine as she could before adding it to a saucepan with cornstarch, brown sugar, and water. Phyllis stirred the mixture until the sauce thickened, and then added the peaches. After the peaches cooked a few minutes, she poured the peach and ginger mixture into a buttered pan, making sure the ginger was evenly distributed with the peaches. Removing the dough disk from the refrigerator, she unwrapped it and worked quickly so the dough would not warm up. Using a floured rolling pin, she rolled the dough disk on a lightly floured surface until it was bigger than the pan. She transferred the dough by carefully rolling it around the rolling pin, lifting and unrolling the dough, centering it over the fruit. With the knife she had used to peel the peaches, she vented the crust and then sprinkled sugar on top. Into the oven it went.

Watching the oven wasn't going to make the cobbler cook any faster, Phyllis told herself. She was about to force herself to pick up a magazine that was lying on the counter and look at it, when the telephone rang.

Phyllis turned off the radio before she picked up the cordless phone and turned it on. "Hello?"

A deep male voice spoke in her ear. "Mrs. Newsom? This is Sam Fletcher."

Phyllis caught her breath. She had been dreading this call, because she didn't know what she was going to do about it. She had to be polite, though, so she said, "Oh, yes, hello. How are you?"

"I'm just fine." Sam Fletcher paused for a second. "I was wondering if this would be a good time for me to go ahead and come over."

There wasn't going to *be* a good time, Phyllis thought, and for a moment she came very close to telling him that something had come up and that they would have to make different arrangements. But then she couldn't do that. She had always been fair, always been a woman of her word. She had made her decision, and now she would have to live with it.

"Of course. That would be fine. We'll be looking for you."

"Thanks. I'll be there in about fifteen minutes. Bye."

"Good-bye," Phyllis said. She put down the phone.

"Who was that?" Eve asked from the hall doorway. Phyllis hadn't heard her come up. Carolyn was behind her. "Who are we going to be looking for?"

Phyllis took a deep breath as she faced them. Now, as the kids in her classes used to say when they thought she couldn't hear them, it was really going to hit the fan.

Chapter 4

"Live with a man?" Carolyn said when Phyllis had explained. "Absolutely not!"

"It's not that terrible, dear," Eve said. "And I should know, if I do say so myself. Of course, this *is* a somewhat different situation."

Carolyn went on. "When I moved in here, Phyllis, you assured me that you intended to have only female boarders."

"That's true," Phyllis admitted. "That was my intention. And when Coach Fletcher expressed an interest in living here, I told him at first that I didn't think that would be possible. But then Dolly Williamson asked me if I would at least put him on the waiting list, as a favor to her."

"It's hard to say no to Dolly," Eve said.

That was certainly true, Phyllis thought. When they were all young teachers, Dolly had been principal at the high school and soon had been promoted to superintendent. It was a little rare for a woman to be superintendent of schools in a large district in those days, but no one had ever doubted Dolly's capabilities. She wouldn't allow anyone to doubt. So she was used to getting her own way, and the teachers who worked under her were used to going along with her. For one thing, most of the time Dolly was right about what she wanted. Going along with Dolly was a hard habit to break.

"How does she know him?" Carolyn asked. "He didn't teach here."

"No, but Dolly knows everyone in education in this part of Texas. So, since she vouched for him, I didn't think it would do any harm to put his name on the list."

"Except that by the time you had an opening here, the circumstances for everyone in front of him on the list had changed so that they didn't want the room," Carolyn said caustically. "Didn't it occur to you that that might happen?"

"To tell you the truth, it didn't."

Eve patted Phyllis's hand. "I understand, dear. You just wanted to get Dolly off your back, so you told her what she wanted to hear. We've all been there."

"Anyway," Phyllis said, "it probably wouldn't be legal to refuse to rent to Coach Fletcher just because he's a man."

Carolyn sniffed. "What's legal and what's right aren't always the same thing. Let him sue you, I say."

"Go to court over it?" Phyllis shook her head. "I couldn't do that."

Carolyn crossed her arms over her chest and glared. "Well, then, if you allow him to live here, you may just lose your other boarders. Isn't that right, Eve?"

"Oh, I don't know." Eve smiled. "Why don't we wait and meet the coach first, before we make up our minds?"

Carolyn rolled her eyes and exclaimed, "You just want to see what he looks like!"

"Well, don't you, dear?"

"No. I don't care."

"You'll be able to see him soon," Phyllis said. "He's on his way over now to look at the room."

Carolyn swung sharply toward her. "You didn't tell us that! You just said he was interested in boarding here."

"Well, of course he wants to look at the room first. . . ."

"Phyllis did tell the coach we'd be looking for him," Eve pointed out.

"Yes, but I thought she meant later. Tomorrow, or . . . or some other day. Not today!"

"Let's not get all worked up," Phyllis suggested. "Maybe

he won't even like the place. He might change his mind about wanting to live here."

"What do you know about him?" Eve asked.

"He coached basketball and taught history at Poolville," Phyllis said, naming a small town northwest of Weatherford. "He retired a couple of years ago."

"An old man, is he?" Carolyn asked.

"No, I think he's about our age. According to what Dolly told me, he retired so that he could take care of his wife while she was ill."

Carolyn's attitude softened slightly. "His wife was ill?"

"Yes. Cancer. She passed away last fall."

"I'm sorry to hear that," Carolyn murmured.

"Poor dear," Eve said.

"That was one reason Dolly was so insistent that I at least consider letting him board here," Phyllis went on. "She said he had been through a lot, and she didn't think it was a good idea for him to be living alone."

"His children are all grown and gone?" Eve asked.

Phyllis nodded. "That's what I understand. Dolly says that he's very much a gentleman."

"He's still a man," Carolyn said. "I don't like the idea of having a man in the house all the time. You know how they get underfoot."

"I gave him my word," Phyllis said firmly. When you got right down to it, that was all that counted, she thought. She didn't want her friends to get upset and move out, but she couldn't go back on a promise, either.

She would just have to hope for the best. Things had a way of working out.

"What's Mattie going to say about this?" Carolyn asked.

Eve said, "I don't think Mattie will care, as long as the coach doesn't get in her way."

Phyllis agreed. Mattie was amazingly active for her age. Actually, she was amazingly active for any age, volunteering at the hospital, the nursing homes, the library, and even substitute teaching at the schools. She was always going places and doing things, even though she didn't drive anymore, and she didn't hesitate to plunge right in when she substituted, even when the subject was something she knew nothing about, like chemistry or French. Mattie would be too busy to worry about something like a man living in the house. She was gone at the moment, in fact. Earlier in the afternoon, Eve had taken her over to the library for one of her weekly volunteer stints.

The doorbell rang, and all three women turned to look at the front door. They stood there for a moment, unmoving. The bell rang again.

Phyllis started toward the door. "I'll get that," she said unnecessarily.

Carolyn and Eve followed her. Sam Fletcher might take one look at the three of them, Phyllis thought, and then turn tail and run. She didn't think she would blame him one bit.

She paused when she reached the door, and glanced through the gauzy curtain over the floor-to-ceiling window beside it at the tall, lanky figure who stood there. He was built like a basketball coach and must have been a player in his day, she thought. He reached for the doorbell again, but Phyllis opened the door before he could press the button a third time, feeling a little bad about leaving him standing in the late afternoon heat. "Hello," she said.

"Miz Newsom? I'm Sam Fletcher. I called a while ago."

For some reason, the voice was even deeper in person than it had been on the phone. His face was not what could be called handsome. It was too craggy and weathered for that. His hair was still thick, dark in places but shot through heavily with silver, as was the mustache he sported. He wore jeans and a short-sleeved blue work shirt. There was nothing fancy about him. If there had been it would have seemed out of place.

"Of course," Phyllis said as she opened the screen door. "Come right in, Mr. Fletcher. Or do you prefer Coach?"

"Actually, I prefer Sam." He smiled as he stepped inside.

Phyllis put out her hand. He took it without hesitation, she noted. Some men of their generation felt uncomfortable about shaking hands with women. That he didn't was a point in his favor, as far as Phyllis was concerned. His hand was big, his handshake firm, though certainly not crushing. And he let go as soon as she did, another good thing.

Phyllis closed the wooden door and half turned to gesture toward Carolyn and Eve. "I'd like you to meet Carolyn Wilbarger and Eve Turner, two of my boarders."

"Ladies," Sam said with a nod. He waited to see if they were going to offer to shake hands, too. Carolyn didn't, but Eve stepped forward and practically grabbed his hand. She didn't let go quickly, either.

"Hello, Coach," she said, her voice practically a purr. "My, you're certainly tall. No one would have to tell me that you coached basketball. I could tell it just by looking at you."

"Yes, ma'am," he said.

"Oh, goodness, don't call me ma'am. I'm just Eve."

"I'm pleased to meet you, Eve." He slipped his hand out of Eve's grip, and Phyllis admired the adroitness with which he escaped. "Pleased to meet you, too, Carolyn," he added.

For a second, Phyllis thought Carolyn was going to point out the fact that *she* hadn't told him to call her by her first name, but she settled for nodding and saying coolly, "Hello."

He grinned as he turned back to Phyllis. "I really appreciate you considering me as a boarder. I've been lookin' to get out of my place. Well, as a matter of fact, I've got to get out, because the house is sold and the new folks want to move in as soon as they can."

"You could rent an apartment," Carolyn said. "There are plenty here in Weatherford."

"There sure are," Sam agreed. "But after living in a house all these years, I just didn't know if I'd ever feel comfortable in an apartment." He looked around the living room, with its hardwood floors, thick rugs, and overstuffed furniture. "This place, now, it looks comfortable."

"It certainly is," Phyllis said. "It's been my home for forty years."

"That's what Dolly told me. She also said all you ladies are retired teachers."

"I taught eighth-grade history," Phyllis said.

Sam's grin widened. "Another history teacher. That was my subject."

"A lot of coaches teach history, don't they?" Carolyn said.

"It seems to work out that way," Sam agreed. "In my case, though, I was teaching history first and sort of got drafted to coach basketball. What with being tall and all, I guess the principal figured I must know something about it."

"You did quite well," Phyllis commented. "Poolville's had good teams for quite a while, haven't they?"

Sam nodded. "The kids always worked hard for me, that was the main thing."

"That's the secret, getting them to try," Eve said. "No one knows what they're really capable of unless they try."

"That's the way I always looked at it," he agreed.

"Well, I suppose you'd like to see the room," Phyllis said. "It's upstairs on the second floor. I hope that's not a problem."

"My knees are a little creakier than they were twenty years ago, but I can still get up and down steps all right."

Phyllis went first, with Sam following her and Eve behind him. Carolyn hesitated; then, obviously unwilling to be left behind, she went upstairs, too.

The vacant room was on the right side of the hall, at the front of the house, a slightly bigger room than the two smaller rooms in the back. The upstairs bathroom and a linen closet took up the rest of the space on the front side of the house. The room was nicely furnished, and Sam was visibly impressed as he looked at it.

"This would be just about perfect for me," he said. "I've got a few things of my own that I'd like to move into it, if that's all right with you, Phyllis. . . ."

She nodded. "Of course. If we need to move any of this furniture out, I have plenty of storage space." She went on, "The bathroom is right next door, and there are stairs at the end of the hall that take you down to a side door and porch, so that you can come and go that way if you like. You'd also have kitchen privileges."

"Within reason," Carolyn said. "With the Peach Festival coming up, the kitchen is going to be pretty busy for a while."

Phyllis's lips tightened. Carolyn was a good one to talk, the way she had hogged the kitchen for half the day.

Sam smiled as he looked around at them. "You ladies wouldn't be entering the cooking contest, would you?"

"Phyllis and Carolyn are involved in that," Eve said quickly. "I never had the skills in the kitchen that those two have. I save my energy for other things."

"Oh," Sam said. "Well, I, uh . . ."

"Don't mind her," Carolyn said. "She's that way with every man who still has a pulse."

That was true, Phyllis thought, although she might have phrased it a bit more delicately. Or not said it at all.

Eve arched her eyebrows. "Well! I certainly hope your recipe this year isn't that sour, dear, otherwise Phyllis is sure to beat you this time."

"I doubt that," Carolyn said.

Phyllis managed to laugh as she wished the tension in the air would go away. She said to Sam, "If we haven't scared you off already, would you like to see the rest of the house?"

"I sure would."

The tour didn't take long. As it was going on, Phyllis explained that there was one other boarder in the house who wasn't there at the moment. Sam didn't press her for the details, and she didn't supply them. If he moved in here, he would meet Mattie soon enough.

They walked back into the living room a short time later. Phyllis began, "I imagine you'll want to think it over—"

"Nope," Sam said. "I've seen enough. This is a beautiful house, and you ladies seem like fine company. I'd be pleased to board here, if you'll have me."

"Well . . ." Phyllis glanced at Carolyn, who still looked disapproving, but maybe not quite as much as she had when she first heard about the possibility. And Eve, of course, was all for the idea. Phyllis tried to think of some reason she should say no, but she couldn't. Sam Fletcher was friendly, polite, and every bit the gentleman that Dolly Williamson had said he was, without being smarmy about it at all.

Phyllis took a deep breath. "When can you move in?"

"I can start bringing my stuff over tomorrow, if that's all right with you."

She nodded. "Of course."

Sam hesitated and then said, "You know, your name sounded familiar to me, Phyllis, and I just remembered where I heard it before. You're the one who found that poor fella under his car, aren't you?"

"I'm afraid so."

"I read about it in the paper." Sam shook his head solemnly. "Must have been a terrible experience."

"Yes, it was, and I don't really like to talk about it." Whenever she thought too much about Mike's visit that morning and the things he had told them, it still made her upset.

"I'm sorry, I won't bring it up again," Sam said quickly. He frowned. "Anyway, don't I, uh, smell something burning?"

Phyllis sniffed, and then her eyes widened with horror. "My cobbler!" she exclaimed as she turned and ran for the kitchen.

Chapter 5

"I never liked funerals," Phyllis said as she straightened the pin on her gray blouse. She wore a black skirt with the blouse. This was her summer funeral outfit. People didn't seem to care as much anymore about wearing something dark to funerals, but to Phyllis anything else would have been a gesture of disrespect for the deceased.

Not that she'd ever had all that much respect for Newt Bishop, but still . . . he was dead, after all.

Mattie leaned over and checked her hair in the mirror that hung in the big house's front hall. "Time you get to be my age," she said, "you'll have been to so many funerals it'll seem like something's missing when you go a week without one."

Eve came along the hall and asked, "Are you sure I shouldn't stay here, Phyllis? Someone should be here while Sam is unloading his things, don't you think?"

"Carolyn will be here," Phyllis pointed out. Carolyn was the lone Methodist among the women. Phyllis, Mattie, and Eve all attended the Baptist church where Newt Bishop had been a member and where his funeral would be taking place in a half hour or so. Newt had shown up for services only occasionally, but he still had a right to have his funeral there. And as loyal church members, Phyllis, Mattie, and Eve all felt like they ought to go.

"Yes, but Carolyn will just hide out in her room, and you know it," Eve said. "She's made it plain that she doesn't want anything to do with Sam. If he needs any help, I'm sure it would never occur to her to offer."

Phyllis said, "Sam Fletcher didn't seem to me like the sort of man who would need any help moving a few things into a house."

A smile spread across Eve's face. "Yes, he did appear quite strong and capable, didn't he?"

Mattie laughed and said, "I want to meet this fella who's got you hens all cluckin' and flappin'."

"Why, I certainly don't know what you're talking about," Eve protested. "I'm not the sort to take on over some man."

That got another laugh from Mattie.

Phyllis picked up her purse from the hall table. "Let's go," she said. "I'll drive."

The other two didn't argue. Mattie had given up driving years earlier, somewhat reluctantly. Her eyesight and her reflexes just weren't up to the task. Eve still drove, but her little foreign car had such a tiny backseat, it was uncomfortable for more than two people. Even the front seat wasn't that big, and Phyllis permitted herself a mental chuckle at the thought of Sam Fletcher trying to fit his long legs into Eve's car. He'd have a much easier time of it in Phyllis's Lincoln.

Not that there was much likelihood he'd ever be riding with either of them, she reminded herself.

The three women went into the double garage and Phyllis hit the button that opened the door behind her car. It rumbled and shook a little as it rose. They got into the Lincoln. The Baptist church was only four blocks away, but what was a pleasant walk at some times of the year definitely wasn't in July.

From the looks of the cars in the church parking lot and at the curbs along the street, there was going to be a good turnout for the funeral. The hearse was already there, parked in front of the building. There was also a police car with a young, bored-looking uniformed officer leaning against the fender. He would lead the funeral procession to the cemetery after the service. Several men in dark suits stood on the church's front porch, talking. Phyllis knew they were from the funeral home. Other people, soberly dressed men and women for the most part, were making their way through the front doors of the church.

Phyllis made a block and drove around back, knowing that there was a small parking lot at the rear of the church property. As she had suspected, it was only half full. She parked the Lincoln there, and then she, Mattie, and Eve got out and walked along the side of the building toward the front, following a concrete walk that led past some hedges.

Just before they got to the corner of the building, Phyllis stopped short. A dark blue pickup had pulled up in the church's driveway and stopped behind the hearse. A tall, slender man got out from behind the wheel and slammed the door hard. A boy climbed out of the truck on the passenger side and closed his door more carefully. One of the men from the funeral home came over to speak to them.

"Phyllis, dear, what's wrong?" Eve asked. "Aren't we going inside?"

"They'll be starting soon," Mattie put in.

Phyllis gave a little shake of her head. "Yes, of course," she said. She had recognized the boy who got out of the pickup. He was Justin Bishop, Newt's grandson who had been helping out at the orchard that day. Which meant the man with him was probably his father.

Quietly, as the three women walked up the side steps to the church's porch, Phyllis said to Mattie, "Isn't that Darryl Bishop over there talking to Mr. McGinley from the funeral home?"

Mattie squinted. "Yes, I believe it is. I suppose I should go talk to him, tell him how sorry I am for his loss."

"We can do that later," Phyllis said, lightly touching Mattie's arm to steer her through the open doors into the church. "He's busy right now."

"All right. They're sure lettin' the air-conditioning out, aren't they?"

Phyllis glanced over her shoulder as they went into the church. Darryl Bishop was in his thirties, with thinning brown hair and a prominent Adam's apple. There was certainly a resemblance between him and the glum little boy who stood with him, surreptitiously tugging at the tie around his neck, but Phyllis didn't see how Mattie could have mistaken Justin for his father. Of course, Phyllis hadn't known Darryl when he was a little boy, either, and Mattie had. People sometimes changed a lot over the years.

The three women found a place to sit in one of the pews on the right-hand side of the auditorium, about a third of the way toward the front. The church was almost full. Perhaps Newt Bishop hadn't had a lot of close friends, but he had been a man with plenty of acquaintances. He also hired a good number of immigrants to work in his orchard, and some of them were on hand. They sat together on the other side of the auditorium, dressed in clean, neatly pressed work clothes, holding their straw Stetsons in their hands as they talked quietly among themselves in Spanish.

Phyllis felt someone sit down beside her, and looked over to see her son. Mike said in a half whisper, "Hi, Mom." He nodded toward the part of the church where Phyllis had been looking and added, "I'll bet at least half of those fellas are illegals."

"You're not going to arrest them, are you?" she asked in surprise.

"Shoot, no. At a funeral? Anyway, they're good, hardworking folks—at least most of 'em are—just trying to do what they can for their families. And they had to put up with working for Newt Bishop, so I figure they've already been punished enough."

Phyllis frowned. Mike's comment came too close to speaking ill of the dead to suit her. She would have a talk with him about that later. At least she approved of his attitude toward the immigrants. Once when he was a kid, she had overheard him laughing with his friends about some "wetbacks." A couple of weeks without any allowance had taught him a little something about not referring to people by hurtful names.

She turned her attention to the front of the church as the organist began to play a hymn. The flowers that surrounded the closed coffin were lovely. Eve was the former English teacher, but a line from some poem came back to Phyllis, something about finding beauty in death. She supposed that might be true, but overall she didn't have much use for it.

The crowd settled down as the organist went through a couple of songs, and then one of the men from the funeral home led the family in through a door to the left of the pulpit. Everyone stood up. Newt Bishop's son and grandson were his only close family, but he'd had some cousins and nieces and nephews. About a dozen people in all filed into the pews reserved for family. The minister came last, stepped up behind the pulpit as the organist finished playing, and said, "Let's all bow our heads in prayer."

Phyllis might not have been to as many funerals as Mattie, but she had been to plenty, enough so that her mind wandered while the minister was eulogizing Newt Bishop and then offering up a short sermon. She looked at Darryl, and though she couldn't see but a little bit of his face, he seemed calm and under control, not broken up as some people might be. Of course, everybody dealt with their grief in different ways. Justin sat beside his father and wiped at his eyes every now and then, obviously trying to be discreet about it. A few of the female relatives let out an occasional sob. But clearly, there wasn't going to be any weeping and wailing over Newt's passing.

One of the ladies from the church got up and sang a hymn, the preacher made a few more remarks, and then the organist played while the men from the funeral home moved the flower arrangement from the top of the casket, opened the lid, and folded back the lining. Everyone stood to file past the coffin for a last look at the deceased, a custom that Phyllis, in her heart of hearts, regarded as somewhat barbaric and morbid. She had already decided that when *she* went, they could darned well leave the coffin closed.

But tradition couldn't be ignored, so she and Mattie and Eve shuffled past along with everybody else. Newt didn't look like himself and didn't look like he was sleeping, no matter what anyone said. Then it was over, and Phyllis was able to step outside with a small sigh of relief.

Mike was behind her. He was in uniform, and as soon as he was outside, he put his hat on. Phyllis touched him on the arm and said, "Are you going out to the cemetery?"

He shook his head. "Nope, I don't think so. I go on duty in just a little while."

"You can wait a minute, can't you?"

"Yeah, I suppose."

Phyllis turned to her friends and said, "Mattie, what happened to Darryl Bishop's wife? The little boy's mother?"

Mattie frowned as she tried to remember the answer to Phyllis's question. "She passed away a few years ago, I know that. Cancer, maybe. Or leukemia. I'm not sure which."

"So it's just the two of them?"

"That's right."

"And now Darryl's lost his father, too," Phyllis said softly.

"Was there something you wanted to ask me, Mom?" Mike said.

She turned back to face him and took a deep breath. "Actually, there's something I want to tell you. That pickup over there, behind the hearse . . ." She nodded toward the vehicles. "That's Darryl Bishop's truck, and I'm pretty sure it's the same one I saw out at Newt's place the other day, just before he was killed."

Chapter 6

"Are you sure about that?" Mike asked a short time later as he sat in the kitchen of his mother's house, a glass of iced tea with lemon on the table in front of him. He had called the dispatcher at the sheriff's office and explained that he was following up on some new information concerning Newt Bishop's death.

"Well, I can't be absolutely certain," Phyllis said as she sat down on the other side of the table. She had a glass of tea, too, but she didn't drink from it, just moved it around a little on the table instead. She frowned. "But if that wasn't Darryl's pickup I saw out at the farm, it was one that looked an awful lot like it."

Mike shrugged. "There are probably a lot of blue pickups in Parker County. I can probably check that through the computer."

Phyllis suppressed a brief flash of irritation. Mike wasn't doubting her word, she told herself. He was just doing his job, which was to consider every possibility and check everything that could be checked. A law enforcement officer had to have proof of things, not just somebody's opinion. Even when that opinion came from the officer's mother.

"I didn't get a real good look at the man who came up and talked to Newt," she said, "but from what I saw, it could have been Darryl. He was certainly taller and thinner than Newt." She held up a hand to stop Mike from saying anything. "And before you point it out, I realize that there are a lot of men around here who are taller and thinner than Newt was."

"That thought did cross my mind," Mike said with a slight smile. "But I believe you, Mom. Don't think for a second that I don't. I'm just a little surprised that you didn't recognize Darryl that day, even seeing him from a distance."

"I'm not. I never knew him all that well, and he wasn't in any of my classes. I haven't seen him to speak to in several years."

Mike nodded. "That makes sense. The man you saw, whether he was Darryl or not . . . you said he was arguing with Mr. Bishop?"

"He seemed to be. I couldn't hear what they were saying, of course, so again, I don't know for sure."

"Did the man seem violent?"

Phyllis concentrated, trying to see the scene again in her mind. "Not violent, really, but definitely agitated. He kept waving his arms around."

"But he didn't try to hit Mr. Bishop?"

"Not that I saw."

Mike took a long drink of the tea and then set the glass down. He frowned, too, and Phyllis began to worry even more.

"You don't think Darryl could have hurt his own father, do you?" she asked.

"You never know," Mike said. "When some folks get mad enough, they're liable to do almost anything."

"But the pickup left," Phyllis pointed out. "And Newt was just fine after that. I know because I saw him several times, moving around the barn."

"Maybe after Darryl drove off, he parked the pickup somewhere close, somewhere you couldn't see it, and then came back on foot. He grew up out there on that farm. He probably knows all the paths and shortcuts. He could've slipped into the back of the barn without anybody seeing him."

"He wouldn't do that unless—" Phyllis stopped short, unable to bring herself to go on.

Mike finished the thought for her. "Unless he planned on doing something he didn't want anybody to know about."

Like killing his father. Mike didn't have to say that part of it. Phyllis knew that was what he meant.

"You seem to have accepted the idea that it *was* Darryl I saw out there that day," she said.

"It's still just a theory, but it's sure worth checking out. I'll talk it over with the sheriff. Somebody needs to go and have a talk with Darryl, I guess." Mike took another swallow of the tea. "Do you know of any reason why he'd be upset with his dad?"

"Upset enough to . . . hurt him, you mean?"

"Just upset in general," Mike said. "Upset enough to yell and wave his arms around."

"I don't know the family that well. I don't have any idea what goes on between them."

Mike nodded. "I guess that's something else we'll have to ask Darryl about."

Phyllis felt a sudden surge of concern. "I almost wish I hadn't said anything. First Darryl loses his wife and is left with that little boy to raise, and now his father's gone, too, and he's suspected of having something to do with it! That poor man."

Mike reached across the table and took hold of her hand. "No, Mom, you did the right thing," he said. "If it turns out that Darryl *did* have something to do with his father's death, you don't need to feel sorry for him. You wouldn't want him to get away with it."

"No," Phyllis said. "I wouldn't."

Before they could say anything else, the doorbell rang in the living room. Eve, Mattie, and Carolyn were in there, and Eve called out, "I'll get it." A moment later, Phyllis heard her say, "Why, Sam! There you are. We were beginning to wonder what had happened to you!"

Sam Fletcher's deep voice rumbled in reply, "Got delayed a little. Nothing to worry about, though."

Mike inclined his head toward the living room and asked, "Who's that?"

"The new boarder," Phyllis said.

His eyebrows rose in surprise. "A *man*?"

"Oh, now, don't you start in on me, too," Phyllis said as she got to her feet. "Next thing you know, you'll be fussing just like Carolyn."

She walked down the hall to the living room and heard Mike following her. As she came into the room, she saw Sam heading toward the stairs with a cardboard box in his hands. Eve was beside him, obviously intent on keeping him company while he moved in. Mattie sat on the sofa, squinting at some needlework and pretty well ignoring the goings-on, while Carolyn was in an armchair, frowning.

Sam stopped when he saw Phyllis and Mike. With a friendly nod, he said, "Hello, Miz Newsom."

"It's Phyllis, remember?" she told him.

There was a twinkle in Sam's eyes as he looked at Mike, said, "Somebody call the law on me?" and then glanced at Carolyn.

"I'm Mike Newsom," Mike said as he stepped forward.

"My son," Phyllis added.

Sam set the box on the floor and extended his hand. "Sam Fletcher. Glad to meet you, Mike. If you grew up in this house, you know what a nice place it is, so I don't have to tell you how pleased I am to be sharing it with your mother and these other fine ladies."

Mike shook hands friendly enough, but he looked at Sam with slightly narrowed eyes. "Don't I know you from somewhere, Mr. Fletcher?"

"From high school, maybe? Poolville never played Weatherford, but we came to some preseason tournaments down here."

Some of the suspicion left Mike's face as he nodded.

"Yeah, I remember you now. You coached basketball at Poolville. You guys always had a good team. I remember being glad we weren't in the same classification." He paused. "So you're going to be living here?"

Eve took Sam's arm. "He certainly is, and it's going to be really nice to have a man around the house."

"Well, I'll try to help out as much as I can," Sam said, and once again Phyllis admired the smooth way in which he disengaged his arm from Eve's grip.

She stepped forward and said, "Sam, you haven't met Mattie yet."

"That's right, I haven't." He joined Phyllis in walking across the room toward the sofa.

"Mattie, here's Mr. Fletcher," Phyllis said. "You wanted to meet him."

Mattie looked up from her needlework with a puzzled expression on her lined face. "I did?"

"Of course," Phyllis said quickly. "He's our new boarder. He's going to be living here."

"Really? Nobody told me about that." Mattie looked up at Sam. "You're a tall one, aren't you?"

"Yes, ma'am, I surely am." He smiled gently at her and reached down to take her hand. "And it's an honor to meet you, ma'am. I've heard a lot about you."

Mattie laughed. "Half of it's probably not true."

"Do I get to pick which half?" Sam asked her, still smiling.

"Just you mind your manners, boy, and we'll get along just fine."

"Yes, ma'am. I intend to behave."

From the bottom of the stairs, Eve said with a laugh, "Not too well, I hope!" That drew a disapproving snort from Carolyn.

Sam didn't pay any attention to them. He said to Mattie, "Now, if you'll excuse me, ma'am, I've got to carry a few things upstairs."

"Sure thing. Nice to meet you, Mr. Fletcher."

Mike leaned over and gave Phyllis a kiss on the cheek. "I've got to run, Mom. See you later." He lifted a hand in farewell to Sam. "See you around, Mr. Fletcher."

"So long, Mike," Sam responded. He went to the foot of the stairs and picked up the cardboard box again.

"What do you have in there, dear?" Eve asked. "It doesn't seem to be very heavy."

If he minded her nosiness, he didn't show any sign of it, Phyllis noted. "Oh, just some pictures." He glanced at Phyllis. "Don't worry, I won't put any nails in the wall to hang them on. They'll sit on the dresser and that chest of drawers."

"That'll be fine," she said with a nod.

Sam went on upstairs, followed by Eve. Phyllis looked back over her shoulder at Mattie, who seemed to have no memory of saying something earlier in the day about wanting to meet Sam. She had certainly been aware that the new boarder was supposed to move in today, but obviously it had slipped her mind entirely. As far as Phyllis was concerned, that was just one more thing to worry about, along with Newt Bishop's death and the fact that the man's own son might be to blame for it somehow.

Things had been a lot simpler back in the old days, when all she'd had to worry about was taking care of a husband, a son, and five classes of unruly eighth graders every day.

Chapter 7

Later in the afternoon, Phyllis went upstairs and down the hall toward Sam's room. The door stood open, but she knocked lightly anyway.

He looked around from where he was straightening a framed picture on the nightstand next to the bed. "Come on in," he said. "It's your house."

"Yes, but I respect my boarders' privacy."

"Good policy," Sam said with a nod.

"I wanted to tell you, though," Phyllis went on, "that you don't have to ring the bell when you come in. This is your house, too, as long as you're living here."

"Mighty nice of you to feel that way. It may take me a little while to get comfortable with that, so you'll bear with me?"

"Of course." Phyllis looked at the photograph on the nightstand, which was of an attractive redheaded woman in her thirties. "Your daughter?"

"My wife," Sam said as he half-turned toward the picture.

"Oh." She should have known that the photo would be of his wife, Phyllis scolded herself. Naturally a widower would want to keep his late wife's picture close by, so that he could look at it whenever he wanted to. "She was very pretty."

Sam picked up the photo and ran a finger along the side of the polished wooden frame. "Yes, she sure was," he said with a touch of wistfulness in his voice. "Her name was Victoria—Vicky, I called her—and I thought she was the most beautiful woman on the face of the earth, right up until the day she couldn't fight that damned disease anymore."

Phyllis felt a tightness in her chest and a catch in her throat at the depth of the emotion in Sam's voice. It was simply stated and there was nothing dramatic about it, but she knew how real and true it was. She knew because she had felt the same way about Kenny.

"I didn't mean to stir up memories . . ." she began softly.

"No, that's all right," Sam said with a shake of his head. Carefully, he replaced the framed photograph on the night-stand. "It's been a while."

"Not all that long, from what I understand. I don't mean to be forward, but I can tell you that eventually it does get better. The hurt fades some."

"But it never goes away completely," he said.

She shook her head. "No. It never does."

He laughed quietly, but there was no humor in the sound. "Makes you wonder, doesn't it, why people go through all the foolishness of falling in love and getting married and raising families?"

"Not at all," Phyllis said without hesitation. "The good times are worth the pain. At least I've always thought so."

"That's a good way to think," he said with a nod, but she couldn't tell if he agreed with her or not.

She changed the subject by saying, "What happened to Eve? I thought she'd still be up here buzzing around you like a moth around a light bulb."

Sam chuckled, and this time he sounded genuinely amused. "I guess she got a little tired of me just saying 'Yep' and 'Nope' like Gary Cooper. I didn't figure she really needed any encouragement, though."

Out of a sense of loyalty to her old friend, Phyllis said, "She just tries to be friendly. You don't like her?"

"I like her just fine. I think she's a fine lady like the rest of you. I guess I'm just not much on flirting. Never did much of it."

That was your wife's loss, Phyllis thought, but she kept the comment to herself. Instead, she said, "I should probably explain about Mattie. . . . She knew you were moving in today, it just slipped her mind."

Sam nodded. "I wondered if it was something like that."

For some reason—probably because he was easy to talk to—Phyllis blurted out, "I'm getting more and more worried about her lately. She forgets things a lot, and sometimes she seems to think that . . . well, she doesn't know what year it is. She thinks it's a long time ago."

"That happens," Sam said. "Have you talked to Miz Harris's doctor about it?"

"Oh, he knows about it. I take Mattie to the doctor for her checkups, and he told me there's really nothing he can do."

"Just be her friend as best you can, for as long as you can."

"Exactly."

"Yeah, I went through that with my dad some years ago. It's a hard road. Folks just have to get through it somehow."

"And we will," Phyllis said. "I just thought you should know, in case Mattie seems a little . . . off to you sometimes."

"I understand." He rubbed his hands together. "Well, I'd better go down and get my rocking chair out of the pickup and bring it in."

"You have a rocking chair?"

"Yeah, but I keep it oiled up so it doesn't squeak. It won't keep you awake nights. I like to sit in it and read."

"I'm sure it won't bother me," Phyllis told him. "I love rocking chairs."

"Thought as much when I saw the ones on the porch," Sam said with a grin. "Nothing like sitting out on the porch on a nice evening."

"Isn't that the truth!" As they left the room, she asked, "Do you need any help?"

"Nope, but I appreciate the offer."

"There you go, imitating Gary Cooper again."

"Aw, shucks—"

She lifted a finger to stop him. "If you call me ma'am, you'll have to move out."

"I'll be careful," he promised, his smile widening into a grin again.

Before leaving for the funeral, Phyllis had put a roast on to cook, knowing that it would take most of the afternoon. She used her mother's recipe and cooked it in Coke, which gave the meat a wonderful, distinctive flavor. "Co' Cola," her daddy had always called it, back when she was a little girl, when he wasn't calling it soda pop. Phyllis had never been one for drinking alcohol, but she truly loved a cold Coke, preferably over crushed ice.

She checked on the roast and found that it was ready to add the cola. She took the cover off and poured most of a twelve-ounce bottle over the roast. She set the timer for thirty minutes, covered the roast again, and put it back in the oven. For a moment, with the cooking contest on her mind, she wondered what a roast cooked in peach soda would taste like. That wouldn't really qualify, of course, since it didn't make use of fresh peaches, but it was still an intriguing idea. She would just have to try it sometime, she decided.

In the meantime, she put some potatoes on to boil. A roast had to have mashed potatoes with it, and she wouldn't use the ones that came out of a box.

Mattie came into the kitchen as Phyllis was opening the oven to baste the roast. "Smells good," she said. "You spend too much time cooking for us, Phyllis. Spend too much time doing for us, all around."

"I like helping people. So do you, Mattie, or you wouldn't be volunteering all the time."

"I've got to stay busy," Mattie said. "Staying busy's good for the mind and body."

Phyllis knew that to be true. Unfortunately, in Mattie's

case no amount of staying busy was going to save her mind from its long, slow descent.

Mattie went on. "That Mr. Fletcher seems like a nice fella."

"Yes, he does, doesn't he?" Phyllis was glad to see that for right now, at least, Mattie's thinking and memory were clear.

"Tall, though. He'll have to be careful going through the doors in this house. Liable to bump his head on 'em."

"I'm sure he'll be careful." Seeing that her friend's mind was sharp at the moment, Phyllis took a chance and said, "Mattie, what can you tell me about Newt and Darryl Bishop?"

Mattie gave a little ladylike snort. "What's to tell? Newt was always surly as an ol' possum. He didn't give me any trouble, mind you. I reckon he knew I wouldn't stand for that. But he was mighty hard on his wife and on that boy. Especially the boy." Mattie shook her head regretfully. "You see kids come to school, and sometimes you just know their folks don't treat 'em right."

"Yes," Phyllis said, thinking of some of her own students. "It's a terrible feeling. You never know what to do."

"That's how it was with Darryl. He'd come into the classroom and be limpin' a little, and with most kids you'd think they just hurt themselves playing. With Darryl, though, it was because his daddy'd taken a strap to him. And Newt's wife, Velma, was a mousy little thing, not the sort to stand up to him, even to protect her child. He didn't beat on her like he did on Darryl, but I'll bet he found plenty o' ways to make her life pretty hard." Mattie sighed. "Of course, times were different then. If a kid misbehaved, his daddy could blister him without havin' to worry about gettin' the law down on him. Problem is, I'm not sure Darryl ever misbehaved enough to deserve all the blisterings he got."

"It seems to me that a child would never forget being mistreated like that."

"Of course they don't forget! Why, many's the time Darryl looked like he wanted to take a strap and get some of his own back from Newt, and he was just a little boy. I worried some about what he'd be like when he grew up. He turned out all right, though, at least as far as I know. Took care of his mama as best he could before she died, and then took care of his wife when she got sick. And he thinks the sun rises and sets on Justin. I don't figure he's ever raised a hand to the boy. That's been good to see, because lots of times when a kid's mistreated, he doesn't treat his own kids very good when he grows up."

Mattie was right about that, too, Phyllis knew. Child abuse was a vicious, self-perpetuating cycle. The fact that Darryl Bishop had been able to break that cycle was admirable.

But she couldn't help but wonder if he had broken it completely. She wondered if all the old hurts—physical, mental, and emotional—had lingered in Darryl all these years. Had he forgiven his father, or was the old resentment he felt toward Newt still there?

Had he hated Newt enough so that something might have set him off and led to . . .

Phyllis pushed the thought away, but she knew she couldn't banish it completely. What she had just learned from Mattie put a different face on the events of the past few days. She hated to think about it, but maybe there was a good reason to suspect Darryl Bishop of having had something to do with his father's bizarre death.

Like it or not, she decided, she was going to have to talk to Mike again, and fill him in on what Mattie had told her about the way Newt Bishop had treated his son all those years ago.

Chapter 8

Phyllis was waiting at Mike's house—a nice brick home in one of the newer residential developments on the north side of Weatherford—when he got home that evening. He came in looking surprised, knowing she was there, because he had seen her car parked out front.

"What is it, Mom?" he asked her. "Something wrong?"

Phyllis laughed. "I ask you," she said to Sarah, her pretty blond daughter-in-law, "is that any way for a son to greet his mother?"

"Absolutely not," Sarah said with a smile of her own. Phyllis got along well with Sarah and thought the world of her most of the time, although there were those very rare instances when she wanted to speak up and offer some unasked-for advice. She always bit her tongue on those occasions, though, and kept her opinions to herself.

"If you two are gonna gang up on me, I'm not even going to try to defend myself," Mike said as he hung his Stetson on a hook near the kitchen door, where he had just come in from the garage. "I'm sorry, Mom. I just didn't expect to see you here tonight."

"Well, I wasn't expecting to come over, but I found out something—about Newt Bishop, I mean—and I wanted to talk to you about it."

That got Mike's interest, right enough. But he paused

long enough to give Sarah a quick kiss and ask her, "Where's Bobby?"

"Getting a little nap before dinner. He was worn out from playing all afternoon."

"He didn't take his first step yet, did he?"

"Not yet. It's going to be soon, though."

"Boy, I hope I'm here for it," Mike said.

"So do I."

Mike came over to the kitchen table where Phyllis was sitting, and took one of the empty chairs. "Now, what's this about Mr. Bishop?"

Phyllis hesitated, still reluctant to stick her nose into the investigation. But what she had found out might be important, she reminded herself.

"I was talking to Mattie this afternoon, after you left," she began, "and I asked her about Newt and Darryl. Darryl was in Mattie's class when he was in second grade, you know."

Mike nodded, not rushing her. She knew he probably felt a little impatient and wanted her to get to the point, but he would never say that.

"Mattie said that Newt was . . . not very nice to his family back then," she went on.

"He was abusive?"

"Well . . . Mattie said that sometimes when Darryl came to school, she could tell that he'd been beaten with a strap. Evidently Newt wasn't quite that physically abusive to his wife, but he made life difficult for her, too."

Sarah said from the stove, where she was stirring a pot of chili, "I wouldn't put up with something like that. Anybody who mistreated my child sure as heck wouldn't be able to feel safe closing his eyes around me ever again."

"It was a different time back then," Phyllis said, echoing Mattie's comment from earlier in the day. "People just felt differently about what was acceptable and what wasn't."

"Right and wrong don't change that much, though," Mike said as his forehead creased in thought. "And a little boy who's abused is liable to grow up to be an adult with a lot of hate in him."

Phyllis said, "That's exactly what I was thinking. And it made me wonder . . ."

"If that was a strong enough motive for murder?" Mike nodded grimly. "People have killed for less, that's for sure. And it's interesting that Darryl Bishop didn't say anything about any of this when I talked to him a little while ago."

"You went to talk to him?" The question came quickly from Phyllis. She realized that the thought of Mike questioning Darryl bothered her, and it took her only a moment to understand why. Darryl was a murder suspect now, and he hadn't been before.

"Yeah, I talked to the sheriff about what you told me earlier—you know, about thinking it was Darryl's pickup you saw at the farm—and he told me to follow up on it. Darryl admitted right off the bat that he was there that day."

Sarah came over and sat down at the table, too. The smell of the chili she'd left simmering on the stove was wonderful, but Phyllis barely noticed it. Sarah seemed worried, too, as she said to Mike, "Did you ask him if he'd had a fight with his dad?" She exchanged a glance with Phyllis that showed they shared the same worry: Killers sometimes turned violent when they were confronted.

Mike seemed pretty casual about the whole thing, though, and obviously he was all right. "I asked him if there had been any trouble between them lately, and he said no. Said he and his dad weren't particularly close, but that they hadn't had any problems."

"That wasn't the way it looked to me," Phyllis said, "and they were close enough so that Darryl's been letting Justin help out in the peach orchard this summer."

Mike nodded and went on, "I didn't press him on his story or tell him that we had a witness who saw him and his father arguing. I didn't want to spook him. Seemed like it might be a better idea to get some more background first, maybe see if I can turn up anybody else who can testify that there was bad blood between them, and tell us the reason why."

"Well, I'm sure you know the best way to handle something like this," Phyllis said. "Lord knows I don't know anything about murder investigations."

"*If* it really was murder," Mike said. "We haven't positively established that yet. There was a scraped place on the locking lever of that bumper jack where something might have hit it and knocked it loose, but we can't be sure when it was put there. Might be totally innocent. We fingerprinted the jack and the tire iron and didn't come up with any prints but Mr. Bishop's."

"So it still could have been an accident?"

Mike shrugged. "With an old jack like that . . . yeah, it could have slipped. But I don't think that's what happened, and neither does the sheriff."

Sarah asked, "What about an alibi? Did you ask Darryl where he went after he left his dad's farm?"

Mike didn't seem to mind the questions. "Yeah, I asked him. He claims he drove home and then went on to work. Problem is, his shift at the truck stop out on the Interstate where he works as a mechanic didn't start until two o'clock that afternoon. He showed up for work when he was supposed to, but he would have had time to park his car out of sight of the barn, circle around on foot like we talked about, knock that old Caddy off the jack, and get out of there and go on to work like nothing happened."

"So he *doesn't* have an alibi," Sarah said.

"Not one that's worth anything."

"It was Justin who found his grandfather," Phyllis said. "Darryl would have to have known that the boy was somewhere right around there. Could Darryl have done such a thing knowing that it was his own son who would probably find the body?"

"Folks who lose their heads and commit murder don't

stop to think it through. They don't think about what the total effect of their actions will be. If they did, there would probably be a lot fewer killings."

"So what now?" Sarah asked. "You'll continue investigating?"

"Yeah. Darryl may be starting to wonder if we're looking at him as a suspect. The sheriff talked to him after Mr. Bishop's body was found, of course, but at the time we didn't have any reason to think that Darryl might have been there that day. And even though he didn't deny it now, he sure didn't volunteer the information then. Now that we've come back to him again and he's had to admit that he was there, he may start to worry. We'll be keeping an eye on him, though, in case he decides to run."

Phyllis frowned. "How can he do that? He has a job, and a son."

"You'd be surprised what desperate people will do, Mom. Darryl could take Justin and leave town, leave the state if he wanted to. He hasn't been charged with anything, or even officially brought in for questioning. There are plenty of cases on record where fugitives have changed their names and dropped completely out of sight for years. Sometimes they're never found."

"And if he tries to get away?"

"We'll try to hold him as a material witness, but even that would be tricky, since we're not officially investigating a crime. Even a halfway decent lawyer would have Darryl sprung in a hurry. What we really need is more evidence . . . but I don't know if we'll get it."

"So if he *did* do it," Phyllis said, "there's a chance he'll get away with it?"

Mike sighed. "That's one of the things that'll drive you crazy about this job. Sometimes guilty people *do* get away with what they've done."

Her son's words stayed with Phyllis as she drove back across Weatherford in the gathering twilight. They mixed

with the things Mattie had told her, and she thought that for a
lot of years, Newt Bishop had gotten away with *his* crimes . . .
the crimes he had carried out against his wife and son.

But in the end, retribution—whether at the hand of God
or man—had caught up with him.

She had to put those thoughts aside and concentrate on
her driving. Her eyes weren't as good as they once had been,
and dusk was a bad time for her. But she reached her house
without any trouble and put the Lincoln away in the garage.

When she came into the house through the kitchen, she
found Carolyn at the stove. The smell of cooking peaches
was in the air, along with something else—the smell of some
ingredient that Phyllis couldn't identify. Carolyn moved
quickly, getting between Phyllis and the stove. "You didn't
need anything over here, did you?" she asked over her
shoulder.

Phyllis knew perfectly well that Carolyn didn't want her
to see what she was cooking. She wasn't going to be pushy
and nosy—even though, technically, this *was* her kitchen—
so she said, "No, not at all," and went on through the dining
room to the living room and the den.

Eve and Mattie were watching an old Cary Grant movie
on one of the cable channels. Eve was watching, anyway;
Mattie had dozed off in her chair. Phyllis didn't want to
disturb her just yet, although later she would see to it that
Mattie got to bed all right. She nodded to Eve and went on
upstairs.

The sound of another TV playing came through the open
door of Sam Fletcher's room. When she looked in, she saw
that he was sitting in the rocking chair, watching the portable
TV he had brought in earlier. The television had a DVD
player sitting on top of it.

Sam smiled at her from the rocker. "Want to join me?" he
asked. He nodded toward the TV. "It's *She Wore a Yellow
Ribbon*. I've got a fondness for the Duke."

"I appreciate the invitation," Phyllis said, "but another time, maybe. Is there anything you need?"

"Nope. That was a wonderful dinner. I don't think I've ever had roast cooked in Coke before. It was mighty good, and that gravy was the best I've ever had. So I'm full, and I've got plenty of movies to watch and books to read. I do believe I'm pretty much set."

"That's good to know. If anything comes up . . ."

"I won't hesitate to holler."

Phyllis smiled. "Good night then . . . Sam."

"Good night, Phyllis."

He went back to watching the movie and rocking slightly. On the TV, John Wayne said, "Never apologize, Mr. Cohill. . . . It's a sign of weakness."

Phyllis walked away, smelling the scent of peaches that filled the house, thinking about Newt Bishop, and wondering if he would still be alive if he'd ever been "weak" enough to apologize for the things he had done.

Chapter 9

It was Mike's case. The sheriff had pretty much said so. And Mike would have been lying if he'd said that he didn't feel any pressure because of it. He had been a deputy for six years, loved the work, loved the people, loved the feeling that he was making a difference in the world.

But a murder case . . . Well, that was different. That was high stakes.

When Mike went to work the next day after his mother's visit, Darryl Bishop was more on his mind than ever. Darryl had a motive now. It wasn't a matter of an unexplained argument anymore. Darryl had good reason to be angry with his father, good reason to hate him, in fact.

But all that had happened a long time ago, Mike reminded himself. Could anybody nurse a grudge for that long and still have it be strong enough to prompt a murder?

Or would the passage of time just make the hate that much stronger?

The Parker County Sheriff's Department was not housed in the historic county courthouse downtown on the square or in the subcourthouse closer to the Interstate, but rather in a compound of its own a few blocks east of downtown that was also the location of the county jail. As Mike walked through the building, he met Sheriff Royce Haney, who jerked a thumb toward his office and said, "Come on in for a minute, Mike."

"Sure, Sheriff," Mike replied. He wondered what Haney wanted with him but wasn't really surprised when the sheriff brought up Newt Bishop's death. The mysteriousness of it weighed on everybody's mind.

"I read your report about your talk with Darryl Bishop," Haney said as he settled into the big chair behind his desk. "You didn't press him about why he went out to his dad's farm that day?"

"He said he was just checking on his son, Justin. The boy's been staying at the farm, helping his grandfather with the orchard. That seemed reasonable enough. Also I didn't want to let on to Darryl that he was under too much suspicion."

"Because you plan on asking more questions of other people who knew them?"

"That's right." Mike explained it as he had to his mother and Sarah the night before. "I want to see if I can turn up any more evidence that there was trouble between them."

Haney nodded. "Good idea. But it might be a good idea, too, not to put all your eggs in that one basket."

"What do you mean, Sheriff?" Mike asked with a frown.

"You don't want to concentrate on one suspect so much that you forget about everybody else. I know that seems to be the way it works in some departments, but I believe in keeping an open mind. If Bishop really was murdered, somebody had to be pretty mad at him. Try to find out if anybody besides his son had a reason to hold a grudge against him."

Mike nodded. Even though sheriff was an elected office, and therefore a politician's job, Royce Haney had been in law enforcement for a lot of years and had plenty of wisdom to pass on. Mike always tried to pay attention to what Haney had to say.

"All right, I'll look into it," he said.

Haney went on. "Folks kill for three basic reasons: love, hate, or greed. Or some combination of those. See what you can turn up."

Mike nodded as he got to his feet. "Will do, Sheriff."

"You don't have to worry about taking your patrol shift while you're doing it, either," Haney added. "I want you to concentrate on the Bishop case."

Mike felt his eyes widen a little in surprise. It sounded like the sheriff was making him an investigator, at least temporarily. He had figured that he would have to balance looking into Newt Bishop's death with the rest of his regular duties. The idea that he could stick to the one case was exciting.

"A lot of people knew Newt," Haney said. "I wouldn't say that we're getting pressure to find out who's responsible for what happened to him, but I'd still like to get it cleared up as quick as we can."

"Yes, sir," Mike said. "I'll get to the bottom of it."

"I know you will." The sheriff's voice hardened slightly. "Don't let me down, son."

Mike didn't intend to.

As he left the sheriff's department, he thought about what Haney had said. *Love, hate, greed . . . or some combination of those three things.* The hate could apply to Darryl Bishop because of the way Newt had treated him as a boy. Mike wondered if greed figured into it as well. Darryl had a decent job at the truck stop but was far from rich. With his father dead, would he inherit the farm and its lucrative peach orchard? The land itself would be worth a lot with the way Weatherford was growing. Cut up, it had to be worth at least a million, maybe more.

Mike knew he would have to find out if Bishop had left a will, and if so, what the terms of it were. Was it also reasonable to ask if anybody else might profit from his death?

Greed meant money, and the best place to find a money trail was the county clerk's office.

Mike headed for the subcourthouse.

Early that afternoon, Mike walked into an office on North Main, about a block from the square. The sign painted on the glass door read LANDERS REALTY. A middle-aged woman with orange hair looked up from a desk and seemed to be a little surprised to see a deputy sheriff. "Can I help you?"

"Is Mr. Landers in?" Mike asked.

Instead of answering, the woman said, "Is this about the real estate business?"

"Well, sort of," Mike answered, "but mostly it's about Newt Bishop's death."

The woman's lips thinned. She looked like she wanted to say that Landers wasn't there, but Mike could see the man for himself through a window into a private office to the left of the woman's desk. She picked up a phone on her desk, pushed a button, waited a second, and then said, "Mr. Landers, there's a deputy here to see you."

Through the window, Mike had seen Landers answer the phone. The silliness of this charade made him want to smile. The man was *right there*.

The woman hung up the phone. "You can go on in."

"Thanks," Mike said. It never hurt to be polite. His mother had taught him that.

Alfred Landers stood up behind his desk and reached across it to offer his hand. He was a tall, thick-bodied man with dark hair and old-fashioned black-framed glasses. "Deputy," he said. "What can I do for you?"

"My name is Newsom," Mike said as he shook hands with the realtor. "I'm investigating the death of Newt Bishop."

"I heard about it," Landers said as he waved Mike into the chair in front of the desk. "Terrible accident, wasn't it?"

"Well, we haven't determined for sure yet if it was really an accident," Mike said as he sat down, "and I'm not sure how terrible it is for you since you can't have felt very friendly toward Bishop these days, what with that lawsuit and all."

Landers frowned as he sank slowly into his chair. "That

lawsuit's over and done with. It's a closed issue as far as I'm concerned."

"You and Bishop sued each other over several hundred feet of prime highway frontage," Mike went on, as if Landers hadn't said anything. "You stood to make a considerable amount of money if you could sell it, especially since you already had a buyer lined up who wanted to put a convenience store and a little strip shopping center there. Bishop claimed that your survey was wrong, though, and that he owned the land."

Landers didn't even make a pretense of being friendly anymore. He glared as he said, "All this is in the court records. I'm sure you've looked it up already, Deputy Newsom. Why are you asking me about it now?"

"Because Newt Bishop won that lawsuit. Your survey *was* wrong."

"It wasn't," Landers snapped, "and if I wanted to take the time and trouble, not to mention the expense, to appeal the decision, I'd prove that sooner or later. It's not worth it, though."

"Mr. Landers, what kind of car do you drive?"

"A Saturn."

"What color is it?"

"Gray." Landers leaned forward. "I can tell that you're dying to ask another question, Deputy. Why don't you go ahead?"

"All right, I will," Mike said, unable to completely suppress the irritation he felt. He instinctively disliked Alfred Landers. "Did you go out to Newt Bishop's farm the day he died?"

"No, I didn't." The answer came quickly, in a flat, hard voice.

"Can you prove that? Were you here in the office all day, say?"

"No, my business keeps me out of the office most of the time. You were just lucky that you caught me here today. I buy and sell properties all over this part of the country. Hell, I don't even remember for sure what day it was Bishop died, but if you give me the date I can check my calendar and tell you where I was."

"You generally go out by yourself when you're doing business like that?"

Landers placed his hands flat on the desk. "That's it," he said. "I'm not saying anything else. If you have any other questions, Deputy, get in touch with my lawyer. His office is right up there on the square. Jerry Hendricks."

Mike stood up. "I think that'll do it for now."

"I hope so. I don't appreciate being accused of things I didn't do."

"Nobody's accused you of anything, Mr. Landers. We're just trying to cover all the bases. If I offended you, I'm sorry."

Landers didn't look mollified. "You can show yourself out."

"Sure. Thank you."

Mike put on his hat when he reached the sidewalk, and paused for a moment to think about what had just happened. He supposed he hadn't handled it very well, but there really wasn't any way he could think of to ask somebody if they'd committed a murder without rubbing them the wrong way. What he had discovered in several hours of digging through courthouse records revealed that Newt Bishop had cost Landers quite a bit of money. That tied in with what Sheriff Haney had said about greed and hate. Bishop's death wouldn't put that money in Landers's pocket—somebody, presumably Darryl Bishop, would inherit the disputed property and Landers still wouldn't have it to sell—but Newt Bishop's death might have been a way of settling the score.

And Landers's car matched the description of the one Mike's mother had seen leaving the Bishop farm in a hurry not long before Newt's body was found.

The sheriff had been right, Mike thought as he got in his

car. While Darryl Bishop still had to be regarded as the strongest suspect, Alfred Landers couldn't be ruled out. That was going to take some more investigation. And there was still the possibility that someone else, someone whose identity hadn't been uncovered yet, had had a reason to want Newt Bishop dead.

Not to mention, accidents sometimes *did* happen. . . .

Not in this case, though, Mike told himself. Maybe it wasn't official yet, but he was more convinced than ever that Newt Bishop's death was murder.

Chapter 10

Life went on, despite the tragedies that were part and parcel of it, and the peach festival was fast approaching. Phyllis hadn't forgotten about Newt Bishop's death, of course, and she had been very interested when Mike told her about the real estate man, Alfred Landers, and the trouble between Landers and Newt. It seemed that at least two people might have had a reason for hating Newt. That didn't mean either of them was a murderer, of course, but still, you had to consider it.

That was Mike's job, though. Phyllis's was to get the recipe for that ginger peach cobbler *exactly* right. . . .

She was in the kitchen several days later when Sam Fletcher strolled in, apparently aimlessly. He stood there with his hands in the hip pockets of his jeans and took a deep breath. "Whatever that is you've got cookin', it smells mighty good," he said.

Phyllis leaned over to look past him down the hallway toward the living room. When she didn't see anyone lurking there—like Carolyn—she said quietly, "It's peach cobbler."

"I knew it had to be something with peaches in it." Sam took another sniff and then frowned in thought. "And something else, maybe. . . ."

"Can you keep a secret?"

"I was a schoolteacher for a lot of years. Had to keep many a secret."

"Some of the worst gossips I've ever known have been teachers," Phyllis said. "I'm serious."

Sam nodded, a solemn expression on his face. "Then sure. Whatever you tell me, it stays between us, Phyllis."

She decided she believed him. "It has candied ginger in it, too," she said. "The cobbler, I mean."

"Ginger, huh?" Sam rubbed his jaw; the faint rasp of beard stubble against his fingertips was a sound that Phyllis hadn't heard in a long time. Not since Kenny's passing, in fact. It struck a chord in her, and she felt an odd fluttering sensation in her chest. You just never knew what you would miss, or what would touch something inside and bring back memories.

He went on, "That sounds like it might be good."

"I hope so. I'm counting on it, in fact. It's going to be my recipe for the cooking contest at the peach festival."

Sam smiled. "Well, if I can help out by being a guinea pig sometime, I'd be glad to—"

"Good," Phyllis said quickly. "Sit down."

Sam looked surprised. "Now, you mean?"

"Yes, sit down there at the table. I'll get you a bowl. I just took it out of the oven a little while ago to cool, and it should be all right to eat by now."

His broad shoulders rose and fell in a shrug. He sat down at the table as Phyllis had told him, while she got a couple of bowls from the cabinet and spoons from a drawer. She had draped a clean dish towel over the quart-sized dish she'd used to bake the cobbler, just in case Carolyn was to come in. When she removed the dish towel, the delicious aroma grew even stronger.

"I don't know where the other ladies are," Sam said, "but that smells so good it's liable to lure folks in off the street."

"Mattie's at the high school, and Eve's gone to pick her up," Phyllis said as she scooped cobbler into the bowls. "Mattie volunteers there as a tutor for the kids who have to go to summer school. And Carolyn's upstairs somewhere. She won't come down."

"You seem mighty sure of that. Is it because of me? I've tried to be nice to her, but she doesn't seem to warm up to people very fast."

Phyllis brought the bowls over to the table. "It's not because of you at all, Sam," she assured him. "Carolyn knows that I'm down here working on my recipe and don't want her skulking around."

"Ah," he said. "So it's like that, is it?"

Phyllis pushed the bowl toward him. "Eat," she said.

Sam dug in, putting a spoonful of cobbler in his mouth and chewing slowly and deliberately, obviously taking his time so that he could fully appreciate the flavor. Phyllis watched him anxiously, forgetting to eat any of the cobbler she had put in her own bowl.

Sam swallowed, and Phyllis said, "Well?"

"A fella can't judge something like this from just one bite," he said. "Let me try another." He dipped his spoon in the cobbler again.

He's doing this on purpose, Phyllis thought. He's teasing me by making me wait.

In an effort to distract herself, she finally thought to take a bite herself. The cobbler *was* good, she decided. The crust was flaky on top but had plenty of body, the amount of sugar she'd put on it was just right, and the filling below was cooked to the proper consistency. A cobbler shouldn't be too runny or too thick and sticky.

Sam swallowed his second bite and said, "You got any vanilla ice cream—"

"No ice cream," Phyllis broke in. "Just the cobbler."

"Well, in that case . . . one more bite. . . ."

She tried not to grit her teeth.

When he had finished the third bite, he said, "The ginger's not real strong, but it gives it a little whang."

"Whang," Phyllis said. "Is that good or bad?"

"Oh, whang is good," Sam said, nodding. "You want a little whang in your food every now and then. Otherwise, everything's all . . ." He searched for a word. "Whangless."

Phyllis took a deep breath. She didn't know the man well enough to dump a bowl of peach cobbler on his head, but right now she was sure thinking about it. "Is it *good*?" she asked, hoping she didn't sound too desperate.

Sam had a mischievous twinkle in his eyes, but he nodded and said seriously, "Yes, Phyllis, it's good. It's really good."

She sat back and blew out a breath of relief. "I'm glad."

"Going after the blue ribbon, are you? And I'd guess that somebody else usually wins it? Somebody in this very house, maybe?"

"I don't like to be petty about things," Phyllis said, "but I would dearly love to win this year."

Sam pointed with his spoon at the rest of the cobbler in his bowl. "I'd say you got a mighty good shot. You mind if I finish this?"

"Oh, no, go right ahead," Phyllis said quickly. "And if you really want some ice cream, I have some in the freezer—"

"No, thanks. I don't want anything to interfere with the flavor of this cobbler."

They sat there for a few minutes in companionable silence, finishing off the cobbler in their bowls. When they were done, Phyllis asked, "Was there anything about it that you didn't like? Anything you can think of that would make it better?"

Sam shook his head. "Can't think of a thing. Far as I can tell, it was just about perfect."

"Just about? But not actually perfect?"

He started to look a little uncomfortable. "What I know about cooking you could put in the tip of your little finger, Phyllis. I never did much of it when I was married, and since Vicky passed away, I've eaten a lot of sandwiches and TV dinners. I can open up a can of something, dump it in a pan, and put it on the stove. That's about the extent of my culinary knowledge."

She felt a little bad about possibly stirring up bad memories for him again, so she tried to keep the moment light by saying, "At least you know the word *culinary*. That's more than some men."

He summoned up a smile. "I suppose so. Seriously, though, if I were you, I wouldn't change a thing in that cobbler. I think you've hit on a winner."

"I hope so." She paused. "Are you going to the peach festival?"

"Well, since I live in Weatherford now, I guess I will. Isn't there a city ordinance or something saying that you've got to go if you live here?"

She laughed. "No, but there might as well be. There's always a big crowd. Have you ever been?"

"Nope. This'll be a new one on me."

"You'll enjoy it. There's a lot to see and do."

She might have told him more about it—she was certainly enjoying sitting and talking to him—but at that moment she heard the front door open, followed by the sound of voices. Eve and Mattie had gotten back from the high school. Phyllis stood up quickly and draped the dish towel over the rest of the cobbler. Sam raised his eyebrows a little at her secretiveness.

He didn't understand, of course. Mattie would never betray her secrets deliberately, but with her mind the way it was, she might let something slip while Carolyn was around. And Eve was something of a wild card, liable to act on a whim. She was friends with both Phyllis and Carolyn, and had been for a long time. Phyllis would never dream of trying to play on that friendship in an attempt to discover Carolyn's plans, and she didn't think that Carolyn would do something like that, either . . . but it never hurt to be careful.

Eve called, "Phyllis, dear, where are you?" and Phyllis

knew right away from the tone of her voice that something was wrong.

"We're in the kitchen," she called back, not specifying that by "we" she meant her and Sam, not her and Carolyn.

Eve led Mattie into the room. Mattie's eyes were red-rimmed, as if she had been crying, but she seemed fairly composed now. Sam shot to his feet instantly and held his chair out, saying, "Why don't you sit down right here, Miz Harris? You look like you need to take a load off your feet."

Mattie sat down without saying anything. Phyllis turned to Eve and asked, "What's wrong?"

Eve looked a little distraught herself. "There was some bad news at the school," she said. "One of the students committed suicide."

Air hissed between Phyllis's teeth in a sharply indrawn breath. "Oh, that's terrible!" she said. "Who was it?"

"A boy named Billy Moser. He would have been a senior when school started again."

Phyllis cast her mind back, trying to remember if she had had a student by that name in any of her classes. After a moment, she shook her head. "I don't recall him."

"He didn't go to junior high here," Mattie said in a dull voice. "His family moved here when he was a freshman."

"I never taught him, either," Eve said. "But I just hate it when something like that happens, when a young person's life gets cut so short before they've even had a chance to . . . to actually live!"

Phyllis and Sam and Eve all sat down at the table, too, Eve next to Mattie and Phyllis and Sam on the opposite side. Sam opened his mouth to say something, then hesitated as if he didn't want to intrude on the thoughts of the others. After all, they were old friends, and he was the newcomer to this group. Sensing that, Phyllis said, "What is it, Sam?"

"I was just thinking about how, as teachers, we get to see too blasted much of things like that, what Eve said about these kids who never have a chance. They get killed in car wrecks, or they get some damn disease that ought to leave youngsters alone . . . or they get so hopeless they throw away the chances they do have."

All three of the women nodded, understanding exactly what he meant. It was a rare school year when *something* tragic didn't happen.

"And if it's so hard on us, when we're just their teachers, I can't imagine what it's like to be their parents," Phyllis said quietly.

"Billy was a pretty good boy," Mattie said. "I've been tutorin' him in English. He failed a couple of classes last year, and he won't graduate this year unless he makes 'em up." She sighed. "Wouldn't have graduated, I ought to say."

"Is that why . . ." Sam began. "Because of his grades, I mean."

Mattie shook her head. "I don't think so. Seemed to me like he was going to pass his summer school courses. But you don't ever know what's goin' on in these kids' heads."

Phyllis heard Carolyn's footsteps on the stairs, and then a moment later she came into the kitchen. Under the circumstances, Phyllis didn't even worry about Carolyn maybe sneaking a glance at what was under that dish towel.

"What are you all sitting around for?" Carolyn asked with a frown.

"We've heard some bad news, dear," Eve said. "Nothing directly related to any of us, but still . . ." She told Carolyn about Billy Moser's suicide.

"That's just awful," Carolyn said as she took the empty chair at the end of the table. "Does anyone know why he did it?"

Mattie shook her head. "We were just talkin' about that."

"How did he . . . I mean . . ."

Leave it to Carolyn to ask an insensitive question like that, Phyllis thought, then instantly scolded herself for being judgmental.

"He hung himself," Mattie said. "From a tree in his own backyard."

They sat there in silence then, and somehow, peach festivals and cooking contests seemed awfully small and unimportant.

Chapter 11

For several weeks beforehand, large banners stretched above the four main roads leading to Weatherford's courthouse square, proclaiming the impending arrival of the peach festival. The local paper was full of stories and announcements about it, and the radio stations played promos for it at regular intervals. Signs were posted in the town's businesses and on the marquee in front of the high school. It was pretty much impossible to even pass through Weatherford during June and the first half of July without being aware of the peach festival.

It loomed pretty large in Phyllis's mind, too, on the Friday evening before it was scheduled to begin, early the next morning.

Carolyn was gone to her daughter Sandra's house, where she would spend the night and cook whatever she was preparing for the contest. That was her habit. Phyllis supposed that she and Carolyn could have shared the same kitchen—after all, it was sort of late for any skullduggery; the weeks of experimentation and preparation were done, and each of them had settled on her recipe—but if that was the way Carolyn wanted to do things, it was fine with Phyllis. It certainly simplified matters.

Sam wandered into the kitchen while Phyllis was standing there gazing raptly at the ingredients spread out on the counter. He watched her for a moment and then said, "You

think if you stare at it hard enough, that cobbler'll make itself?"

"Hush," she said, having grown comfortable enough in
his presence to talk to him like that. "I'm just going over
everything to make sure I don't need to run to the grocery
store one last time."

"Oh. That makes sense. Got everything you need?"

She nodded slowly. "Yes, I think so."

"Well, if anything comes up, I'm pretty good at makin'
last-minute shopping runs . . . if somebody gives me a list,
that is."

Phyllis smiled. "I believe I've got it covered. But I appreciate the offer."

"Eve and Miz Harris sort of drafted me to help out with
those quilts that Miz Harris made. She's supposed to have
'em on display at one of the booths, and I got volunteered to
carry them down there and help set 'em up."

"I imagine that was Eve's doing," Phyllis said. "She was
going to help Mattie herself, but she's a firm believer in not
doing anything that she can charm some man into doing for
her."

"Why, Miz Newsom," Sam said with a grin, "if I didn't
know better, I'd say that was sort of a catty remark."

"Oh, no, Eve admits it. She's very open about how she
likes to have men wait on her."

"Yeah, come to think of it, she did say something about
strong backs and weak minds . . . I guess I qualify."

Phyllis couldn't help but laugh, and it felt good. After the
past two weeks, with all the bad news they had contained,
anything that brought a smile to her face was welcome.

"I don't think it's a matter of a weak mind," she said.
"More like a good heart."

Sam shrugged. "I try." He changed the subject by saying,
"So, what's the plan for tomorrow?"

"Well, the cooking contest judging isn't until two o'clock
in the afternoon, so I'll wait until in the morning to fix the

cobbler I'll be entering. I'll probably go downtown with Mattie and Eve for a while when the festival opens, then come back here and get everything ready."

"I hear there's music at these things."

"Oh, yes, it goes on all day, and then there's a street dance in the evening."

"You ever go to the dance?" Sam asked.

There was a look on his face that seemed vaguely familiar to Phyllis, and after a second she was able to place it. She had seen it on the faces of countless adolescent boys who had finally worked up the courage to dare all the unutterable terrors of the universe and ask some girl on a date.

She shook her head and said, "No, I don't dance. I'm a Baptist, after all."

"So am I, but I thought it was all right now for Baptists to do a little boot-scootin'."

"No, I don't think so." She was a little annoyed with him but tried not to show it. Why had he picked a time like this, when her mind was already packed with worry over the contest, to broach such a subject? I swear, she thought, if men didn't have bad timing, they wouldn't have any timing at all.

"Well, maybe I'll just listen to the music," he said. His face, rugged and grizzled with years, bore the same sort of crestfallen expression those adolescent boys exhibited when the objects of their desires explained that they were already dating high school boys—with cars. "I don't figure even W. A. Criswell could find anything wrong with that, if he was still around."

Phyllis threw him a bone by saying, "Yes, it might be nice to listen to some of the music." He brightened up at that. She added, "And I know Eve would be happy to dance with you."

"Yeah, I expect she would." He started drifting toward the doorway. "You let me know if there's anything I can do to help you."

"Don't worry, I will."

Sam nodded and left the kitchen. Phyllis turned back toward the counter and resumed her study of the ingredients. What had just happened here was at most a minor problem, and she soon put it out of her mind completely. There were much more important things to think about.

She had a contest to win.

The big day was here at last. Phyllis got up early, having slept surprisingly well the night before. She had expected to be nervous and restless, but instead she just felt confident. She didn't know if that was a good sign or not.

Since she was already up, she got started fixing breakfast for everyone, getting the coffee perking and the pancakes and bacon cooking. Mattie and Eve and Sam came into the kitchen one by one, drawn by the delicious aromas. Phyllis poured the coffee and served the food. The air had a festive atmosphere to it, like this was a holiday. In a way, it was. It was certainly one of the biggest days of the year in Weatherford and Parker County.

As one of the exhibitors, Mattie would be allowed into the fenced-off downtown square early, along with anyone who came to help her set up. After breakfast, Sam loaded the three big cardboard boxes containing the quilts Mattie had made into the back of his pickup. Mattie and Eve got into Phyllis's car, and she said to Sam, "Just follow me on downtown."

He nodded. "Will do."

Even though it was early, the parking spaces, along the streets that were still open, were already filling up as they approached the square. Later in the day, things would be so crowded that people would have to park in the lots at the junior college and take a shuttle bus downtown. Now, though, Phyllis was able to find a couple of places on a side street two blocks away. Sam pulled his pickup in behind her Lincoln.

"Will this be too far for you to carry those quilts?" she asked as they all got out.

"Nope," he said. "Strong back, remember?" Stacking the boxes on top of each other, he lifted them out of the pickup with a slight grunt of effort. "Somebody else may have to navigate, though, since I can hardly see over these boxes."

"I'll be glad to help you find your way, Sam," Eve said quickly. She stepped up beside him and took his arm. "Just come this way."

The sidewalks were already getting crowded, too. Phyllis went first, to clear a path, and Mattie brought up the rear. Portable fencing had been brought in and set up, and brightly painted ticket booths sat at all the entrances to the festival area. A man at one of the gates saw them coming and opened it for them, ushering them in. "Good mornin', good mornin', Miss Phyllis," he boomed heartily. "And Miss Eve, lookin' as pretty as ever. And Mattie, I swear, you're just as pert and spry as you were sixty years ago."

"Well, why wouldn't I be?" Mattie shot back crisply. "You're as old as I am, Donnie Boatwright, and you're here workin' this festival."

"Where else would I be?" Boatwright spread his arms to encompass all the growing hubbub around them. "I've been comin' to the peach festival my whole life!"

Donnie Boatwright was more than a local character in Weatherford. He was a local legend. As a businessman, he had made small fortunes in several different enterprises, as varied as a funeral home and a drive-in theater. As a politician, he had served lengthy terms on the city council and as the mayor. As a civic leader, he had been the president of the Lions Club and the Rotary and had held seats on various boards and commissions. He'd been on the school board and headed up the Chamber of Commerce. Now retired, he poured most of his considerable energy into the peach festival—and more importantly to Phyllis, Donnie

Boatwright was the head of the judging committee that would select the winner of the cooking contest.

Like Mattie, whom he had dated briefly many, many years earlier, Phyllis recalled, Donnie was a firm believer in keeping busy to ward off advancing age. He had to be well over eighty, but he was still a big, vital man with thinning, snow-white hair worn rather long and sweeping white mustaches that had been his trademark for years. He looked past Mattie at Sam and said, "I don't believe I know you, son."

"He's with me," Mattie said.

"I can see that. Those your quilts in those boxes, Mattie?"

"That's right."

Donnie leveled an arm. "The Quiltin' Society's booth is right over there."

As the four of them walked past, Sam nodded to Donnie and said, "I'm Sam Fletcher, sir. I'd shake hands, but mine are sort of full right now."

Donnie laughed. "Come on by and say hello later, Sam. I'm glad to meet you."

"Likewise, and I'll do that." Guided by Eve, Sam walked on across the square, past the towering limestone courthouse that was built in 1886, when Weatherford was still a wild frontier town.

They came to an area set up with folding chairs and large, easel-like frames over which the quilts would be draped for display. Some of the ladies from the Quilting Society sold their work at the festival, while others just put it up for people to look at and admire. Mattie fell into the latter category. Phyllis happened to know that most of the quilts Mattie made wound up being donated to local charities, which provided them to underprivileged families in the area. That was just one more way Mattie tried to serve the community where she had spent her entire life.

In what Phyllis regarded as an admirable display of patience and tolerance, Sam let Eve and Mattie boss him around as he unloaded the quilts and arranged them on the display stands to the women's satisfaction. When that was done, he tucked the boxes safely in a corner so that they could be used to carry the quilts back to Phyllis's house when the festival was over.

Mattie took a seat in one of the folding chairs. Big beach umbrellas had been set up over the chairs to provide some shade, an absolutely necessity on a sunny July day in Texas. Even under the umbrellas, it would be plenty hot before the day was over.

"I'll stay here with Mattie," Eve said. "I know you have to get back home and get started on your secret project, Phyllis."

With a nod, Phyllis said, "I'll see you later."

Sam started to leave, too, but Eve latched on to his arm again. "Why don't you stay a while and keep us company, Sam, dear? This is the best spot on the square. You can sit right here and see the whole panoply of humanity go past."

"If I didn't already know you were an English teacher, that vocabulary'd give it away," Sam said with a smile.

That brought a laugh from Eve. "Yes, I know all sorts of words. And all sorts of things."

Sam glanced at Phyllis and raised his eyebrows, but she just shook her head. He should have made his escape while he had the chance.

As for Phyllis, she had work to do. It was time to cook. Time to, as the kids said, take names and kick . . . well, she supposed she wasn't going to kick anything.

But there was a peach cobbler waiting to be baked, and a blue ribbon to be won.

Chapter 12

If Phyllis hadn't known someone who lived just a few blocks from the square, she would have had to park at the junior college and take the shuttle when she returned to the festival right after lunch. As it was, she was able to leave the Lincoln in her friend's driveway and walk the rest of the way downtown, carrying the dish that contained her cobbler. The dish was still warm, but not too hot to handle.

The preparation and cooking had gone off without a hitch. She had practiced so much, both in reality and going over everything in her mind, that by now she knew the recipe by heart, and her movements as she put the cobbler together were like the muscle memory of a highly trained athlete. Her confidence was still high, too. She had a good feeling about the way this day was going to turn out.

Several long tables were set up on the courthouse lawn, just east of the imposing edifice. Red-white-and-blue striped awnings on metal posts shaded them. Numbers were taped onto the front of the tables, marking off the spots for each contestant. Those numbers corresponded to the entry forms that had been turned in earlier to the contest coordinator, who was also the head judge, Donnie Boatwright.

In addition to the cobbler, Phyllis carried a cardboard stand-up with her name printed on it, and a stack of recipe sheets she had done on the computer. It wasn't a requirement of the contest that the entrants had to provide their recipes to the public, but most of them usually did, including Phyllis. She would set the sheets next to the cobbler, and anybody who wanted one could pick it up.

She didn't see Donnie as she approached the square, but the clip-on badge she wore identifying her as one of the participants in the contest got her past the man at the gate where she entered. She circled the courthouse to get to the area where the tables were set up.

Not surprisingly, the first person she saw there was Carolyn, who already had her entry sitting on the table in front of her. Phyllis tried not to stare as she walked past, but curiosity compelled her to check out what Carolyn had prepared for the contest. It was some sort of cheesecake/pie with a white cream covering the fruit layer, and a graham cracker crust. Carolyn had also put a few decorative slices of peaches on top. The cake/pie sat enticingly in a pie plate layered in another plate filled with crushed ice, and covered by a clear plastic cover that kept bugs off it but still let it be seen.

Carolyn had brought a sign, too, a fancier one than Phyllis's, with her name on it and the name of her creation: PEACHES-AND-CREAM CHEESECAKE. She didn't have a stack of recipe sheets, though, since she tended to be a little territorial about such things. Phyllis had to admit that the dessert *looked* awfully good.

"What have you got there?" Carolyn asked as Phyllis walked past.

Phyllis didn't hesitate in answering, since it was much too late for secrecy to make any difference now. "Peach cobbler," she said.

Carolyn smiled. "Peach cobbler," she repeated. "Well, it's hard to go wrong with the old standbys," she added in a condescending tone.

Phyllis smiled, too, and went on, "Spicy peach cobbler, with candied ginger."

That made Carolyn's superior expression waver a bit.

"Spicy peach cobbler with ginger," she repeated. "That sounds interesting."

"And delicious," Phyllis said.

"Well . . ." Carolyn sniffed a little. "That will be up to the judges, I suppose."

Phyllis didn't make any retort to that comment, but instead walked along the tables until she came to the spot assigned to her. She went behind the table and set her cobbler down. She had a clear lid on the dish, and while she had to admit that her entry wasn't as visually appealing as Carolyn's, the true test was in the taste. That was what would win or lose this contest.

The toe-tapping sound of bluegrass music came from the bandstand set up on the other side of the courthouse. The air was also filled with voices, as people thronged around the square. The festival spilled over into some of the side streets as well. There were face-painting booths and games for the kids; dozens of arts and crafts displays, including the one set up by Mattie and the other members of the Quilting Society; and an almost endless array of food vendors, many of them featuring peach ice cream and peach smoothies in addition to corn dogs, chili dogs, pretzels, barbecue sandwiches, popcorn, giant dill pickles, cotton candy, and funnel cakes. Several radio stations were doing remote broadcasts, and a TV satellite uplink truck was parked near the square, so that a features reporter could do a live report. The peach festival was a human interest extravaganza and had a little something for just about everybody.

Phyllis stood there and took it all in. Later, after the judging, she would wander around and get a better look at all the displays, as she usually did. For the moment, though, most of her attention was focused right here on these tables. Trying not to be too obvious about it, she stole glances at the other entries.

As usual, there were several peach pies, and she hoped none of the other cooks had hit upon the idea of adding ginger to their recipes. One contestant had an ice chest under the table, and the sign at her spot announced that her entry was a peach icebox pie. She would keep it on ice until the actual judging took place. There was also a peach pizza, and some other dishes that Phyllis couldn't identify. They didn't look any too appetizing, but it was hard to tell how something would taste just by looking at it.

She spotted Sam Fletcher making his way through the crowd, coming in her general direction. When he saw her, he grinned and raised a hand in greeting. It took him a few minutes after that before he finally reached the contest area.

He came to Carolyn first and said to her with a smile, "Afternoon, Miz Wilbarger. My, that is one fine-lookin' dessert."

Sam was a smart man, Phyllis thought. He knew how proud Carolyn was of her cooking. Most of his other overtures toward friendliness had been met with indifferent or even chilly receptions by Carolyn, but this time she returned his smile and said, "Thank you, Mr. Fletcher. Perhaps you'll come back by for a taste—after the judging, of course."

"Of course," Sam said with a nod. "I'm looking forward to it."

He moved on down the line of tables, stopping here and there to comment on one of the entries. When he reached Phyllis, she said, "Are you really going to eat some of Carolyn's cheesecake?"

He glanced around as if to see whether or not Carolyn was watching. She was engaged in conversation with some other festivalgoers, though. In a voice loud enough for Phyllis to hear but quiet enough to be lost quickly in the hubbub of the crowd, he said, "I don't know. It looks good, but to tell you the truth, Phyllis, I'm so blasted stuffed already I don't know if I'll be able to eat again for a week."

"I take it you've been sampling all the food around the square?"

Sam rubbed his stomach and groaned. "I never could

resist chili dogs and homemade ice cream. Not to mention cotton candy and pretzels and . . ." He stopped and shook his head. "Lord, it's making me more full just to talk about it."

Phyllis laughed. "I suppose you won't be wanting any of my peach cobbler, then."

"Oh, after that dish of it I had before, I want it. I just don't know if I can handle it. But we'll see. I have amazin' recuperative powers."

She just smiled and shook her head. After a moment, she asked, "How's Mattie? Have you seen her lately?"

"Yeah, she said she'd be over here to wish you luck before the judging starts. She seems to be having the time of her life showing everybody her quilts."

"I'm a little surprised you don't have Eve hanging on your arm," Phyllis said.

"I think she's workin' the crowd."

Phyllis raised her eyebrows. "Mr. Fletcher!"

Instantly, a flush spread over Sam's face. "I mean, she's fillin' up her dance card for the street dance tonight," he said hastily in his embarrassment. "I've already promised her a few dances myself."

"I'm sure you'll find it enjoyable. Eve's quite a dancer . . . despite being a Baptist."

They chatted for a few more minutes and then Sam moved on, saying that he wanted to see all there was to see at the peach festival. Phyllis glanced at her watch. It was a little less than half an hour until the judging was to begin.

She heard Donnie Boatwright's booming voice and looked around to see him working his way along the tables, speaking to all the contestants and looking at their entries. Visual presentation wasn't an official part of the contest, but a good-looking dish just somehow seemed to taste better, Phyllis knew. She thought her peach cobbler was quite attractive, for a cobbler.

"There's Donnie, the center of attention as usual."

The voice made Phyllis look around. She saw that Mattie

had come up and was standing there, hands on her hips, half glaring at Donnie Boatwright as he approached.

"I thought you and Donnie were old friends," Phyllis said.

"Oh, we are," Mattie said, "but that doesn't mean he's not loud and obnoxious sometimes."

"Well, I guess that's true of everyone."

Mattie snorted. "True of Donnie Boatwright, that's for sure."

Donnie carried a large bottle of water. All the judges did, because they took a drink or two between tasting each entry. Clearing the palate, Donnie called it, like he was at some fancy wine-tasting or something instead of a cooking contest. When he came to Phyllis's place, he set the bottle down on the table next to the cobbler and said, "What have we here?"

"Spicy peach cobbler," she said proudly. "With candied ginger." She patted the stack of printed recipes. "Here's how you make it."

"Oh, I don't need one of those," he said with a laugh. "I'm an expert at tastin' things, not cookin' 'em." He turned to Mattie. "I saw your quilts a while ago, Mattie. They're beautiful, as always."

"Thank you, Donnie," she said.

"But not as beautiful as you, of course."

Mattie crossed her arms and said, "You hush up your flattery, Donnie Boatwright. It doesn't mean a thing to me."

"Feisty as ever," he said with a chuckle. To Phyllis, he added, "I'll be back with the other judges later."

"You won't be disappointed," she promised.

Donnie moved on to chat with the other contestants, and several minutes later Phyllis noticed that he had gone off and forgotten his water bottle. She picked it up from the table and called his name. When he turned to look at her, she held up the bottle so he could see it.

Chuckling, he came over to retrieve it. "Thank you,

Phyllis," he said. "It's like the old saying: I'd forget my head if it wasn't fastened on."

A few more minutes passed, and Phyllis caught herself tapping her toe restlessly. Time was short now; soon the judging would begin. The confidence and anticipation she had felt earlier evaporated like spilled water in the hot Texas sun and was replaced by worry. She couldn't help but look at her common cobbler and compare it to Carolyn's beautiful peaches-and-cream cheesecake. Why hadn't she come up with something better? Carolyn was going to beat her again, and even though they were friends, that wouldn't stop Carolyn from gloating over her victory all year, until the next summer and the next peach festival rolled around again, and then it would happen all over again and Carolyn would win. . . .

Phyllis drew in a sharp breath and told herself to stop it. This was just a silly little cooking contest. It didn't matter a hill of beans who won it. Probably in a year's time no one would even remember who won this year.

No one except Carolyn. And Phyllis, who knew somehow that no matter what the outcome, she would never forget how this year's cooking contest at the Parker County Peach Festival ended.

Chapter 13

Mike and Sarah Newsom walked slowly around the square, Mike holding his son, Bobby's, right hand, Sarah holding Bobby's left. The little boy could walk with somebody holding his hand, but he was being stubborn about taking that first step on his own. Of course, in the middle of a crowd like this, Mike and Sarah didn't want him even trying. They held on tightly to him. Mike had been carrying Bobby earlier, but the boy had wanted down, and kicked his legs until Mike lowered him to the ground.

"I don't know where he gets that stubborn streak," Mike said.

Sarah laughed. "I do."

"Hey! What do you mean by that?" The grin on Mike's face showed that he didn't take any real offense at the comment.

"Let's get a smoothie at that booth over there," Sarah said, instead of answering the question.

"I think I'll get a frozen lemonade and share it with Bobby."

"He won't want it. It'll be too sour. But I can give him some of my smoothie."

"Okay." The crowd was getting thicker, so Mike leaned down and got hold of his son under the arms. "C'mon, hoss," he said as he picked up the boy. "Don't want you getting trampled in this sea of humanity."

Bobby didn't fuss this time about being carried. He had walked enough, so that he was probably tired.

Mike and Sarah bought a frozen lemonade and a peach smoothie and went in search of a relatively quiet place to enjoy them. That wasn't going to be too easy to find in Weatherford's town square on this particular day. Sarah suggested, "Let's go around on the other side of the courthouse where they're having the cooking contest. It'll probably be a little more peaceful over there."

"Good idea," Mike agreed. "We can give my mom some moral support, too. The judging ought to be starting soon."

"You think she'll win this year?" Sarah asked.

"I hope so. I think the contest means more to her than she'll admit, especially since it seems like Miz Wilbarger nearly always wins."

As they made their way across the courthouse lawn and around the big limestone building, Mike spotted Darryl Bishop and his son, Justin, getting some popcorn at one of the booths. Justin looked like he was enjoying himself, but Darryl wore his usual hangdog expression. He just had the look of somebody who had been beaten down by life until he didn't want to fight it anymore.

Over the past couple of weeks, Mike's investigation of Newt Bishop's death hadn't turned up any new information that amounted to anything. He had talked to quite a few people who had known both Newt and Darryl, and while the consensus was that father and son had never been close, nobody knew of anything that might have driven Darryl to murder, either. Of course, Mike had been careful not to come right out and tell people that Darryl was a suspect, but some of the folks he had questioned had probably gotten that idea, anyway.

Nor had he found any fingers of guilt pointing toward Alfred Landers. As had been the case with Newt Bishop, the real estate man wasn't particularly well liked, but lots of people were acquainted with him, and none of them had anything really bad to say about him. Mike had checked all the records and found that Landers had never been in trouble with the law. Not only that, but he didn't have a history of suing people, or being sued. The legal tussle with Newt Bishop was the only litigation in which Landers had been involved. He was hardly your typical murderer.

But there was really no such thing as a typical murderer, Mike reminded himself. Anybody, no matter how spotless his background or sterling his reputation, could snap and lash out under the right circumstances. Anybody could have gotten angry enough to knock that jack out from under the bumper of Newt's Cadillac. It was just that most folks, when they saw what they had done, would have been horrified and tried to help the man pinned under the car.

To do such a thing and then walk away from it . . . that required cold blood, rather than hot.

Mike pushed those thoughts out of his mind. He was at a festival where hundreds of people were having a great time, he had his son in his arms and his pretty wife at his side, and this just wasn't the time or the place for dwelling on morbid things like murder. He had come to the peach festival to have fun. It was just pure chance that he had seen Darryl and Justin and started thinking about the Bishop case.

They walked behind the tables where the cooking contest entries were set up. Phyllis saw them coming and smiled. "Let me see that grandbaby," she said eagerly as she held out her hands. Mike gave Bobby to her and she snuggled the boy against her. "Hello, Bobby. Can you say *Grandma*? *Grandma*?"

Bobby just gurgled.

"He's not saying much of anything yet," Mike said. "And he still hasn't taken that first step on his own, either."

"It'll come, don't you worry," Phyllis said.

Sarah asked, "Wasn't the contest supposed to start before now?"

A worried expression appeared on Phyllis's face. "Ten

minutes ago, in fact," she said. "I don't know what the
holdup is, but I wish they'd go ahead and get on with it. I
don't like this waiting. It's too hard on my nerves."

"There's nothing to be worried about, Mom," Mike told
her. "You're a lock to win this year."

"I wish I felt as sure of that as you do." Phyllis looked
along the row of tables and stiffened. "Here they come now.
The judges, I mean."

"I'll take Bobby," Sarah said. She lifted him out of Phyllis's arms.

Mike leaned over and kissed his mother on the cheek.
"Good luck, Mom."

"I'll need it," he heard her mutter.

There were four judges: Donnie Boatwright, of course;
Marcia Hannigan, a home economics teacher at the high
school; Bud Winfield, the publisher of the local newspaper;
and Harley Sewell, a disc jockey from one of the radio stations, who had been playing oldies since those particular
records were brand-new. Phyllis knew all the judges, although
none of them that well, and she watched as they moved along
the line of tables, stopping to eat a small sample of each contestant's entry. They made notes, conferred with each other,
drank some water, and went on to the next contestant.

Phyllis knew from experience that once they had tasted
all of the entries, they might go ahead and declare a winner
then and there, or they might go back and taste a few of the
dishes a second time if they were having trouble reaching a
decision. She hoped they wouldn't draw out the torture for
too long.

Her heart sank a little when the judges lingered over Carolyn's peaches-and-cream cheesecake. Bud Winfield even
exclaimed how good it was, and the others nodded. The
smile on Carolyn's face was huge. She glanced along the tables toward Phyllis, and Phyllis thought she saw the gleam
of triumph in Carolyn's eyes.

It's not over yet, Phyllis told herself grimly. There was still her peach cobbler to be eaten, along with peach strudel, peach preserves, peach fritters, peach salsa, and all the other entries that hadn't been sampled so far.

Donnie Boatwright took a big swallow of water from his bottle and moved on, the other judges following him. He paused to pull a handkerchief from his pocket and mop sweat off his high forehead. He downed another long drink of water.

"Well, well, what have we here?" he said as he paused in front of the next contestant. His voice was as loud and hearty as ever, but Phyllis thought she heard a slight note of strain in it. Maybe the heat was getting to Donnie, or his stomach wasn't reacting well to all the different peach dishes he was eating. She hoped he wouldn't get sick before he had finished judging the contest.

At last Donnie and the other judges arrived at Phyllis's spot. Donnie smiled at her and said, "Now we get to try this nice-lookin' peach cobbler. Spicy peach cobbler, isn't that right, Phyllis?"

"That's right," she said as she dipped small servings of the cobbler into bowls that she had ready. She added a plastic spoon to each one and handed them to the judges. "Spicy peach cobbler with candied ginger."

"That sounds good," Marcia Hannigan said. "I'm eager to try it."

"Well, let's dig in, folks," Donnie said. He began spooning the sample into his mouth.

Phyllis waited anxiously. She glanced around and saw that Carolyn was watching the judges' reactions. To Phyllis's surprise, Carolyn looked nervous, too. Maybe she wasn't as confident of victory as she sometimes acted.

Sam had joined the crowd looking on, too, along with Eve and Mattie, and Mike and Sarah and Bobby were still there. She certainly didn't lack for people rooting for her, she thought. She just hoped that she wouldn't let them down.

Donnie finished his cobbler and set the empty bowl on the table. "Mighty good, Phyllis, mighty good," he said, but then he gave a little shake of his head and put a hand on the table to steady himself.

"Donnie, are you all right?" Phyllis asked.

"Yeah, yeah, just a little dizzy. Must be the heat." He lifted his water bottle and drained the rest of the liquid in it. "I'll be all right in a—" he began.

But then he stopped abruptly, and his eyes rolled up in their sockets. The water bottle slipped from his fingers, hit the table, and bounced off to fall on the ground. He lurched back a step.

"Donnie!" Harley Sewell shouted. "What's wrong?" Marcia Hannigan let out a choked cry, and Bud Winfield lunged toward Donnie, reaching out in an attempt to grab his arm and steady him.

Bud missed because Donnie staggered into a half turn, stiffened, and then pitched forward onto his face, toppling like a felled tree. He hit the ground hard, without any attempt to catch himself. Startled yells came from the men in the crowd, and one woman even screamed.

Phyllis just stood there behind the table, shocked into motionlessness by Donnie's sudden collapse, but Mike's emergency training took over and sent him hurrying to Donnie's side. He rolled the old man onto his back, and Phyllis recoiled in horror as she saw Donnie's glassy eyes staring sightlessly up at the red, white, and blue canopy over the table.

Donnie was dead. Phyllis knew that as surely as she had known it about Newt Bishop on that other terrible day.

And to make things even worse, in the middle of all the sudden commotion and chaos, she heard Carolyn exclaim as plain as day, "Oh, my God! Phyllis's peach cobbler killed Donnie Boatwright!"

Chapter 14

Phyllis was so stunned that all she could do was stare at Donnie's drawn, lifeless face and wonder if somehow her cobbler *had* killed him. But then she realized that wasn't possible. The other judges had eaten it, too, and they were standing there just fine, other than being as surprised and upset as everyone else.

Police and emergency personnel were on duty at the festival, of course, and the uproar caused by Donnie's collapse quickly caught their attention. Mike had been kneeling at Donnie's side, checking futilely for a pulse, but he stood up and stepped back as a couple of EMTs from the Weatherford Fire Department came running up. Even in her rattled state, Phyllis recognized them as Calvin Holloway and Ted Brady, two former students of hers and friends of Mike's.

Calvin was six-foot-six and almost three hundred pounds and had been all-state on both the offensive and defensive lines for the Weatherford High School Kangaroos before going on to Grambling State University over in Louisiana. He had played a year for the Cowboys as an undrafted free agent before coming home to Weatherford and becoming an EMT.

Ted was about half the size of his partner, with red hair and a multitude of freckles, a terrier to Calvin's Great Dane, as Phyllis often thought of them. Or Mutt and Jeff, although come to think of it she hadn't seen a Mutt and Jeff comic strip for thirty years or more, and didn't think the newspapers even published it anymore.

"What happened?" Calvin asked Mike as Ted dropped to a knee beside Donnie and started checking his vitals, even though it was obvious the man was dead.

"Mr. Boatwright just collapsed," Mike replied. "I didn't find a pulse. I guess it was probably a heart attack or a stroke, something like that."

He glanced at Phyllis, and she knew suddenly that he had heard Carolyn's ridiculous accusation, too. But he had to realize how crazy the idea was. A bowl of peach cobbler couldn't kill anybody.

Could it?

"Was he showing any signs of distress before he collapsed?" Calvin asked.

Mike shook his head. "Not that I noticed."

Phyllis felt like she had to speak up. "He was sweating," she said. "And he said he felt dizzy."

"It's hot out here," Mike pointed out. "Everybody's sweating."

Determinedly, Phyllis said, "Yes, but it seemed a little worse with Donnie. And he was drinking a lot from his water bottle, like he was dehydrated."

Calvin frowned. "Heatstroke, maybe."

From his kneeling position beside the body, Ted said, "Heatstroke victims are usually flushed. Look at his face, Calvin. It's got a bluish tinge, not red."

"Blue?" Calvin repeated as he knelt at Donnie's side, too. "That's usually an indication of . . ."

He didn't go on, and Phyllis said, "An indication of what, Calvin?"

The big EMT didn't answer. He just looked up and said, "Mike, can you get some other cops and move all the people back? We're gonna have to get an ambulance up here."

"Sure." Several officers from the Weatherford Police Department were on the scene by now, and Mike relayed

Calvin's request to them. The officers spread out and began urging the crowd to step back and give the emergency personnel some room.

"What about the contest?" Carolyn asked. "The judges hadn't announced a winner yet. They hadn't even tasted all the entries yet."

Harley Sewell said, "It looks like there won't be a winner this year, Miz Wilbarger. I don't see how we can go on without Donnie."

Carolyn looked like she wanted to argue, but then she clamped her lips tightly shut. Clearly she didn't like the decision, but it would have looked awfully insensitive if she insisted that the contest go on even though one of the judges had just dropped dead.

The terrible thing, Phyllis thought, was that *she* almost felt the same way. Of course she was sorry about what had happened to Donnie, whether it turned out to be a stroke or a heart attack or some other medical problem, but after all the weeks of preparation, it was a terrible letdown to know that there wouldn't be a winner this year. She understood why the other judges didn't want to continue, though.

For one thing, they might be afraid that whatever had happened to Donnie would happen to them, too. They didn't want to be taken down by a killer cobbler. Phyllis noticed that none of them had finished the samples in their bowls, but had instead placed them back on the table and unobtrusively pushed them away.

Sam, Eve, and Mattie made their way to Phyllis's side, although they had to go around quite a distance because of the large area directly in front of the tables that had been cleared by the police. When they reached Phyllis, Eve clutched her hand and said, "This is just terrible, dear."

"My cobbler didn't do it," Phyllis said.

Eve stared at her. "What?"

"I said, my cobbler didn't kill Donnie." Phyllis's jaw tightened. "No matter what Carolyn says!"

Sam said diplomatically, "Well, I don't guess she meant it *quite* that way—"

"You all heard her," Phyllis cut in. "She accused me of killing Donnie Boatwright with my cobbler!" Phyllis knew her voice had risen a little, but she couldn't seem to do anything to stop it.

Sarah was still standing there holding Bobby. She said quickly, "Nobody thinks that, Phyllis. We all saw it with our own eyes. It was just a coincidence that—"

"That Donnie fell over dead just as he finished eating Phyllis's contest entry?" Carolyn asked as she came up.

Phyllis's eyes narrowed and she traded glares with Carolyn. She couldn't believe what she was hearing. Sure, there was a rivalry between them over the cooking contest. An intense rivalry, a person could call it. Maybe even, on occasion, a bitter rivalry. But the two of them were friends for the rest of the year, and had been for a long time. For goodness sake, Phyllis thought, Carolyn even lives in my house! Why was she trying to hurt her and ruin her reputation by saying those terrible things about her cooking killing somebody?

"Dear, perhaps you'd better not say anything else," Eve told Carolyn.

"I'm just saying what we all saw with our own eyes," Carolyn said stubbornly. "Donnie ate Phyllis's cobbler, and he dropped dead!"

Mike stepped up and in an unusually formal tone said, "That's enough, Mrs. Wilbarger. Everyone's upset already, and there's no point in making things worse."

Carolyn leveled a cold stare at him. "Are you speaking as a sheriff's deputy, Mike . . . or as Phyllis's son?"

"Take it whichever way you want, ma'am."

Phyllis admired Mike for sticking up for her, but she didn't want him to be rude and disrespectful to Carolyn—no matter how obnoxious Carolyn was being.

The loud wail of a siren made all of them turn to look as an ambulance with its lights flashing circled the courthouse, bumped up over the curb, and came across the lawn toward the tables. When it came to a stop, more paramedics hopped out, and they all gathered around Donnie's body, lifting it onto a stretcher and then placing it in the back of the ambulance. Calvin shut the doors and shook his head solemnly.

He motioned for Mike to come over and join him and Ted. The three of them huddled together, and after a minute they were joined by Weatherford Chief of Police Ralph Whitmire, who had just reached the scene. Since Donnie's death had taken place within the city limits—about as much in the city limits as you could get, Phyllis thought, since they were in the middle of the downtown square—Chief Whitmire would be in charge of whatever investigation was carried out. Phyllis assumed there would be an autopsy, since Donnie's death had been not only sudden but also unexplained, but she was sure that would uncover the reason for his unexpected collapse. He had been over eighty years old, after all. Such things happened, sad though they were.

The ambulance pulled away and with its siren still howling, headed down South Main Street toward the hospital. There was no real hurry, of course, since it was much too late to do anything for Donnie, but Phyllis supposed the driver was anxious to get there, anyway.

She realized that the other three judges had wandered off somewhere. They had probably left deliberately so that nobody could pressure them to continue with the contest. She sighed and said, "I guess everybody might as well pack up their contest entries and go home." She reached for the glass lid, intending to put it back on the dish that contained the rest of the cobbler.

Mike saw what she was doing and stepped quickly away from Calvin, Ted, and Chief Whitmire. "Wait a minute, Mom," he said. "You can't do that."

Phyllis frowned. "Well, why in the world not? I don't want to leave the rest of this cobbler sitting around uncovered."

"You can't disturb any of that stuff." He raised his voice

and called to the people behind the tables, "Everyone just leave your contest entries right where they are, please."

Sam motioned toward the half-eaten samples that the judges had set on the table. "What about those?" he asked. "I was just about to gather them up and put them in one of the garbage cans."

Mike shook his head. "You can't do that, either. Everything has to stay just like it is."

Sam's eyes narrowed, and he studied Mike suspiciously for a few seconds before he said, "You know, Mike, it sounds to me a whole lot like you're treating this as a crime scene."

"A crime scene!" Eve said. "But that's ridiculous."

Phyllis thought so, too, but she knew Sam was right. Mike didn't want them touching the food because it might be evidence, and you couldn't have evidence without a crime. Well, you could, but that certainly wasn't the way Mike was acting. For that matter, Calvin and Ted and Chief Whitmire were awfully grim-faced, too, as they came over to the table.

The chief nodded to her and touched the brim of his hat politely, then said, "This cobbler right here was what Mr. Boatwright was eating before he collapsed?"

"He had finished his sample," Phyllis said. She pointed to the table. "There's the empty bowl right there."

"Yes, ma'am. You'll have to leave everything here until we've finished our investigation."

Phyllis felt a little dizzy herself, but not for the same reason Donnie had. She just couldn't believe what she was hearing. If she didn't know any better, she'd think that the police chief was taking Carolyn's crazy comments seriously.

Forcing herself to remain calm, Phyllis said, "Why are you doing this, Chief? Donnie Boatwright was an old man. I know you have to find out what caused his death, but surely you can't suspect any sort of . . . of foul play!" She hated the way that sounded, like she was on one of those police TV shows.

Chief Whitmire just looked across the table at her and said, "I'm sorry, Mrs. Newsom, but from what Holloway and Brady tell me, there's a good chance Mr. Boatwright was poisoned."

And that, Phyllis thought as she struggled to calm her clamoring mind, would make it murder.

Chapter 15

An uneasy silence hung over the living room of Phyllis's house later that afternoon as the four women—and Sam—sat there. Mike had promised to drop by as soon as he could, to let them know how the investigation into Donnie Boatwright's death was going, but they had no way of knowing when he would get there.

Down on the square, the peach festival continued. One tragic death, even that of someone as well-known as Donnie, wasn't enough to make the festivities come to more than a temporary halt. Once the ambulance was gone, everybody had returned to what they were doing before the commotion broke out. The only indications that something had happened were the yellow police department tape strung around the site of the cooking contest and the presence of an unusual number of officers in that area.

Finally unable to stand the awkward silence any longer, Phyllis declared to the room at large, "I didn't poison him, you know."

"Of course you didn't, dear," Eve said quickly.

"I'm not a murderer." Phyllis leveled a glare in Carolyn's direction.

Carolyn glared right back. "I never *said* you were a murderer. I never even thought that. It must have been an accident. You put something in your cobbler you shouldn't have—"

"There was nothing in that cobbler that could kill anybody!" Phyllis insisted.

Mattie spoke up, saying, "All this fussin'. It just doesn't make sense. Donnie was an old man. His heart gave out, more than likely. No sense in fussin' over it."

"That makes the most sense to me, too," Sam put in. "You'll see. When Mike gets here, he'll tell us they've decided that Mr. Boatwright died of a heart attack or something like that."

Carolyn gave a dubious snort.

Phyllis tried to ignore her. "I don't know. Donnie was acting awfully strange just before he keeled over. And not once did he grab his chest or anything like that. Isn't that what you do when you have a heart attack?"

"That's what people do on TV," Sam said. "It might not always be like that in real life."

"There's not really any point in speculating," Eve put in. "We'll just have to wait and see what the police and the doctors find out."

Phyllis knew Eve was right, but waiting was hard. Especially when, no matter how much she denied it, deep down a part of her worried that she *had* somehow caused Donnie's death. As she sat there, she went over in her mind again and again the steps she had taken and the ingredients she had used in preparing the cobbler that morning. . . .

There was nothing, she finally decided, nothing in it that could have hurt anybody. The other judges had eaten it, too, and they hadn't died. At least, they hadn't gotten sick there at the festival, and she hadn't heard anything about any of them falling ill later.

A heart attack, a stroke, things like that were the only possibilities that made any sense, no matter what color Donnie's face had been.

The sound of a car door slamming outside made everyone look up. Phyllis got to her feet and went to the front door, opening it to look out. It was late afternoon by now—

evening, really—and shadows had started to gather under the big trees in the front yard. There was still plenty of light, though, to reveal the worried expression on Mike's face as he came up the concrete walk toward the house.

Phyllis pushed the screen door open as Mike climbed the steps to the porch. "Come in," she said. "Can I get you something?"

"No thanks, Mom," he said as he stepped into the living room. "Sarah will have supper waiting for me by the time I get home. I just wanted to stop by, like I told you I would, and let you know what we found out."

"Sit down." Phyllis realized just how nervous she really was as she steered Mike toward one of the sofas and then perched on the front of the cushion next to him. Everyone else in the room leaned forward, anxious to hear what he had to say. Phyllis couldn't stop herself from asking, "Was it a heart attack?"

Mike shook his head. "No, the autopsy ruled out a coronary. Dr. Lee said Mr. Boatwright's heart was in good shape for a man his age. It wasn't a stroke, either."

"Then what was it?" Carolyn demanded.

Mike sighed and said, "Poison, just like we thought. Cyanide, to be precise. That blue tinge to his face was a strong indicator of cyanotic poisoning, and that turned out to be right."

Phyllis closed her eyes for a second and felt dizzy again. But when she opened them, she took a deep breath and forced herself to remain calm. "There's no way I put any cyanide in that cobbler," she said. "I know *every ingredient* that went in it, and cyanide just wasn't one of them!"

Mike let himself smile a little. "No, the poison wasn't in your cobbler, Mom," he told her. "You can stop worrying about that. We gathered up all the contest entries and tested them, and there was no cyanide or anything else bad in any of them."

Phyllis turned her head to look at Carolyn, as if to say *See?*

Carolyn got the message, because she said indignantly, "Well, what did you expect me to think? The way Donnie fell over as soon as he finished that cobbler of yours, any reasonable person might think that it killed him."

"I didn't," Sam said, and Phyllis could have kissed him for it. "The thought never crossed my mind."

Eve added, "I never believed it, either." Mattie just shook her head solemnly.

"I see," Carolyn said. "You're all ganging up on me, are you?" She got to her feet. "Well, I don't have to sit here and take it." She started to march toward the stairs.

Phyllis wanted to stop her. She felt a little vindicated, of course, but she didn't want it to ruin her friendship with Carolyn. Even though she was still a little mad at her for saying those things, she had seen the hurt in Carolyn's eyes and knew that to her, at least, it did seem like they were all turning on her.

But before Phyllis could say anything, Mike spoke up again. "Uh, Miz Wilbarger, if you could sit back down, please? I still need to talk to all of you."

Carolyn paused at the bottom of the stairs and asked, "What about?"

"About Mr. Boatwright's death. It's going to be officially declared a murder, and everybody who was there has to be questioned."

"Everybody at the peach festival?" Phyllis said. "That's going to be an awfully big job!"

"No, not everybody who was at the festival. Just the folks who talked to Mr. Boatwright or were around him when he died." With a rueful expression on his face, Mike shrugged. "And yeah, even that is going to be a big job. But I told Chief Whitmire I'd take statements from the five of you. The Weatherford police and the sheriff's department will be working together pretty closely on this."

Reluctantly, Carolyn went back to her chair and sat down. "I don't see why you need to question *me,*" she said. "I can't tell you anything that will help. Donnie was past my place in the contest before he collapsed."

Sam leaned forward and clasped his big hands together between his knees. "Let me ask you a question, Mike, if that's allowed."

"Sure, Mr. Fletcher, go ahead."

"You said the poison wasn't in any of the contest entries. If that's true, how did it get into Donnie Boatwright?"

Phyllis's eyes widened as a thought occurred to her. "His water bottle!" she exclaimed.

Mike turned his head to look at her and nodded. "That's exactly right. We found amygdalin in the little bit of water that was left in the bottle."

"I thought you said he was poisoned with cyanide," Eve said.

Mike nodded again. "It was hydrogen cyanide that killed him, all right, but that was because he had ingested a lot of amygdalin. That converts to hydrogen cyanide in the human digestive system." With a humorless chuckle, he spread his hands and continued, "I'm no chemist or forensic scientist, you understand. I'm just repeating what Dr. Lee told us."

Phyllis knew that Dr. Walt Lee was the county coroner, as well as being in private practice. He was Phyllis's doctor, in fact, as well as Mattie's and Eve's. She had faith in whatever conclusions he drew.

Sam asked, "Where'd this amygdalin stuff come from?"

"Well, that's sort of interesting," Mike said. "It's a chemical that's used to make the cancer treatment drug called laetrile. It's found in various nuts and in the pits of certain fruits. The apricot pit has the most amygdalin in it . . . but the peach pit comes next, right after it."

"Peach pits!" Carolyn said. "Good Lord, at this time of year there are peaches everywhere you look around here. How can they be poisonous?"

"The peaches themselves aren't. Just the pits. And even they won't hurt you unless you eat a bunch of them, like fifty or sixty, Dr. Lee said."

Phyllis shook her head in confusion. "This doesn't make sense. Donnie didn't eat peach pits. Even if there were a little of this chemical in the fruit, how many peaches would a person have to eat to get sick from them?"

"More than anybody reasonably could," Mike assured her. "The doctor wasn't sure how it was done, but he thinks somebody managed to extract the amygdalin from a bunch of peach pits and then somehow doped Mr. Boatwright's water with it. Everybody knows he carries around a big bottle of water all day at the peach festival, and he's always drinking from it." Mike corrected himself, "He *did,* anyway."

Sam said, "This stuff doesn't have any taste or smell to it?"

"Odorless, tasteless, and colorless, the doc said," Mike confirmed. "The cyanide that it converts to smells like bitter almonds, but the original form doesn't have that smell."

"I've heard of laetrile, of course," Phyllis said. "For a while there, a lot of people were using it as a cancer treatment."

Mike said, "Yeah, the government never approved it, though, and by now there's been enough research to show that it's really not effective. The theory was that the small amounts of cyanide created by it in the human system would attack just the cancer cells and kill them off." He shrugged. "It didn't really work out that way, and not nearly as many people use it now. But some people with cancer still believe it works, and you can get it in Mexico."

"There's no chance Boatwright was taking the drug and maybe got an accidental overdose?" Sam asked.

"No. He didn't have cancer, and that's the only reason anybody would use laetrile. Besides, patients who are taking it are warned not to eat peaches or apricots or anything like that, just on the off chance they'd get too much of the stuff in their systems that way."

It was quiet again for a moment as they all thought about

what Mike had told them, and then Phyllis said, "You wanted to ask us some questions?"

"Yeah. Did any of you see anybody messing with Mr. Boatwright's water bottle during the festival?"

Silence reigned again as they pondered the question. Finally, Carolyn said, "I didn't see anything like that."

"Neither did I," Phyllis said. "But Donnie carried that water bottle around all the time and sometimes set it down while he was talking to people. I even picked it up and handed it back to him when he was about to walk off without it." Her eyes widened suddenly as a thought occurred to her. "That means my fingerprints are on it!"

"We'll check on that," Mike said, "but there are probably a lot of fingerprints on it, mostly Mr. Boatwright's. I don't know if any of the others will be usable."

"Someone must have been able to get hold of it, just for a minute or two, and dumped that chemical into it," said Phyllis. Then they could just put it back and Donnie would never know the difference."

Mike nodded. "That's what we think happened, all right. And it must have been not long before the cooking contest started, because he was drinking a lot from it then. If somebody had doped the water earlier in the day, Mr. Boatwright would have collapsed before it was time for the contest." He looked around the room. "What about the rest of you? Did you see anything suspicious?"

Sam said, "I never even met the fella until yesterday morning. If I saw him during the day, I didn't really pay any attention to what he was doing or what was going on around him."

"I didn't talk to him," Mattie said. "I was sitting there at the Quiltin' Society show."

"I saw Donnie several times during the day," Eve said. "I even got him to promise me a dance later on." She shook her head. "But I didn't notice anything odd, and now I won't get that dance, or any of the others I was promised. After what happened, I just don't feel like it." She sighed.

After a moment, Mike asked, "Do you know of anybody who had a grudge against Mr. Boatwright? Somebody who might have wanted him dead?"

"Donnie Boatwright was an institution in Weatherford," Phyllis pointed out. "Everybody knew him. We certainly all did."

"Just because everybody knew him doesn't mean everybody *liked* him," Mike said.

Sam grunted. "Somebody sure didn't. Unless . . . Is there any way this could have been an accident, Mike?"

"No, sir," Mike replied with a shake of his head. "It was deliberate."

With a frown, Phyllis asked, "What if somebody just wanted to make him sick? Maybe whoever put that stuff in his water didn't actually mean to kill him."

"I don't understand, Mom. Why would anybody do that?"

"Well, I don't know. I was just trying to think of some other explanation for what happened. But if Donnie had gotten sick just then, instead of dying, it would have interfered with the judging. And it certainly would have looked bad for whoever's entry he had just sampled, which turned out to be mine . . ."

As her voice trailed off, Phyllis turned her head to look at Carolyn.

"My God!" Carolyn burst out. "Now you're accusing *me* of murder?"

"Not murder," Phyllis said. "But if you wanted to ruin my chance to win the contest, having one of the judges get sick right after he ate my cobbler would do it."

Carolyn came to her feet. "This is outrageous! How dare you accuse me—"

Eve broke in, "The first thing you said after Donnie collapsed, dear, was that Phyllis's cobbler had killed him. That's an even worse accusation."

Phyllis shook her head, stricken by Carolyn's expression

and wishing now that she hadn't brought up the subject. "I'm sorry, Carolyn. Please forgive me, and forget I said anything. I was just thinking out loud. I didn't really mean to accuse you."

"Well, that's certainly what it sounded like!"

Mike looked at Carolyn and said carefully, "Miz Wilbarger, if something like that *did* happen, everybody would know that it was purely an accident—"

"I didn't do it, I tell you!"

"No, she didn't, Mike," Phyllis declared without hesitation. "That would have required Carolyn to consider the possibility she might lose to me, and I don't believe that thought ever entered her mind."

"Of course it didn't!" Carolyn said.

Mike held up his hands to bring the discussion back under control. "For what it's worth, Miz Wilbarger, I don't believe you'd do such a thing, either. But my job is to consider all the possibilities."

Carolyn sniffed and still looked offended, but she settled back into her chair.

"I think we've hashed this out enough for now," Mike went on. "If any of you think of anything you saw or heard, anything at all that's the least bit suspicious, or even puzzling, please let me know." He put his hands on his knees and pushed himself to his feet. "I'd better be going."

Phyllis got up and went with him to the door. She stepped out onto the porch with him and said quietly, "Carolyn really couldn't have done it, you know. I don't know what made me say that."

"Like you said, you were just thinking out loud, Mom." He put a hand on her shoulder. "Are you going to be all right? I know it was a mighty bad day for you."

"I'll be fine," Phyllis said. "But you're right . . . it should have been a wonderful day, but it didn't turn out that way at all."

Especially for Donnie Boatwright, she thought.

Chapter 16

The atmosphere in the house was very strained for the next couple of days. Carolyn had been hurt by the accusations leveled at her, but so had Phyllis. They sort of tiptoed around each other, not talking much, and when they did speak, it was in carefully polite, neutral tones. Phyllis was glad Carolyn hadn't gotten so mad that she wanted to move out. Phyllis didn't want to lose her as a boarder—or a friend.

Time would heal the rift; Phyllis was confident of that. But it might help, she thought, if the police caught Donnie Boatwright's murderer. It would be easier for both her and Carolyn to put their hurt feelings behind them, once they were in the clear.

Donnie's funeral was held at the Methodist church. The services for Newt Bishop had been well attended, but this funeral was in a whole other category. The big sanctuary in the church was packed, and several hundred people crowded into the fellowship hall next door, to listen to the service as it was piped in on the church's public address system. Representatives from the news media in Fort Worth and Dallas were there, too. Since Donnie's death had officially been ruled a homicide, while Newt's still could have been an accident, that provoked more interest, too. Donnie's decades-long career as a local politician, businessman, and celebrity made the story that much more intriguing.

Phyllis was well aware of all that, but it still seemed like a circus to her, and that made her uncomfortable. A person's final farewell shouldn't be a mob scene.

But she felt like she ought to attend, even though she just added to the mob. She, Carolyn, Mattie, Eve, and Sam filed in and found seats in the church early, before the auditorium completely filled up. A short time later, Carolyn's daughter, Sandra Webster, and her husband, Jerry, came in and sat down beside Carolyn, filling up the pew. Sandra had worked for Donnie Boatwright at one time, Phyllis recalled. That was probably why she was here.

Donnie had a younger brother and sister, Charles Boatwright and Sally Boatwright Hughes. Both were in their seventies. Donnie himself had been a bachelor his whole life. This day and age, that sometimes prompted whispered speculation about a man's sexuality, Phyllis knew, but not among her generation. They had known perfectly well that a man could fail to marry and still not be, well, like that. Anyway, Donnie had been quite a dashing figure in his time, and had always had plenty of lady friends. Mattie had been among them in her younger days, in fact. Phyllis recalled Mattie talking about how Donnie had taken her dancing once at the Casino Ballroom over in Lake Worth.

Phyllis bowed her head as the minister offered up a prayer to get the service underway. This was the second funeral she had attended this summer, she thought briefly, and she hoped it would be the last.

The Methodist minister was more long-winded than the Baptist preacher who had done Newt Bishop's funeral, and the service began to grate on Phyllis before it was over. She sat there with her face solemn and composed, however, not letting her impatience show. Finally, the minister wrapped things up, and Phyllis joined the hundreds of others in attendance in filing past the casket. Whoever had prepared the body had taken great care to get Donnie's sweeping mustaches just right. They bristled as if Donnie were still alive. Phyllis was surprised that the sight of that affected her more than the music or the minister's words, causing a pang of regret and the awareness of her own mortality to go through her. Donnie Boatwright hadn't been her friend, but she had known him for so long that she regarded him as a fixture of sorts in Weatherford, someone who had always been there and it seemed always would be. Despite his age, he had been a vital personality. But now he was gone, his life ripped away from him, and it just seemed wrong.

When they reached the sidewalk in front of the church, Phyllis turned to Mattie, thinking that perhaps the older woman would be upset. Mattie never cried at funerals, though—she claimed she had been to too many of them for that—and her eyes were dry now. Phyllis had thought it might be different, as Mattie and Donnie were old friends, but obviously not.

Nor was Carolyn crying, or her daughter Sandra, for that matter. Eve dabbed at her eyes with a lacy handkerchief, though. Phyllis suddenly found herself wondering if anything had ever gone on between Eve and Donnie. Their breezy, sometimes earthy personalities had certainly been similar, and the fact that Donnie was twenty years older probably wouldn't have mattered to Eve, especially back when Eve was, say, forty and Donnie was sixty.

Phyllis pushed those thoughts out of her head. Such things were none of her business.

Sam put his hands in the pockets of his black slacks and watched the mourners as they continued to pour out of the church and join the crowd that spilled for more than a block along the sidewalk. "Mr. Boatwright must've been one heck of a popular fella," he said.

"I'm surprised you never met him," Phyllis commented. "Everyone in Parker County seemed to know him."

Sam shrugged. "I knew who he was because I saw his name in the paper all the time. But our paths just never crossed, I guess."

Sandra Webster heard him and said, "You were one of the lucky ones, then."

The curtness of the comment took Phyllis by surprise. She looked more closely at Sandra and saw no sign of grief at all. Sandra was in her early forties, a little heavy but still an attractive woman with reddish-blond hair that had just started to be touched with gray here and there. Not only did she not look upset about Donnie's death, Phyllis was shocked to see what looked almost like a certain degree of satisfaction in Sandra's eyes.

Jerry Webster put a hand on his wife's arm and said quietly, "Let's go, honey."

Sandra nodded, gave Carolyn a quick hug, and then moved off along the sidewalk with her husband. Phyllis frowned as she watched them go. What had that unexpected comment been about? Under other circumstances, Phyllis might have asked Carolyn what Sandra meant, but given the tension between them, she didn't think that was a good idea right now. Carolyn didn't volunteer any explanations, either.

None of them were going to the cemetery for the graveside service, so they headed for Phyllis's house. She was eager to get out of her churchgoing clothes and into a pair of blue jeans.

When they got there, Carolyn went straight to her room and shut the door. Phyllis tried not to sigh. She still hoped that everything would work out sooner or later, but it was beginning to look like Carolyn might not ever get over being angry. If that turned out to be the case, it would be a real shame. Phyllis had already apologized for her thoughtless comments, though, so she didn't see what else she could do.

Murder, it seemed, changed everything, and sometimes the damage just couldn't be repaired.

Mike was surprised when he came into Sheriff Royce Haney's office and found Weatherford Chief of Police Ralph Whitmire sitting there in front of the sheriff's desk. Of course, there was no reason why the two top law enforcement officials in the county shouldn't get together, and Mike happened to know that Haney and Whitmire got along well, unlike the situation in some places where there was friction between the sheriff's office and the police department. But it was rare for them to have such a summit meeting as this appeared to be.

"Sit down, Mike," Sheriff Haney invited. "You know the chief?"

"Yes, sir," Mike said. He shook hands with Whitmire and then took the other chair in front of the sheriff's desk.

"Of course Deputy Newsom and I know each other," Whitmire said. "I keep my eye out for good young officers, and Mike's got a job waiting for him in my department any time he wants it."

"No offense, sir," Mike said with a slight smile, "but I'm happy right where I am."

"Yeah, so stop trying to steal my deputies, Ralph," Haney said with a smile of his own. He grew more serious as he went on. "I asked you in here to talk about Donnie Boatwright's murder, Mike."

That took Mike by surprise, too. He had written up statements for his mother and her friends—recounting their assertions that they hadn't seen anybody messing with Donnie's water bottle, or anything else suspicious—taken the paperwork by the house for them to sign, and then turned them in for the sheriff to pass along to whoever from Chief Whitmire's department was in charge of the investigation. Given the high profile of the victim, and the case, that might well be the chief himself.

He hadn't put anything in the statements about the wild accusations his mother and Carolyn Wilbarger had traded, because it was just crazy to think that anybody would commit murder over a cooking contest, but now he thought maybe that had been a mistake. He shouldn't have let loyalty to his mother color his judgment.

"I thought the Weatherford police have jurisdiction over that case, Sheriff," he said.

"They do. But as you know, we're trying to help out any way we can." Haney laced his fingers together and rested his hands on his stomach. "I'll tell you the truth, Mike. There's a lot of pressure to make an arrest and clear this case."

Chief Whitmire nodded in solemn agreement with the sheriff's statement.

"Donnie Boatwright was an important man, even though he didn't hold public office anymore. The district attorney, the mayor, the city councilmen, and the county commissioners . . . everybody knew Donnie. Everybody wants his killer caught."

"So do I, sir," Mike said. "I don't have any idea who it is, though."

"We're hearing from Donnie's family, too," Haney went on as if Mike hadn't spoken. "His brother and sister are mighty upset, as you can imagine. What makes it worse is that there was a large insurance policy on Donnie's life, and the insurance company isn't going to pay off as long as there's a cloud hanging over his death."

"That doesn't make any sense," Mike protested. "Mr. Boatwright's death has been ruled a homicide. What else does the insurance company need?"

Whitmire said, "They don't want to take a chance on paying a bunch of money to somebody who might have been responsible for Donnie's death."

Mike sucked in a sharp breath. He knew he was staring, but he couldn't help it. "The insurance company thinks Mr. Boatwright's brother or sister killed him?"

"They consider it a possibility. Not only that, but just because the death was ruled a homicide doesn't mean that Donnie couldn't have put that poison in his water bottle himself."

"Now that *is* crazy. He wouldn't have committed suicide. The doctor said he was in good health."

Haney shrugged. "People have killed themselves before

when it didn't seem like they'd have any reason to do such a thing."

Mike shook his head. "I don't see it. The insurance company is just looking for excuses to drag its feet about paying off."

"Maybe," Haney agreed. "But even if that's true, they'll have to settle once the case is closed. Charles Boatwright and Sally Hughes know that, and that's why they want us to make an arrest."

"There can't be an arrest until we know what happened," Mike said stubbornly.

"Of course not," Haney agreed. "There's not going to be any rush to judgment about this. But you can see why we can't afford to overlook any possibilities."

This *was* about the statements he had taken from his mother and her boarders, he thought. He had begun to hope that the sheriff and the chief wanted him to probe some other angle of the case.

Sheriff Haney leaned forward. "Mike, I hate to ask you this, but are you certain your mother and her friends didn't have any reason to hurt Donnie Boatwright?"

"Of course they didn't," Mike responded without hesitation. "They all knew him, of course, but so did half the people in Parker County. And just about everybody in the county knew *of* him."

"None of them had any reason to hold a grudge against him?"

"Not that I'm aware of," Mike said, and that was a totally honest answer.

"What if there was some other reason?" Chief Whitmire asked. "When somebody's murdered, you always have to take a look at who was close to them when it happened. Maybe Donnie was just in the wrong place at the wrong time."

"You mean maybe he was killed because somebody tried to sabotage the cooking contest?" There, he had said it. And it sounded unbelievable even to his ears, and he'd been there when his mother and the others were talking about it.

"We're just trying to cover all the bases," Haney said. "Do *you* think that might be what happened?"

Mike shook his head. "For what it's worth, Sheriff, I've known my mother my entire life and Miz Wilbarger almost that long, and I just don't believe either of them would do that. I *know* my mother wouldn't. I couldn't say about all the other women in the contest, but I even know some of them and they don't strike me as killers."

"Well, it was a long shot," Haney said with a sigh, "and even though we can't rule out the other contestants entirely, based on the evidence, I don't think they should be a focus of the investigation. What do you say, Ralph?"

"I never believed it, either," Whitmire said. "But maybe one of the contestants . . . say, Mrs. Wilbarger . . . had a reason to want Donnie Boatwright dead that didn't have anything to do with the cooking contest itself."

"That still doesn't seem possible to me," Mike said, but inside him, a feeling of unease stirred.

Haney and Whitmire looked at each other for a second, and then the sheriff said, "That's because you don't know what we've found out, Mike. But we're about to tell you. . . ."

The morning after Donnie Boatwright's funeral, Phyllis did some shopping. When she got back to the house and started to put the groceries away, she paused as she looked into the refrigerator and saw the fresh peaches that were still sitting in the crisper. After a moment, she took them out and dropped them in the garbage can. It went against the grain for her to throw away perfectly good food—she had been raised never to waste anything—but she knew good and well that she wasn't going to feel like fixing anything with peaches in it for a long time. These particular peaches would be rotten before she would ever use them, and she didn't feel up to freezing them.

Right now, she didn't care if she ever ate a peach again.

Taking a deep breath, she got back to work and put away the rest of the groceries. The house was quiet. Eve and Mattie had gone out to the high school for their tutoring sessions with the summer school students. Carolyn was probably upstairs in her room. Sam's pickup had been gone when Phyllis came in from the store, so she didn't know where he was.

The silence made the knock on the front door sound even louder than usual—and somehow ominous. Phyllis frowned and gave a little shake of her head. There was nothing sinister about a knock on the door, she told herself. She was just being silly because it had been such a hectic, upsetting summer.

She went up the hall and through the living room, touching her hair out of habit as she went to make sure it was in good order. A smile spread across her face when she looked through the curtains over the window beside the door and saw Mike standing there.

"Come in," she said as she opened the door. "What brings you by?"

"Business, I'm afraid." He stepped into the house, holding his Stetson. He was in uniform, and his expression was solemn. Phyllis felt an immediate stirring of apprehension when she saw the look on his face.

"This is about Donnie Boatwright, isn't it?" she asked tensely, lifting a hand to the throat of her blouse.

"Yeah." Mike glanced around. "Is Miz Wilbarger here?"

"I think she's upstairs. Why do you—" Phyllis stopped and began to shake her head. "Oh, no, Mike. I told you, that was just a crazy moment on my part. Carolyn would never have poisoned Donnie just to make me look bad. Not even by accident."

"It's not that. It's not about the contest at all. But it looks like Miz Wilbarger might've had another reason to hold a grudge against Mr. Boatwright. The investigation has uncovered some information about her daughter—"

Phyllis stiffened as she remembered the way Sandra

Webster had looked at Donnie's funeral and the odd comment she had made afterward. Neither Sandra nor Carolyn had seemed particularly upset that Donnie was dead.

Mike had noticed her reaction. He said quickly, "Mom, what is it? Do you know something about Miz Wilbarger's daughter?"

"No!" The shout came from the top of the stairs before Phyllis could say anything. "No, she doesn't know anything."

Phyllis and Mike both turned their heads to look up the stairs. Carolyn stood there, gazing down at them with a rather stunned expression, and as they watched, she raised her hands, covered her face, and began to sob in total misery.

Chapter 17

For one awful moment there, Phyllis had been convinced Carolyn was about to confess that she had murdered Donnie Boatwright. It was a horrible, unbelievable, unsettling feeling.

But after Mike had gone up the stairs and gently but firmly brought Carolyn downstairs to the living room, Carolyn sank down in an armchair, wiped away some of her uncharacteristic tears, and said bluntly, "I didn't kill him. I didn't have anything to do with his death, and neither did Sandra. I won't lie to you and say that we were sorry to see him dead, though. After the things he did, he deserved it. After what he did . . ."

"Why don't you tell us about it, Miz Wilbarger?" Mike suggested quietly.

Phyllis thought that she should probably leave the room, that whatever Carolyn was about to say was really none of her business. But Carolyn didn't ask her to go—in fact hardly seemed to know that Phyllis was even in the room—so she stayed as Carolyn began to talk in a halting voice.

"At first we all thought it was a good thing Sandra had gone to work for Donnie Boatwright. Jerry . . . well, Jerry's had trouble at times holding a job. . . . He's doing fine now, he's been at Home Depot for a couple of years and is doing really well, but back a few years ago Sandra's salary came in really handy."

"What did she do for Mr. Boatwright?" Mike asked.

"She was his secretary and bookkeeper. He had an office down on the square, you know, where he kept up with all of his various businesses. That's where Sandra worked, in the office. It was just the two of them. I guess . . . I guess that's why Donnie thought he could . . . could . . ."

"Just take your time," Mike told her gently. "What did Mr. Boatwright do?"

"He was always *touching* her," Carolyn said. "He'd put a hand on her shoulder or come up behind her and rub her neck, and more than once while she was at the filing cabinets, he'd reach past her to get something and his arm would brush up against her . . . her breast. She thought it was just an accident at first—it was a small office—but it didn't take her long to realize that there was nothing accidental about it."

As she listened, Phyllis thought that what Carolyn was saying didn't sound at all like the Donnie Boatwright she had known. Sure, he was loud and boisterous, but she had never seen him acting in such a crude, offensive manner.

Of course, she had never been alone with him, either, she realized, and she hadn't been close to anyone who worked for him.

Mike nodded. "What did Sandra do?"

"Well, she put up with it, of course. She and Jerry needed the money. But after a while it got so bad . . . He started touching her even more, and he suggested that she come to his house so they could *work* there. . . ." Carolyn sniffed angrily. "As if Sandra didn't know exactly what he meant by work. . . . Anyway, she asked him to stop it, and he acted like he didn't know what she was talking about. But things got better for a little while, and Sandra started hoping that he'd gotten the message."

"But things didn't stay that way, did they?" Mike guessed.

Carolyn shook her head. "No. A few weeks later, Donnie said he had to go to Corpus Christi on a business trip. He wanted Sandra to go with him. She told him that she couldn't do that, and he said that if she wanted to keep her job, she'd go with him and do whatever he wanted. Well, that was the last straw."

Phyllis felt anger burning inside her. Even though Carolyn's story was at odds with Donnie's public personality, her words rang with utter conviction, and Phyllis knew that she was telling the truth. Donnie should have been ashamed of himself. The old goat! Phyllis couldn't blame Sandra for being upset or Carolyn for being mad, even after all this time.

"What did Sandra do?" Mike asked.

"She told him to back off or she would go to the police and have him charged with sexual harassment."

Mike frowned. "That's usually an internal matter within a company, isn't it?"

"Donnie *was* the company. There was no one else for Sandra to complain to. But sexual harassment is against the law. She could have filed charges against him. At the very least she could have sued him, and that would have brought it all out into the open. Donnie couldn't allow that to happen. Not the great Donnie Boatwright."

"So what did he do?"

"He framed her!" Carolyn burst out. "He changed the books and made it look like she was stealing from him. He said that if she didn't drop the whole sexual harassment thing, he would have her arrested for embezzlement!"

That accusation was just as shocking as the ones Carolyn had already leveled at Donnie, Phyllis thought. Donnie's behavior had gone beyond being crude to being downright criminal.

"If it was a frame-up, why didn't she go to the cops herself?" Mike wanted to know.

"Oh, come on!" Carolyn said disgustedly. "Who were the police going to believe, my daughter or the great Donnie Boatwright? I can tell by looking at Phyllis here that she doesn't want to believe Donnie would do such a thing. The police certainly wouldn't have."

Phyllis said, "For what it's worth, I *do* believe you, Carolyn. I never knew Donnie was like that, but I know you're telling the truth."

"I certainly am. Sandra told me all about it when it happened. I got so mad I wanted to—"

"Wanted to what, Miz Wilbarger?" Mike asked quietly.

"You know good and well what I was about to say, Mike. I wanted to kill him."

"Did you kill him?" Mike's voice was so hushed that it was almost a whisper. Phyllis didn't want to believe it was possible Carolyn could have done such a thing, but after what she had heard in the past few minutes she didn't know what to think anymore.

"No." Carolyn's answer *was* a whisper. "No, I didn't kill him."

The room was silent for a long moment as Carolyn's denial of guilt hung in the air. Then Mike said, "What happened with the trouble between your daughter and Mr. Boatwright? How was that resolved?"

"Well, Sandra had no choice," Carolyn said with a shake of her head. "She had to promise that she would drop the whole matter, and in return Donnie wouldn't go to the police about the embezzlement. The phony embezzlement, I should say, because Sandra never stole a penny from him. Not one penny." Tears began to roll down Carolyn's cheeks again. "But then he . . . oh, Lord, that vengeful bastard . . . he had Sandra arrested anyway."

Phyllis's eyes widened in shock. "My God, Carolyn, why didn't I know about all this? Why didn't you tell your friends?"

"You think I wanted my friends to know that my daughter had been arrested for embezzlement?" Carolyn took a deep, shuddery breath. "Some things you do your best to keep in the family, Phyllis." Her tone softened a little. "Besides, it hadn't been all that long since you'd lost Kenny. I didn't want to burden you with my worries."

Phyllis reached out and caught hold of Carolyn's hand, squeezing it. "It wouldn't have been a burden," she said. "I would have helped you any way I could."

"But there was nothing you could do. There was nothing anybody could do. He was . . . Donnie Boatwright. He was untouchable." Carolyn's breath hissed between her teeth. "But somebody touched him, all right. Somebody touched him real good."

Phyllis glanced at Mike, who was watching and listening intently, taking in everything Carolyn said, and the way she said it. Carolyn certainly wasn't making her earlier denial sound any more believable with statements like that.

"Was your daughter ever prosecuted?" he asked after a moment.

Carolyn shook her head. "No. In fact, Donnie dropped the charges less than twenty-four hours later. I don't think he really wanted Sandra to go to jail. He was just . . . *punishing* her for daring to defy him."

"She never lodged a sexual harassment complaint against him?"

"What would have been the point?" Carolyn asked with a shrug. "Donnie having her arrested was like a, what do you call it, a preemptive strike. By putting his charge on the record first, he made it look like anything she said would just be a lie to get back at him."

"She didn't work for him after that, of course."

"No, he fired her, and since she had the arrest on her record, she had a terrible time getting work for a long time after that. Things have gotten a little better now. Sandra works in the medical records office at the hospital. But she's never forgotten what Donnie Boatwright did to her . . . and I've never forgiven him for it."

Stop it, Phyllis thought. You're just digging yourself a deeper and deeper hole.

But that was the way Carolyn was. She had always been blunt and opinionated, never hesitating to tell anybody what was on her mind. In a way, Phyllis was shocked that Carolyn had managed to keep Sandra's troubles with Donnie a secret for all this time.

Carolyn dabbed at her eyes and said again, "I didn't kill him. I don't know if you believe me or not, Mike, but it's the truth."

"You've been using a lot of peaches in the past few weeks, getting ready for the contest, haven't you?"

"So has your mother," Carolyn responded with some of her more characteristic testiness. "I don't see you accusing her of murder."

Mike shook his head. "I'm not accusing you of murder, Miz Wilbarger. I'm just trying to gather information."

"Well, here's some information for you—there are a lot of other people around here who have been handling peaches lately. For God's sake, this is Parker County. *Everybody* has peaches."

"That's true," Mike said, "but not everybody had a good reason to hate Donnie Boatwright."

"Look harder," Carolyn said flatly. "If he was the sort of man who would do what he did to my Sandra, he must have done terrible things to a lot of other people."

That was a good point, Phyllis thought. Maybe Donnie had more enemies than anyone knew about.

"I promise you, there'll be a complete investigation," Mike said. "We're not going to overlook anything. That's the reason I had to come and talk to you today, Miz Wilbarger, even though I didn't really want to bring up all those old troubles. Sheriff Haney and Chief Whitmire thought it might be a little easier on you if it came from somebody you knew."

"Well, I'm not sure that it was," Carolyn said. "But I don't blame you, Mike. You're just doing your job."

"Yes, ma'am."

She wiped away the rest of her tears. "Was there anything else?"

"No, not right now."

"Will . . . will you have to talk to Sandra?"

"I'm afraid so."

"She didn't even go to the peach festival, you know," Carolyn said quickly. "I happen to know she drove over to Fort Worth on Saturday, to go shopping at Ridgmar Mall."

Phyllis was shocked to realize that Carolyn was trying to establish an alibi for Sandra. But that made sense, she mused, because if Carolyn was a suspect because of what Donnie had done to Sandra, then Sandra herself had to be under suspicion, too.

"I'll sure ask her about that," Mike said. "In the meantime, you're not planning on leaving town any time soon, are you?"

"Mike!" Phyllis couldn't contain the exclamation. "What a terrible thing to ask!"

Carolyn lifted a hand. "No, it's all right, Phyllis. Mike was always such a nice, polite boy. I know he doesn't like this any more than we do."

"No, ma'am," Mike said fervently. "You've sure got that right."

"I'm not going to be leaving town. You can find me right here, any time you need to talk to me."

Mike got to his feet and nodded. "Thank you. We'll be in touch."

Carolyn stood up, too, and said, "Now, if you'll excuse me, I think I'm going to go upstairs and lie down for a while."

"Can I get you anything?" Phyllis asked.

Carolyn shook her head. "No, I . . . I just want to rest."

Phyllis and Mike stood there as Carolyn climbed slowly up the stairs. When she was gone, Mike sighed.

"I sure didn't want to do that," he said.

Phyllis felt like giving him a maternal thump on the back of the head for upsetting Carolyn like that. At the same time, though, she knew it was true what Carolyn had said—Mike was just doing his job.

She followed him onto the porch, well out of Carolyn's earshot. "You knew about all of that before you got here, didn't you? That didn't just come out of the blue."

He shrugged. "I knew some of it. Chief Whitmire turned up the arrest record for Sandra Webster. That happened before he came to Weatherford, but the record of the arrest warrant was still in the computer. Since the charges were dropped, they never made it as far as court records."

"What about the sexual harassment charge?"

"Now, that I didn't know about," Mike said. "We only had half of the story—the half that said Sandra Webster embezzled money from Donnie Boatwright." He hesitated. "I've got to say, the things that Miz Wilbarger told me just make it look worse for her."

"Michael, you know good and well Carolyn Wilbarger never killed anybody. She's been my friend for thirty years."

His eyebrows rose in surprise, and she knew it was because she had called him Michael, which she hardly ever did—only when she was really mad or upset. "I'm sorry, Mom," he said, "but she's been Sandra's mother for even longer than that. And what would *you* feel like doing if somebody did their dead level best to ruin my life?"

"Why, I'd—" Phyllis stopped short, frowned, and then said, "I wouldn't *murder* anybody because of that."

"No, but you'd feel like it, wouldn't you?"

Phyllis just looked at him for a long moment and then finally said, "I don't believe it. I can't believe it. Carolyn wouldn't do such a thing."

"I hope it turns out you're right." He turned his hat over in his hands. "You know, I really shouldn't even be talking to you about all of this. The details of an investigation are supposed to be confidential."

"I'm your mother. If you can't talk to me, who can you talk to?"

He put his hat on and smiled. "I'll remember to tell that to the sheriff if he ever calls me on the carpet about this."

Phyllis folded her arms and said firmly, "You just tell Sheriff Haney to talk to me if he has any problem with you. I'll set him straight."

She just wished that settling this whole awful murder business could be that simple, and that she could make everyone else see what was so plain to her.

No matter what her faults might be, Carolyn Wilbarger was no killer.

Chapter 18

Phyllis was still upset by the time Eve and Mattie got back from the high school, but she didn't say anything to them about Mike's visit or Carolyn's shocking revelations. Obviously, Carolyn didn't want the story of her daughter's troubles with Donnie Boatwright getting out, and Phyllis intended to honor that wish to the best of her ability.

Sam came in a short time later and found Phyllis in the kitchen. "I was wondering if I could ask you about something," he said.

"Of course. What is it?"

"I notice there's a workbench in the garage. Was it your husband's?"

Phyllis smiled. "What makes you think it's not mine? A woman can work a saw, too, you know."

Sam looked embarrassed as he said hastily, "I'm sorry. The bench just looked like it hadn't been used for a while, and I figured—"

"You figured correctly, Sam," Phyllis broke in. "I was just teasing you. That was Kenny's workbench."

"Oh. Well, I'm glad I didn't put my foot too far in my mouth. What I was wondering was—"

"If you could use it? Of course. I'd be glad to see someone getting some use out of it."

"If you don't mind my asking," Sam went on, "what did your husband use it for?"

"Kenny collected model trains," Phyllis explained. "He had quite a setup in one of the upstairs bedrooms. He designed all the layouts himself and built all the little buildings." She smiled at the memory of all the hours of painstaking work Kenny had put into his hobby. "They were very detailed. He was quite good at it."

"I'm sure he was. What happened to all the trains?"

Phyllis's smile was touched with sadness as she said, "After he passed away, I donated everything to a children's hospital. That was what Kenny wanted done. He liked to think that after he was gone, his work could bring some enjoyment to children and parents who needed cheering up."

"Sounds like he was quite a fella," Sam said quietly. "But I already knew that."

"How could you know that?"

"Because of the lady he married," Sam said.

Phyllis didn't say anything, and at that moment the timer on the oven went off, telling her it was time to take out the meatloaf she was cooking. She had never been more glad for an interruption in her life.

Sam didn't leave, though, so after she had taken the meatloaf out of the oven, she changed the subject, sort of, by saying, "What do you intend to build?"

"Oh, I thought I might knock together a bookshelf or two. Most of my books are boxed up in storage, and I'd like to get some of 'em out. That is, if you don't mind my cluttering up the room with shelves."

"It's your room as long as you're here, Sam. You should feel free to do whatever you want."

"Okay. I've got some boards out in the pickup. I'll go, uh, unload 'em."

Phyllis laughed. "You don't lack for confidence, do you, Sam? You knew I'd let you use the workbench."

"Well, I didn't exactly *know* . . . but I was hopin'."

He went out, and Phyllis continued getting supper ready. She wondered if Carolyn would come down to eat.

As it turned out, the answer was no. Phyllis knocked on her door, but Carolyn said she didn't feel like eating. At the table, Eve wanted to know what was wrong, and Phyllis said, "I think she's just a little under the weather."

"Hope it's not anything catchin'," Mattie said. "I've got a bunch to do these days. Can't afford to get sick."

Phyllis wasn't sure how Mattie kept up with all her volunteer efforts anyway. Tutoring the summer school students took up most of her time, but she also put in stints at the library and the senior citizens' center.

"I don't think it's contagious," Phyllis said. "Maybe I'll take a tray up to her later, if she feels like it."

The conversation turned to what was going on at the high school these days. Even though it was summer vacation, things never really stopped completely at the school. There were the summer classes, of course, but there were also early band and football practice and other summer activities going on. It was less than a month until regular school started again, in fact. For most of Phyllis's teaching career, school had started in September and lasted until the end of May. These days, though, the trend was to start the school year earlier and earlier. Phyllis didn't like it, and was glad she didn't have to teach classes when it was well over a hundred degrees outside.

According to Mattie, a pall still hung over the school, caused by Billy Moser's suicide. While he hadn't been the most popular kid in school, he had been well liked.

"And of course, kids all think they're immortal to start with," Mattie said. "It really knocks 'em for a loop when something bad happens to one of their friends. Of course, they get over it fairly quick, at least on the surface, but I think it lingers in their minds for a long time. Once actual school starts, though, they'll be too busy to think about it much."

After supper, Phyllis went upstairs again and knocked softly on Carolyn's door, intending to ask if she wanted her to bring up a tray. When there was no answer, a frown creased Phyllis's forehead.

She didn't believe for an instant that Carolyn would ever do anything to, well, hurt herself, but with the talk of Billy Moser's suicide fresh in her mind, it was difficult not to at least consider the possibility. Phyllis caught her lower lip between her teeth and hesitated as she looked down at the doorknob. Respecting the privacy of her boarders was one of Phyllis's ironclad rules, but if something was wrong with Carolyn, and she just walked away and let it happen, she would never forgive herself. She was just looking out for her friend's welfare, she thought as she reached for the knob.

She turned it slowly and quietly and found that the door wasn't locked. Easing it open, she leaned forward and looked into the room. The blinds were closed and the curtains were drawn, but enough of the evening afterglow seeped in so that Phyllis could make out the shapes of the furniture. She saw Carolyn lying on the bed, fully dressed except for her shoes. Phyllis listened intently and heard her deep, regular breathing. Relief went through her as she realized that Carolyn was just sound asleep. That was probably the best thing in the world for her right now.

Carefully, Phyllis pulled the door closed so that it didn't make any noise. She turned away—

And stopped short as she saw Sam Fletcher standing in the hall at the head of the stairs, his hands tucked into the hip pockets of his jeans and a quizzical expression on his face.

Phyllis lifted a hand. "I can explain—" she began.

"No need," Sam said. "This is your house, after all."

"Listen, Sam, I was . . . worried about Carolyn."

He nodded slowly. "Yeah. You said she was feeling poorly."

"It's not just that she's sick." Phyllis felt an almost overwhelming compulsion to explain herself. More than that, she realized suddenly that the knowledge she had gained today was a heavy weight. She wanted to share it with somebody, but she couldn't tell Eve or Mattie. They had known Carolyn for too long and were too close to her. Carolyn would be humiliated if she ever found out that two more of her friends knew her daughter's secret.

But Carolyn barely knew Sam. Odd though it might seem, she would probably be bothered less if Sam knew about Sandra's troubles than if Eve or Mattie found out.

And it wasn't like Sam would ever have any reason to mention the matter to Carolyn, either. The two of them hardly spoke. Anyway, if Phyllis swore Sam to secrecy, she knew instinctively that he would keep his word.

"Were you going to your room?" she went on.

"Yeah, but just to get my work gloves. I thought I might get started on those bookshelves we talked about."

"Do you mind a little company? Or does it bother you to have someone around while you're working?"

His graying eyebrows lifted in surprise. "I'd be glad for the company," he said.

"Good. I'll meet you in the garage."

Sam nodded, still looking a little puzzled, and went past her toward the door of his room.

Phyllis went downstairs and was waiting in the garage when Sam got there a few minutes later. Eve and Mattie were in the living room watching some reality show on television, so Phyllis didn't think she and Sam would be interrupted.

Sam was pulling on his gloves as he came into the garage. Phyllis said, "I know it looked like I was snooping, but—"

"Hold on a minute," Sam said. "I figured you wanted to talk about that, but let me get a board up on the bench first."

He selected a board from a stack of one-by-sixes he had unloaded from his pickup earlier, and placed it on the workbench. Then he took a folded piece of paper from his shirt pocket, unfolded it, and smoothed it out on the bench.

"Plans I drew up," he explained. "Architecture's beyond

me, but I can design some bookshelves." He took a short pencil from his pocket and laid a four-foot metal ruler on the board. "Go ahead, Phyllis. Tell me whatever you want to tell me . . . and I'm guessing you want me to keep it under my hat."

"I'd appreciate it."

"You've got my word on it," he said simply, and that was good enough for her.

"Mike was here this afternoon. He had some questions for Carolyn . . . about Donnie Boatwright's murder, and about Carolyn's daughter, Sandra."

Sam started to look surprised, but he managed to confine the reaction to one quirked eyebrow. He lined up the ruler on the edge of the board and marked off four feet. Then he moved it and marked off two more feet for a total of six. "Go on," he said as he used a square to draw a straight line across the width of the board.

Phyllis sketched in the details of what she had learned that afternoon. Sam listened impassively as he took a circular saw from the cabinet underneath the workbench. Obviously, he had investigated to see what tools were stored there. Phyllis paused in her story and felt a funny little twinge inside when she saw one of Kenny's tools in Sam's hands, but then a feeling came over her that told her it was all right. Just as Kenny had wanted his work on the model trains to be put to good use, he wouldn't have wanted perfectly good tools to just sit in the cabinet and rust.

Phyllis resumed the story, and when she had finished, she said, "So you can see why I was worried about Carolyn. I thought she might have done something . . ." Her voice trailed off. She couldn't even say it, the idea seemed so ludicrous now.

"You thought maybe she really did poison Donnie Boatwright, and she was takin' the easy way out instead of waiting to get caught," Sam said.

"Well, yes. I know it's ridiculous. Carolyn would never

do either of those things. But I guess my worry just got the best of me for a minute."

"No crime in worryin' about a friend. I'm not sure I agree with you completely, though."

"Oh? What don't you agree with?"

"I can see Carolyn gettin' mad enough to try to even the score with Boatwright, but if she ever did something like that, I don't think she'd kill herself over it, or even deny it. Seems more likely to me that she'd stand up straight, spit in the eye of whoever accused her, and say that heck, yes, she did it, and Boatwright had it comin' to him."

Phyllis couldn't help but smile at that description. "That *does* sound more like Carolyn, all right."

Sam shook his head and said, "I never have thought that she did it. She might slap somebody silly, but she wouldn't poison 'em." He plugged in the saw. "Innocent or not, though, she's still got a mighty big problem on her hands."

"Why do you say that?" Phyllis asked with a frown.

"Because Boatwright's murder has got the whole town stirred up. Mike may not have said anything to you about it, but I'll bet the cops are under a lot of pressure to arrest somebody."

"You don't think they'll really come after Carolyn, do you?"

Sam raked a thumbnail along his jawline. "I don't know. Sounds to me like she's their main suspect. And you've got to admit, she's got a good motive. She's been up to her elbows in peach pits lately, too, and that's where the cops think the chemical that killed Boatwright came from. On top of that, she was around the festival all day, and she could have slipped the stuff into his water bottle. In a big crowd like that, you'd think somebody would notice something that unusual, but that's not necessarily the case. Most folks don't pay any attention to anything that's not right in front of their noses."

"I've had a lot of peach pits in the house, too," Phyllis pointed out, "and I was around the festival enough that I could have poisoned Donnie's water. That's true of dozens of other people."

Sam shook his head. "You didn't have any motive. Carolyn did."

"What about all those other people, especially the ones in the contest?"

"That's what the cops ought to be trying to find out." Sam slipped a pair of safety goggles over his head. "I don't know if that'll happen, though. Once they start looking hard at a particular suspect, they sometimes tend to neglect all the others."

Phyllis didn't think that would happen, especially with Mike being involved in the investigation . . . but you could never tell about these things. If Chief Whitmire and Sheriff Haney decided that Carolyn was guilty, they might try to push the case through the system in a hurry. What was that old expression? Railroaded? Phyllis respected both lawmen enough to hope that they wouldn't do such a thing, but they were, after all, politicians. . . .

"Somebody killed Donnie Boatwright," she declared firmly, "and it wasn't Carolyn. They'll just have to find out who it really was. *Somebody* will have to find out the truth."

"Uh-huh," Sam said, and then he bent over and set the saw on the board he had clamped to the end of the workbench. He pulled the trigger and the circular blade began to revolve with a high-pitched whine. It bit into the wood, shearing smoothly through it as Sam followed the line he had drawn. The blade cut the end of the board off cleanly, and it dropped to the concrete floor of the garage. Sam set the saw aside, straightened up, and pushed the goggles up on his head as he turned to look at Phyllis. "Somebody meaning you?"

She returned his level gaze but didn't answer. Her heart pounded in her chest, as if she were standing on a high place, looking down at empty air just waiting for her to step out into it. . . .

Chapter 19

The idea was still nibbling around the edges of Phyllis's brain the next day. On the face of it, it was ridiculous. She couldn't investigate a murder. She was just a retired schoolteacher.

But she had taught history for all those years, she reminded herself. That meant she knew about cause and effect, and how one incident followed another and another and another, all of them linking together to form a single, far-reaching chain of events. Of course, random violence sometimes occurred in the world—all too often, in fact—but she didn't believe for a minute that there was anything random about what had happened to Donnie Boatwright. The decision to kill him had been prompted by something that had happened in the past.

And what was history if not the study of the past and how it affected the present?

Mike would be furious if she started messing around in his case, she told herself. But if it was true what Sam had said about the authorities feeling considerable pressure to solve Donnie's murder, if she could help Mike to do just that, it would be a good thing. Wouldn't it? Being the mother of a deputy sheriff, and well-read to boot, she knew a few things about criminal investigations. She wouldn't do anything to interfere with the official investigation, and she wouldn't compromise any evidence.

She would just . . . ask a few questions here and there.

That was all. If she found out anything interesting, Mike could take it from there.

Once her mind was made up, she knew she had to get started before she thought better of it. She got her car keys and stepped out into the garage.

Sam was already at work again on his bookshelves, cutting the shorter boards that would form the shelves. His plan was to cut all of them and then stain them before he put them together. He set the saw aside, pushed the goggles up, and asked, "Goin' somewhere?"

"Just to run a few errands," Phyllis said.

She thought he looked a little suspicious, but he nodded and said, "I guess I'll see you later, then."

Phyllis just smiled and nodded back to him as she got into the Lincoln. Being casual, that was the ticket. Whatever she did, it would just be a little something, nothing to get all worked up about.

But she couldn't sit by and do nothing, she thought as she drove away from the house. Carolyn was still refusing to eat this morning. Something had to be done to clear her name, and Phyllis was no longer sure that the law was interested in that.

She drove out the old highway to the newspaper office on the edge of town. A few years earlier, she'd had Bud Winfield's twin daughters in her class, so she was acquainted with the editor and publisher of the paper. She knew him from the cooking contest at the peach festival, too, since he was usually one of the judges.

Bud was in his office when Phyllis got there; she saw him through the window between the office and the reception area. The woman behind the counter asked if Phyllis needed help, but before she could answer, Bud came to the door of his office and said, "Hello, Miz Newsom. Something we can do for you?"

"I was hoping I could talk to you for a few minutes, Bud."

"Sure, come on in and sit down."

Phyllis accepted the invitation. She sat down on an old

sofa in Bud's office as he closed the door. He went behind his desk and sank into a swivel chair.

"I'm sure sorry about the way that contest turned out," he told her. "Your cobbler was mighty good. What was that secret ingredient again? Cinnamon?"

"Ginger," Phyllis said, "and it wasn't a secret. I even had the recipe printed up to give to people."

"Oh, yeah, I remember that. It's a real shame, what happened to Donnie."

"That's what I wanted to ask you about."

The lanky, redheaded Bud raised his eyebrows. "Me? I don't know anything more about it than what the police have said in their official statements."

"You haven't heard if they're close to making an arrest?"

Bud shook his head. "Not that I know of. I'm not sure they even have any suspects."

Then do I have a scoop for you, Phyllis thought, or at least I would have if I could reveal what I know about Carolyn and Sandra.

But she would never do that. Instead she said, "I was more interested in talking about Donnie himself. You've known him for a long time, haven't you?"

"Oh, yeah, more than twenty years. Ever since I moved to Weatherford and bought the paper in, what was it, '84. You can't cover local events in this town and not run into Donnie Boatwright. He had a finger in every pie you can think of." Bud grinned. "Not just the peach ones."

"Yes, if there was ever a man whom everybody knew and liked, I guess it was Donnie," said Phyllis.

"Well . . . I don't know that I'd go so far as to say that *everybody* liked Donnie. He was a businessman, after all, and you can't do business without getting crosswise with somebody every now and then."

"Really?" Phyllis tried to look and sound interested without letting Bud know just how strong her interest really was. "Are you saying he had enemies?"

"He had one, anyway," Bud said pointedly. "Whoever slipped him that poison."

"I guess that goes without saying. But who could have hated him that much?"

Bud shrugged. "I don't like to gossip, but . . ." He broke into a grin. "Ah, who am I trying to kid? I'm a newspaperman. I love to gossip." He leaned forward. "Donnie was quite a ladies' man, you know, and he didn't slow down much when he got older. In a week's time, you might see him out for lunch or dinner with two or three different women. Heck, I'm surprised he never called you up after your husband passed away."

With a smile, Phyllis said, "Maybe he just hadn't gotten around to me yet."

"Maybe so. But all I'm saying is that a guy who plays the field like that has to leave a few broken hearts behind him. And traditionally, poison *is* a woman's weapon."

"I suppose that's possible. Maybe money was at the root of it, though. You said Donnie might have made enemies in the business world."

Bud frowned in thought and then said, "Yeah, but I can't think of anybody he screwed over—pardon my French— bad enough to make them want to kill him. Unless, of course, it was his brother and sister."

Again Phyllis struggled to control her reaction. She didn't want Bud to see how shocked she was by what he had just said. "His brother and sister?" she repeated calmly.

"Yeah. Now I really *am* telling tales out of school. But from what I've heard—and this is just rumor, mind you, because it all happened before I came to town—Donnie had a falling out with Charles and Sally a long time ago because of what happened with their mother's will."

"I never heard anything about that."

"No reason you would have. It was Boatwright family business, after all. But as I understand it, the old lady had quite a bit of money, and Charles and Sally both expected that they'd get an equal share along with Donnie when she passed away. That's not how it happened, though. Donnie had her power of attorney, and he managed to get his hands on most of her funds before she died. Then, to add insult to injury, she changed her will at the last minute and left everything to him anyway. That was the real slap in the face to them." Bud shrugged. "Of course, that was a long time ago, and even without that inheritance they were expecting, Charles and Sally did all right for themselves. Charles has that car dealership, and Sally married Kent Hughes, who had that restaurant out on Highway 80. So neither of them ever hurt too much for money."

"I imagine they still resented what Donnie did, though."

"Yeah, but to think either of them would have held a grudge that long. . . ." Bud shook his head. "I just don't see it. Besides, they were pretty broken up at the funeral. I think they forgave Donnie a long time ago. He could be a scoundrel, but you couldn't help but like him."

Maybe that was true, Phyllis thought, but their demeanor at the funeral didn't have to mean anything. She recalled the line from Shakespeare about how a man could smile and smile, and still be a villain. She supposed that was true for crying at funerals, too.

The picture of Donnie Boatwright that was starting to form in her mind was considerably different from the image he projected to the public. Womanizer, sexual harasser, blackmailer, a man who would take advantage of his own family. . . . That was a far cry from everybody's friend, the sort of surrogate grandfather or uncle to the whole town that Donnie had pretended to be.

Or maybe he really was those things, too. Everybody was a mixture of good and bad, and Phyllis knew personally of quite a few ways that Donnie Boatwright had benefited Weatherford and Parker County. But the flaws had been there as well, and there was no doubt that one of them was responsible for getting him killed.

"Phyllis, let me ask you a question," Bud said, breaking

into her thoughts. "Why did you come here today to talk about Donnie?"

"Well . . . I was right there when he died," she said. "That really bothered me, and not just because it looked for a minute like my peach cobbler might have killed him. I guess I just wanted to understand Donnie a little better, in hopes that maybe I'd understand why it happened."

Bud nodded slowly. "Yeah, I see what you mean. It was a real shock to all of us. Seeing him die like that, well, it's made me think a lot about my own life."

"I appreciate you talking to me—"

"Oh, I have an ulterior motive," Bud said.

"What could that be?"

"Your son's a deputy sheriff, and I know the sheriff's department and the Weatherford police are cooperating on this case. Maybe if Mike were to hear something about the investigation . . . and if he just happened to mention it to you . . . you could maybe give me a call. . . ."

"You want me to be a source for you," Phyllis said. "What is it the newspaper stories always say? A source close to the investigation?"

Bud smiled. "I'm just saying that could work out well. And Sheriff Haney would never find out where the information came from. I protect my sources."

"I'll think about it, Bud," Phyllis said, "but I can't make any promises."

"Oh, sure, I understand. The subject might not ever come up. But if it does, keep me in mind, that's all I'm asking."

Phyllis got to her feet. "I enjoyed our talk. Thank you, Bud."

"No problem. I'm convinced my girls got through Advanced Placement History in high school because of what they learned in your class. So I owe you for that."

"Not at all. It's my job to teach. Or rather, it was my job, I should say."

"None of us are ever too old to learn." Bud's expression

grew more solemn as he stepped over to the door. "I probably shouldn't say this, since big stories are good for the paper, but I hope there aren't any more murders around here for a while. Two of them are plenty."

Phyllis paused. "You're talking about Newt Bishop, as well as Donnie?"

"Yeah. There's never been an official finding in his death, but I'm convinced somebody knocked that jack out from under his car on purpose."

"So am I," Phyllis said.

Bud's eyes widened suddenly. "Say, you were the one who found Newt's body. And you were right there when Donnie collapsed. That's sort of strange, isn't it?"

Phyllis smiled. "Do you think *I'm* the killer, Bud, or just a jinx?"

"No, no, I don't mean anything like that," he said quickly. "It's just . . . weird."

"Well, for the record, I'd just as soon not see any more dead bodies, either."

"Yeah." Bud laughed. But Phyllis thought it sounded a little weak, and he watched her with what looked like a mixture of interest and apprehension as she walked out of the newspaper office.

She knew he didn't seriously believe that she was a serial killer, murdering first Newt Bishop and then Donnie Boatwright. But it was certainly true that she had been on hand for both of those mysterious deaths.

And as she drove away, she suddenly asked herself if there could be any connection between them. As old-timers in Parker County, Donnie and Newt had known each other. Donnie had known just about everybody of any importance in the county, and with his successful peach orchard, Newt had qualified for that distinction. But for the life of her, Phyllis didn't see how their deaths could be related.

It was sure something to think about, though.

Chapter 20

"What can I do for you, Miz Newsom?" Charles Boatwright asked as he and Phyllis stood in the showroom of Boatwright Motors, surrounded by the gleaming shapes of new cars.

"Well, I was thinking about getting another car," Phyllis said. "That Lincoln of mine is more than a few years old now."

"Yes, but they're good cars, built to last. How many miles do you have on it?"

"Oh, goodness, I don't know for sure," Phyllis said. "Around seventy thousand, I think."

Charles waved a hand. "It ought to do just fine for you for a good while yet. If you'd like, though, I can have the fellows in my service department look it over for you, just to make sure there aren't any mechanical problems developing."

Phyllis couldn't help but laugh a little. "This is the first time I've ever had a car salesman try to convince me *not* to buy a car."

Charles laughed, too. He was short and stocky, and despite being in his seventies, his hair was still thick and mostly brown. His hands and the lines around his eyes showed his age more than anything else.

"I just want everybody to drive what they need to be driving," he said. "I firmly believe there's a right car for everybody, and if you're happy with what you have, you don't go messing with it."

"Those sound like words to live by."

Charles smiled. "I try to."

"Well . . . I have to admit that my car's not really giving me any problems, and if you think I ought to stick with it a while longer, I will."

"Just remember who gave you that good advice, and when you need to replace your Lincoln, you come see me again."

"Oh, I will." Phyllis hesitated. "While I'm here, I'd like to tell you just how sorry I am about what happened to your brother."

A solemn expression appeared on Charles's face, and he nodded slowly. "It was a terrible shock, all right. I appreciate your words of condolence, Miz Newsom." He paused. "Although I suppose under the circumstances, what happened was almost as shocking for you as it was for my sister and me."

"It was horrible," Phyllis admitted. "For a moment there, I . . . I really did think that I might have been to blame for . . . for what happened."

Phyllis blinked her eyes and raised a hand to cover them, as if trying to conceal the fact that she was about to cry. She had never thought of herself as any sort of an actress, but she must have been convincing, because Charles Boatwright stepped toward her quickly, touched her arm, and said, "Oh, no, Miz Newsom, please don't blame yourself. We all know now that you had nothing to do with it."

"Yes, but . . . he had just eaten some of my cobbler. . . ."

Charles looked around the showroom. A couple of his salesmen were talking to other customers, and there were people out in the service area, but other than that, the place wasn't busy. He said, "Why don't you come into my office and sit down for a minute? I don't like for anyone to leave Boatwright Motors upset."

"I . . . I think I would like that," Phyllis said. "Thank you, Mr. Boatwright."

He took her arm and steered her toward a door that led off the showroom floor. "Please, call me Charles," he said. "Would you like a cup of coffee, or a cold drink?"

"Some coffee would be very nice."

"We'll get you settled in the office, and I'll bring you a cup."

Phyllis felt a twinge of guilt as Charles took her into his spacious, wood-paneled office and set her down in a comfortable leather chair in front of his desk. Here she was, putting on a big show of being upset, and he was trying to be nice to her.

But she wanted to find out more about the relationship between Donnie Boatwright and his brother and sister, and this was the only way she'd been able to think of.

Charles said, "I'll be right back," and left her sitting in the office. Phyllis frowned at the desk, wondering if she ought to take this opportunity to rifle through it. That was one of the things detectives did, wasn't it?

But she realized that she wouldn't really know what she was looking for, and anyway, Charles probably kept any important documents locked up. And since the poison that had killed Donnie probably had come from peach pits, it wasn't like she could open a desk drawer and find a bottle of arsenic or something like that in it. Locating the murder weapon wouldn't be that convenient in this case.

Maybe she could find something that would indicate the car dealership was going broke. That would strengthen Charles's motive. His brother had cheated him out of his inheritance, and now his business was failing. That would be a reason to get mad enough to kill, wouldn't it?

But for one thing, all you had to do was take a look around the dealership to know that it was doing just fine. The place practically reeked of success. That could be a sham, of course, a cleverly constructed façade, but Phyllis didn't think that was the case. And for another thing, she didn't want to get caught searching the desk. So she stayed where she was in the leather chair, although she did have the presence of mind to take a lacy handkerchief from her purse and clutch it in her hand as if she had been using it to dab at her eyes.

Charles came back into the office a minute later, so Phyllis was glad she hadn't tried to get into his desk. He carried a Styrofoam cup of coffee in one hand, along with packets of sugar, artificial sweetener, and nondairy creamer in the other hand. "I didn't know how you take your coffee," he said, "so I brought some of everything."

"Thank you, Mr. Boatwright. I'm sorry to be such a bother."

"No bother at all," he said as he handed the cup to her and placed the other things on the front edge of the desk where she could reach them easily. "And I told you to call me Charles."

Phyllis summoned up a smile. "Then thank you, Charles." She set the cup on the desk and emptied some creamer and artificial sweetener into the coffee. She lifted it to her mouth, took a sip, and said, "That's very good."

"Well, you just take your time with it."

"I hate to keep you from your work. . . ."

He sat down behind the desk and gave another of those expansive hand waves that seemed to be a habit with him. "You're not keeping me from anything." He smiled. "I'll let you in on a little secret. . . . This place practically runs itself. The key is hiring good people."

"I know several people who say they wouldn't buy a car from anybody else."

"Why, that's mighty nice to hear. It's been a pleasure serving the good people of Weatherford and Parker County for all these years."

He sounded a little like a TV commercial, Phyllis thought. She supposed that when you were in the business of selling cars, that became a habit, too. She took another couple of sips of coffee and then said, "I'm really glad you don't hold a grudge against me because of what happened to your brother. I hesitated about coming here today because of that."

"Goodness, why in the world would you feel that way?" Charles asked with a frown. "You didn't have anything to do with his death."

"If you don't want to talk about it, I certainly understand, but . . . do the police have any idea who was responsible?"

What looked like anger flashed in Charles's eyes. "If they do, they haven't told me about it," he said, his tone growing sharp. "And I don't mind saying, my sister and I are rather upset about it. They won't tell us if they have any suspects, or anything else about the investigation."

Phyllis felt a flash of relief. That meant the police were keeping their suspicions of Carolyn to themselves, at least for the time being. She was convinced Carolyn was innocent, so there was no point in the story of what Donnie had done to Sandra ever getting out to the public.

"That must be terribly frustrating," she said.

Charles nodded. "It is. I've heard that with every day that goes by in a murder case, the chances of catching the killer go down. I just hate to think that whoever killed Donnie might get away with it."

"I don't see how anybody could want to hurt your brother. He did so much for Weatherford and for Parker County, and I'm sure he did that much or more for his family."

"Well, I wouldn't say—" Charles stopped himself. After a moment, as Phyllis looked at him with a puzzled expression on her face, he went on. "There are little spats in every family. And Donnie was my big brother, after all. Brothers always fight sometimes."

Phyllis allowed herself a smile. "Mine certainly did."

"I remember a time . . ." Charles leaned back in his chair and smiled a little. Phyllis knew that people seemed to like talking to her. She supposed she had developed that ability during her years as a teacher, because sometimes you needed the students to open up to you. Charles went on. "We were swimming over in the Clear Fork, before they ever built the lake, and Donnie kept dunking me. He thought it was so funny, and he just wouldn't stop. I got so aggravated at him I could have just—"

Phyllis expected Charles to say *killed him,* but instead he stopped short, and to Phyllis's surprise a tear welled from the corner of his right eye and ran down his cheek. "I'm sorry," he went on as he brushed it away. "I don't mean to get all maudlin. It's just that talking about Donnie brings back so many memories."

"I understand," Phyllis said.

"When you lose somebody, even the memories of them that aren't so good become precious in their own way."

Phyllis nodded. "I know exactly what you mean. There were days when I wanted to strangle my husband, but since he's been gone, even those times mean so much to me."

"Exactly," Charles said. "Even when Donnie would pull some stunt that you didn't like—and he could pull some doozies, let me tell you—once you got over being mad you'd see that he was, well, just being Donnie. You couldn't stay upset with him. I know I never could."

Was he telling the truth, Phyllis asked herself, or was he just trying to cover up the rage he had felt for years—the rage at the injustice of it all, which had built up until Charles Boatwright finally snapped and did something to get even with his older brother?

"Ah, well," Charles went on after a moment of silence, "you didn't come here to listen to me reminisce about Donnie. I'm sure you must have better things to do."

"No, that's fine," Phyllis said quickly. "If our conversation made you relive some good times, I'm glad. And I know talking to you has made me feel better."

"Well, good. I guess I had better get back to work, though. . . ."

Phyllis took one more sip of coffee and then set the cup on the desk. "Thank you. I'm sorry if I was a bother."

"Not at all, not at all." Charles came to his feet as Phyllis stood up. "Now, you remember what I told you about coming to see me when you do get ready for a new car. I'll see to it that you get the best deal in Parker County."

"Thank you, Charles." Phyllis tucked her handkerchief back in her purse. She hoped he hadn't noticed that her eyes weren't red, as they would have been if she had really been crying. Probably not, she decided, since the very idea of a woman crying gave most men the fantods. They were too busy feeling uncomfortable and wondering what they should do to pay much attention to what was really going on.

With a smile, Phyllis left the office. She walked across the showroom and out the door to the parking lot, where she had left her car. To her left was the service area, and in front of and beyond it was the large lot where late-model used cars were parked. To her right was the sweeping lot full of new vehicles. Just looking at all the cars made Phyllis realize that her thoughts about the dealership possibly going under had been foolish. Charles Boatwright was doing very well. He might harbor some resentment toward his brother for the fast one Donnie had pulled when their mother passed away, but was it likely he hated Donnie enough because of it to poison him?

Phyllis didn't think so.

And yet there had been that moment when Charles had spoken of the incident in the Clear Fork of the Trinity River, when he and Donnie were young. True, the moment had been a fleeting one, but for a second there Phyllis had been convinced she saw a lot of long-forgotten anger in Charles's eyes. She was leaning away from regarding him as a strong suspect in Donnie's murder, but she couldn't eliminate him entirely.

As she drove away, her mind went back to the story of Cain and Abel. While it was hard for her to even conceive of one brother hating another enough to kill him, there was plenty of precedent. Cain had murdered Abel out of jealousy, and down through the ages, time and again, brother had slain brother for that reason, and for all the other possible combinations of greed and lust and ambition you could think of. It happened sometimes, and maybe Charles Boatwright was just a darned good actor.

She supposed she needed to keep digging. She had done enough gardening to know that to get the results you wanted, most of the time you had to get your hands dirty.

Chapter 21

When Phyllis got home, she found Mike waiting for her on the front porch. He and Sam Fletcher were sitting in two of the rocking chairs, glasses of iced tea in their hands. Phyllis saw them as she drove past the house and turned into the driveway. When she got out of the Lincoln, instead of going into the kitchen, she left the garage door open and walked out into the driveway, then followed the path of round cement blocks across the grass to the front walk.

"You gentlemen look like you're taking life easy," she commented as she climbed the steps to the porch.

"That's the only way to take it," Sam replied with a smile. He lifted his glass of tea as if he were toasting her with it.

"Where have you been, Mom?" Mike asked.

For a second, Phyllis wondered how he would react if she said she'd been out trying to find a killer. She glanced at Sam. Had he called Mike and told him that his mother had decided to play detective? He couldn't have, she decided, because she hadn't confided her plans to him before she left. She had figured out already, though, that Sam was pretty shrewd, especially for a man. There was no telling what *he* had figured out.

Those thoughts flashed through Phyllis's mind in an instant, as she smiled and said, "Oh, just out running around. Shopping and things."

"You don't have any packages," Mike pointed out.

"You never knew that pretty little wife of yours to go shopping without buying anything?"

"Well, now that you mention it . . ." Mike said with a shrug. He took a drink of tea and went on. "I came by because I thought you'd like to hear how things are going with the Boatwright investigation."

Phyllis sat down in the rocker next to him, her purse on her lap. "Can you do that?" she asked. "I mean, can you tell me about it without getting in trouble?"

He chuckled and said, "You're already mixed up in it." Once again she felt a surge of worry. "You were there when Mr. Boatwright died, and one of your friends is the leading suspect. I'd say that gives you a right to hear about it, and if the sheriff doesn't like it, he can go jump in the lake."

Phyllis smiled. Despite being a grown man with a family of his own, there were times when Mike still seemed just like a little boy to her, and this was one of them.

Sam made a motion to get up. "I'll go on in the house, since I reckon you'll want to talk to your mom alone, Mike."

"No, that's all right, Mr. Fletcher," Mike said quickly. "I know you're trustworthy, or my mother never would have let you live here in the first place."

Sam settled back in the rocker. "I appreciate that. I like to think I can keep my mouth shut when I need to."

"Go ahead, Mike," Phyllis urged, glad that Sam was staying. It made her feel somehow like less of the burden was on her. "What have you found out?"

"Not a lot, unfortunately," Mike said with a little sigh. "Sandra Webster's alibi checks out. She and her husband didn't go to the peach festival. They were over in Fort Worth, and they've got the credit card receipts from the stores where they shopped, with the date and time on them to prove it."

"Just because one of them was there using a credit card doesn't mean the other one was," Sam said.

"It does when one of them signed the receipts in some

places and the other signed at the other stores. Plus we talked to the employees at the various places and found several of them who remembered both Sandra and Jerry Webster being there on Saturday."

"Kids who work minimum-wage jobs in mall stores remembered *two* customers out of the hundreds who come through on a Saturday?" Phyllis asked. She wasn't trying to destroy Sandra's alibi, but that still struck her as unlikely.

"Well," Mike said with a smile, "evidently Sandra Webster is the sort of customer who likes to complain about anything and everything. That would make her more memorable."

Phyllis supposed that was true. Anyway, she didn't believe that Sandra had killed Donnie Boatwright any more than she believed that Carolyn was a murderer. If Sandra had a legitimate alibi, that was a good thing. It meant she was in the clear.

But it also meant that Carolyn was still the chief suspect in Donnie's murder. Phyllis supposed that the way she felt now was what people talked about when they referred to mixed emotions. She couldn't be too glad about Sandra's alibi, because it made things look even worse for Carolyn.

What she needed was for someone else to be revealed as Donnie's murderer, so that both of them would be cleared.

"What else have you found out?" she asked. "Have you looked into Donnie Boatwright's background? Surely there was somebody else besides Carolyn who had a good reason not to like him."

Maybe that little nudge would point Mike, and by extension the rest of the officers investigating the case, in the right direction, Phyllis thought.

"Mr. Boatwright's life was pretty much an open book," Mike said. "He never had any serious trouble with anybody, never got arrested, never pressed charges against anybody except Sandra Webster—and those were dropped—and he was never involved in any lawsuits. He was about as squeaky-clean as anybody you'll ever find."

No, he wasn't, Phyllis wanted to say, but then she would have had to explain how she had discovered the things she had learned. If Mike found out that she was conducting an investigation of her own, she knew good and well he would tell her to stop it, to leave those things to the proper authorities. She was afraid that if she did, though, sooner or later Carolyn was going to be arrested for murder, or at least taken in for questioning. They had no way of tying her directly to the dangerous chemical that had been put in Donnie's water, nor did they have any witnesses who had seen her tampering with the water bottle. That meant the case against her was purely circumstantial, and in the end the district attorney might decide not to go ahead with it.

But by then it would be too late. Everyone in town would know that the police thought Carolyn had killed Donnie Boatwright. That would be enough to convict her in the minds of many people. She would be humiliated, and for the rest of her life she would be known as the probable killer of one of Parker County's leading citizens.

Then there was the worst-case scenario: that Carolyn would be arrested, charged, and put on trial, and a jury would decide that there was enough evidence against her to send her to prison. Phyllis couldn't let that happen. She believed in her friend's innocence, and Carolyn couldn't wind up behind bars for something she didn't do.

"Maybe you'd better keep looking," she said grimly to Mike. "Nobody is *that* squeaky-clean. Donnie must have had some enemies besides Carolyn and Sandra."

Mike shrugged. "It's not like we've given up on all the other possible angles. We have to pursue the most likely leads, though."

Phyllis wanted to snap at him, but she held her tongue. Getting angry wouldn't do any good. And she knew her son well enough to know that he *would* do the best job he could. But he wasn't the only one involved in the investigation, and before it was over, the whole thing might be taken out of his hands. When Ralph Whitmire thought he had enough evidence to make an arrest, he'd do it, no matter what some deputy sheriff who didn't even work for him thought about the matter.

"I guess I'd better be going," Mike said as he got to his feet. "I'm on duty, but I didn't think it would hurt anything to stop by here for a little while." He set his empty tea glass on the railing that ran along the front of the porch and leaned over to kiss Phyllis on the cheek. "So long, Mom."

"Give my love to Sarah, and hug Bobby for me," she told him.

He smiled. "I will."

Phyllis stood there, her hands on the railing, watching as he got into his car and pulled away from the house.

Behind her, Sam said, "You got a mite put out with the boy, didn't you?"

She turned to look at him. "What makes you say that?"

"You want Carolyn to be innocent, and you're afraid that Mike's leanin' toward thinking that she's guilty. I'll bet you the sheriff thinks she is, and that's got to be rubbin' off on Mike a little."

"My son is very fair and open-minded."

"Well, of course he is," Sam said. "You wouldn't have raised him to be any other way. But he's human, too, and when his boss and everybody else he works with are convinced about something, he wouldn't be human if he didn't start to thinkin' that they might be right."

Phyllis wanted to deny it, but she knew that Sam was correct. Barring a miracle—like the real murderer stepping forward to confess—the only way to save Carolyn was to give the authorities something they couldn't ignore, something concrete that would at least point the finger of suspicion elsewhere.

And Phyllis had the sinking feeling that nobody else was going to even try to do that except her.

"Maybe something will come up," she said. She started toward the front door. "I've got to fix lunch—"

Sam stopped her by asking, "Where were you this morning, really? Out asking folks questions about Donnie Boatwright?"

Phyllis stiffened, and her voice was chilly as she said, "I don't think I have to account to you for my whereabouts, Mr. Fletcher. I'm a grown woman, after all."

"Yes, ma'am, I know that, but lately I've had the feelin' that you think you need to go out and do the cops' job for them."

She couldn't stop herself from saying, "Maybe somebody needs to."

"Maybe," Sam agreed, "but there's one thing you've got to consider. . . . If you go looking for a killer, you just might find one. And if that happens . . . what'll you do then?"

Phyllis stood for a long moment, not saying anything. He was right. She *hadn't* thought it through all the way. Chances were, Donnie Boatwright's killer wouldn't want his or her identity known. If Phyllis was on the verge of uncovering incriminating evidence, and if the murderer found out . . .

Well, whoever it was had already killed once.

But as frightening as that prospect might be, Phyllis knew she couldn't abandon the task she had set for herself. Somebody had to find out the truth, and if she was the only one willing to do it, then that was the way it would have to be.

"Don't have an answer, do you?" Sam said.

"What would you suggest?" she asked coolly.

His answer surprised her. He looked her straight in the eye and said, "Let me play detective with you."

Chapter 22

At least Sam hadn't suggested that they play doctor, Phyllis thought later. Although in a way, that would have simplified matters. In that case she could have just slapped his face, told him to behave himself, and been done with it.

As it was, she had to seriously consider his offer to join her in her quest to find the evidence needed to clear Carolyn.

Phyllis postponed the decision until after lunch. For a change, Carolyn came downstairs to eat. That was a welcome sign of life on her part, Phyllis thought. Carolyn had eaten very little since Mike's visit the day before.

When Eve and Mattie came in and took their places at the table, it was almost like old times. The only difference was that Sam was there. Phyllis didn't know how she felt about that anymore. So far, having him in the house had worked out well. Eve and Mattie seemed to like him, even if Carolyn didn't. And Phyllis would have been lying if she had said, even to herself, that she didn't enjoy his company.

But wasn't that just like a man to come in and try to take over? She knew that he was worried about her safety, and to be honest, now that she had thought about it, she realized what she was doing held the potential for danger. Having Sam at her side while she did her poking around in Donnie Boatwright's less-than-savory history probably would make her feel safer.

Even so, she had a hard time believing that she would be

in any serious danger in her own hometown. This was Weatherford, for goodness sake, not Dallas or Houston or someplace like that.

Then she reminded herself of what had happened to Donnie, and a little shiver went through her. Weatherford had been *his* hometown, too, but that hadn't saved him from a clever murderer.

To get her mind off the dilemma while they ate lunch, Phyllis said to Mattie, "Summer school will be over pretty soon, won't it?"

"Another week," Mattie replied. "Kids'll get a little break before regular school starts, but not much of one."

"I suppose you'll miss tutoring them."

"I always enjoyed bein' around kids. Some of 'em are just little brats, of course, but most of them are pretty nice, even in this day and age. They really want to learn, but Lord, they've got a lot of distractions. People and things crowdin' in on 'em all the time. They're always in a hurry to experience everything." Mattie shook her head solemnly. "If you ask me, they grow up too fast these days. They don't have enough time to just be kids anymore, and that's not fair to them."

"That reminds me," Eve said. "Phyllis, can you take Mattie to school and pick her up tomorrow? I have to be gone for the day."

Phyllis nodded. Eve had mentioned to her several days earlier that she would be busy and would need help driving Mattie. Eve was going to Dallas for a doctor's appointment and would be gone all day, Phyllis was sure. Anytime anybody had to go to Dallas, it was almost always an all-day trip. There was nothing wrong with Eve, as far as Phyllis knew, but she went to Dallas every year for tests because of a cancer scare some years earlier. Knowing that Eve wouldn't want her personal medical history discussed at the table, Phyllis didn't say anything about the reason for the trip. She just said, "I'd be glad to."

"Thank you, dear. I don't know what any of us would do without you. You certainly seem to hold everything together around here."

Sam smiled and put in, "I haven't been living here all that long, but even I already know that's true."

"Now, Sam, there's no need for flattery," Phyllis said, but at the same time, it felt good to be appreciated.

"It's not flattery if it's true. 'No brag, just fact,' like Walter Brennan used to say on that old TV show."

Phyllis wasn't sure what TV show he was talking about unless it was *The Real McCoys,* and she didn't recall Walter Brennan saying anything like that when he was on that show, but it didn't really matter.

And there wasn't time to think about it anymore, because Carolyn surprised her by saying, "I know I never would have made it though the past few days without you, Phyllis." She looked around the table. "Without all of you. You've all been good friends to me."

"Why, of course we're your friends, dear," Eve said. "We always stuck together as teachers, and nothing's really changed."

"I wouldn't go that far," Carolyn said heavily. "It seems to me like a lot has changed. People dying, and all of us getting older, and all the ugliness in the world . . ." She stopped and took a deep breath. "Things just aren't like they used to be."

Mattie said, "They never are. Things change all the time. We may not like it, but . . . that's the way it is."

A moment of silence descended on the room. Mattie was certainly right, Phyllis thought. Things had changed for all of them, and not necessarily for the better. She had lost Kenny, and Sam had lost his wife, and with every day that went by, Mattie was losing more of her memories and the things that made her uniquely Mattie. Eve probably worried that she was losing her looks and her ability to attract men. And as for Carolyn . . .

The way things were going, before too much longer Carolyn might well lose her reputation and gain a new one as a killer. She could even lose her freedom.

But not if Phyllis could do anything about it. She decided, then and there, to accept Sam Fletcher's offer of help. With two of them trying to find the real killer and clear Carolyn, maybe teaming up would double their odds.

Still, if Mr. Sam Fletcher thought he could just waltz in and start telling her what to do . . . well, he had another think coming, and that was all there was to it.

After lunch, when Eve and Mattie had gone back to the high school and Carolyn had retreated upstairs to lie down for a while in her room, Phyllis found herself again sitting on the front porch with Sam. They rocked for a few minutes in companionable silence. The big post oak trees, which were all well over a hundred years old, cast enough shade over the house and the front yard so that the air wasn't too hot to be unpleasant yet. Late in the afternoon, anybody with any sense would be inside somewhere in the air-conditioning, but right now, sitting out on the porch wasn't bad.

"I've been thinking about what you said this morning," Phyllis finally said. "I believe you're right, Sam. I probably shouldn't be doing what I've been doing alone."

He nodded slowly, not seeming to take any particular pleasure in the fact that she was agreeing with him. It was as if he didn't see it as vindication of his position, just as practicality on her part, and she liked that about him. He didn't have to win all the time.

"Why don't you tell me what you've come up with?" he suggested. "Get me up to speed, as they say."

For the next few minutes, that's what Phyllis did, explaining what she had learned from first Bud Winfield and then Charles Boatwright.

"Are you sure this newspaper fella is right about Donnie

rookin' his brother and sister out of their inheritance?" Sam asked when she was finished.

"Well, Bud said it was a rumor, so I'm not a hundred percent certain. That's why I thought I'd go to the courthouse and see what I can find out. Wills are public documents, so there should be a copy of it on file in the county clerk's office. If Donnie *was* his mother's sole heir, that would prove something."

"But not that either of his siblings killed him."

"No," Phyllis admitted. "It wouldn't prove that. But it would give them a motive."

"Something to create some reasonable doubt where Carolyn is concerned."

"I don't want to just create reasonable doubt to keep her from going to prison," Phyllis said grimly, "but I suppose if things came down to it, I'd settle for that outcome."

"What you really want to do is find the killer."

"I don't think the police will do it. Not as long as they have their sights set on Carolyn."

"You're probably right about that." Sam rested his big hands on his knees, which looked a little knobby even through his blue jeans. "Well, let's go to the courthouse."

"I'll drive," Phyllis said as she got to her feet.

"Fine with me."

That was another point in his favor: that he didn't mind a woman being behind the wheel.

As they drove off in the Lincoln, he commented, "This is a good-sized car."

"We got in the habit of buying them because Kenny had long legs. Mike did, too, as a boy, although he sort of grew into them and you can't tell it as much now. And he always had a lot of friends who we were taking to Little League baseball games and peewee football practice, so we needed the room."

"What you're sayin'," Sam said with a smile, "is that you

were a soccer mom before the media knew there was such a thing. Only you drove a Lincoln instead of an SUV."

"And the kids back then didn't play soccer." She smiled, too, but didn't take her eyes off the road. "Every new generation that comes along thinks they've invented everything, without considering what people did before."

The county clerk's office was in the sprawling, one-story subcourthouse on Santa Fe Drive, rather than the old courthouse on the square, which was used mostly now for criminal trials and county commissioners' meetings. Phyllis parked out front, and she and Sam went inside. A woman behind the counter smiled a greeting and said, "Can I help y'all?" Before Phyllis could answer, the woman added, "Say, aren't you Miz Newsom?"

"Yes, I am," Phyllis said. She had a pretty good idea what was coming next.

"I had you for history in the eighth grade. I'll bet you don't remember me, do you?"

Phyllis was already searching through the sea of fourteen-year-old faces in her mind, trying to match one of them to the thirty something-year-old face smiling at her over the counter. "Doris Moody," she said, the name popping out of some mental recess.

"That's right!" the woman said, obviously excited and pleased that Phyllis had recognized her. "Only it's Doris Threadgill now. I married Gary Threadgill. Do you remember him?"

Phyllis did indeed, and the thought flashed through her mind that Doris Moody had been smart enough and pretty enough to do better than Gary Threadgill, who had always sat in the back of the room and talked and cut up and barely passed the class. But he had been a football player, and Phyllis supposed that had been enough for sweet, shy little Doris. And she supposed she wasn't being fair, because sometimes even the Gary Threadgills of the world grew up to become fine, upstanding adults.

None of which she said to Doris. Instead she said, "Of course I remember him. How's he doing?"

"Just fine. He's an engineer over at Lockheed. We've got three kids. You want to see their pictures?"

"Of course."

Once Doris had fetched her purse from one of the desks on the other side of the counter and shown off the photos of her children, she laughed and said, "My, I've just been rattling on, when y'all probably came in here for something important. What can I do for you? Marriage license?"

"Good Lord, no," Phyllis exclaimed before she could stop herself. She was immediately embarrassed, and so was Doris.

Sam just kept a pleasant smile on his face, though, as Doris said hastily, "I, uh, remembered that your husband passed away a few years back, Miz Newsom, and I just thought . . . I mean, since you came in with this gentleman—"

"Sam Fletcher," he said, coming gallantly to Doris's rescue. He reached over the counter and shook hands with her. "Pleased to meet you, Doris," he went on with the easy familiarity that seemed to come naturally to him. "Phyllis and I are friends. We're working on some . . . genealogical research."

"Oh," Doris said, clearly relieved that no one was offended. "Well, you've come to the right place. We've got records here stretching all the way back into the eighteen hundreds."

"We don't need to go back that far," Phyllis said. She didn't know exactly when old Mrs. Boatwright had died, and she supposed they should have come armed with that knowledge. "Maybe fifty years or so."

"Any records in particular?"

"Last wills and testaments," Phyllis said.

Doris lifted a gate in the counter. "Well, come on back. I'll show you where those record books are."

When Phyllis saw the long rows of file cabinets, she realized what a daunting task she and Sam had set for themselves. It might take days of looking through the record books before they found the last will and testament of Donnie Boatwright's mother.

"Any particular year you want to start with?" Doris asked.

Sam took his cell phone out of his pocket and said, "Hold on a minute."

Phyllis hadn't heard the phone ring, but maybe he had it set to vibrate. But rather than answering a call, he opened the phone and appeared to make one, poking at keys on the keypad for a good five minutes instead of talking into the blasted thing. Doris looked like she was starting to get a little impatient when Sam finally closed the phone and said, "Nineteen sixty-eight. Starting with May of that year, if you need it narrowed down more."

Doris nodded and turned to the file cabinets, opening one of them and running a fingertip along the spines of the large, leather-bound books that were filed inside it. While she was doing that, Phyllis tried not to stare at Sam.

"Here you go," Doris said as she hauled out one of the books. "What you're looking for should be in this volume. It covers April, May, and June of that year, and then the volumes continue on after that if you need any more of them." Again she ran her finger along the line of books.

"Thank you for your help," Sam said.

"Oh, it was no problem. And I'm sorry about that marriage license mix-up before."

"Don't you worry about it," Sam told her.

"Y'all can use this table right here," Doris added. She set the book on the wooden table in front of the filing cabinets.

"Thank you, Doris," Phyllis said. "You've been a big help."

"Not as big a help as you were to me, Miz Newsom. I always enjoyed your class."

"That's nice to hear. You were a good student."

Doris smiled, nodded, and went back to the front counter, leaving Phyllis and Sam there with the record book. As they sat down, Phyllis opened it, but before she began looking through it, she asked quietly, "How in heaven's name did you do that?"

He tapped his shirt pocket where he had slipped the cell phone. "Oh, I got Wi-Fi on this phone, so I Googled Donnie Boatwright and found out his mother's name, then Googled her and got an obituary for her, and that gave me the date of her death, May 27, 1968. We can figure it took a while after that for her will to be probated, but it ought to be within the next few months. That'll cut down some on our looking."

"It'll cut down a lot," Phyllis said. "Oh, and by the way . . . I was lost after you said *Wi-Fi*."

Chapter 23

Phyllis's comment hadn't been completely true. She had understood some of what Sam said. She knew that Google was a search engine on the Internet, and she *thought* Wi-Fi meant that he had wireless access to the Internet on his phone. But she wouldn't have had the slightest idea how to accomplish what Sam had done in a matter of minutes. That made her feel a little resentful at first, as if he had been showing off, until she told herself that he probably couldn't have come up with a recipe for spicy peach cobbler, nor could he have cooked it and made it fit to eat. Everyone had their own particular talents, she had always told her students, and she believed that.

They sat side by side, their blue-jean-clad legs almost touching but not quite, and leaned forward in their chairs to peer at the documents in the massive book. These were only photocopies; the actual documents were probably in the files of the various attorneys who had handled these wills. But copies would do just fine for their purposes.

Phyllis recognized quite a few of the names she saw as they paged through the volume. Back in the sixties, she had been a young teacher and had known many of the families in town due to her associations with her students. Weatherford had seemed like a much smaller place back then, the sort of town where everybody knew everybody else. That hadn't been true, of course, even then, but that perception had been a lot closer to accurate in those days. Now, with the town sprawling out in all directions and new housing developments springing up seemingly overnight and new businesses pouring in, Weatherford was . . . well, it was getting to seem a lot like Fort Worth or Dallas. That unique small-town atmosphere still existed, but it was fading.

Like Mattie said, you couldn't stop change. Most of the time, you couldn't even slow it down.

By the time they reached the end of the book, they hadn't found Oletha Boatwright's will. Sam got up, carried the volume back over to the filing cabinet, replaced it, and took out the next one in line. He set it in front of Phyllis, who opened it and began turning the pages as Sam sat down again.

This volume covered the third quarter of 1968, and when they came to the pages for August of that year, they found what they were looking for. Mrs. Boatwright's last will and testament included enough legalese to fill up three pages, but once Phyllis and Sam waded through all the verbiage and figured out what it meant, the upshot was pretty simple: Mrs. Boatwright had directed that her outstanding debts be paid, had made a couple of small bequests to charities, and then had left the balance of her estate to her son, Donald Wilson Boatwright.

Sam sat back in his chair and shook his head. "Not even a mention of the other two kids. It's like Donnie was her only child."

"That would make me mad," Phyllis said. "Wouldn't it bother you?"

"I'd probably be pretty peeved," Sam agreed. "Maybe not so much about the money, but more about being ignored that way. I don't hardly see how a parent could do that."

"I got the impression that Mrs. Boatwright relied on Donnie to take care of her. He had her power of attorney, after all."

"You know how much money was in the estate?"

Phyllis shook her head. "No idea, and the will doesn't

say. But Donnie's always been well-to-do, as far back as I remember him. I have only a vague memory of his mother being alive, but I think she lived in the same house where Donnie does now . . . where he *did,* I should say. It's a beautiful old place on the western edge of town—not quite what you'd call a mansion, but close."

"So it was probably a valuable estate?"

"The house had to be worth a lot. From what Bud Winfield said, Donnie had already gotten his hands on a lot of the other assets. But I'll bet the estate added up to quite a bit, anyway." Phyllis studied the photocopied document and then placed a slender finger on the date the will had been written. "May 21. A week before Mrs. Boatwright died. That's changing your will at the last minute, all right."

"Wonder what the terms were of the will this one replaced," Sam mused.

Phyllis shook her head. "There's no way of finding that out. Unless . . ." She turned back to the final page of the document and found the signature of the lawyer who had prepared it, feeling a sudden surge of excitement when she recognized it. "William Kinnison. He's still alive, Sam. I think he's mostly retired, but he still has a law office down by the square."

"You think he'd talk to us?"

"I don't know," she said, "but I think it's worth a try."

There was a coin-operated photocopy machine near the table. They took the book over to it, made two copies of every page they needed, and then put the book back in the filing cabinet. As they were leaving, Doris Threadgill smiled at them and asked, "Y'all find what you were looking for?"

"I hope so," Phyllis told her.

They drove toward downtown, Phyllis handling the big Lincoln easily in the traffic. They went past the First Monday grounds and the farmer's market, then Phyllis found a parking place on the square. William Kinnison's law office was on one of the side streets, less than a block off the square, she explained to Sam.

"He may not be there," she said. "I don't know how often he comes into the office these days."

Luck was with them. The secretary inside the well-furnished office told them, "Yes, Mr. Kinnison is here. Do you have an appointment?"

"I'm afraid not," Phyllis said. "We just need to talk to him for a minute, though."

"Could I ask what this is about?"

"It's about a will."

The secretary, who was in her fifties, shook her head. "I'm sorry, Mr. Kinnison doesn't draw up wills or other documents anymore. He doesn't take any new clients, either. He's semiretired and only handles a few matters for his existing clients."

"That's what we want to ask him about—one of his existing clients."

The secretary got a stern look on her face. "I'm afraid Mr. Kinnison can't help you. He can't discuss any legal matters pertaining to his clients. That would be privileged information."

Sam held up the copies they had made of Oletha Boatwright's will. "This is public information, right out of the county clerk's office."

The secretary frowned and started to say something else, but before she could, the door to the inner office opened and a tall old man with a white beard stepped out. "I heard someone come in, Debbie," he said. "Who—?" The man stopped and smiled at Phyllis and Sam. "You're Mrs. Newsom, aren't you?"

"That's right. I don't think we've ever met, Mr. Kinnison—"

He waved a gnarled hand. "No, but I know you. Saw your picture in the paper last week after Donnie Boatwright keeled over dead when he ate your peach pie."

Phyllis bristled. Trying to control her annoyance, she said, "My cobbler didn't have anything to do with it."

"No, no, didn't mean that it did. What can I do for you?"

"We'd like to ask you about Donnie," Phyllis said, "and the will his mother made that left everything to him."

Sam held up the photocopies again.

Kinnison's eyes widened a little in surprise. "Lord, I hadn't thought about that in years," he muttered. "Come in, you two, come in. I don't believe I know you, sir."

Sam introduced himself and shook hands with Kinnison, as he ushered them into his office. The secretary looked on in apparent disapproval, but Phyllis pretty much ignored her.

Kinnison had to be close to ninety years old, but he was still spry for his age. He wore a brown, Western-cut suit and a string tie with turquoise and silver decorations, and he looked like he could still climb into a saddle if he wanted to. When he was settled down behind his desk and Phyllis and Sam were in the leather chairs in front of it, he said, "You must be mighty interested in the past to go to the trouble of digging up that old will."

"I was a history teacher before I retired," Phyllis told him. "The past has always held a great deal of interest for me . . . especially the way it affects the present."

Kinnison took a long black cigar out of a humidor on his desk. For a second Phyllis was afraid he was going to light it, and she knew a stogie like that probably smelled terrible. He put it in his mouth and left it unlit, though, preferring to chew on the end and roll it from side to side occasionally. He held out a hand and said, "Mind if I take a look at those papers?"

Sam hesitated but handed them over. Kinnison studied them for a few moments, frowning as he read over the words he had written nearly forty years earlier.

"Lawyers have always been long-winded," he finally said as he dropped the papers on his desk. "I was just as guilty as any of 'em. What do you want to know about this will?"

"It was drawn up just a week before Mrs. Boatwright passed away," Phyllis said.

"That's not a question, but I know what you're getting at. It's not that unusual for someone to have a will made when they know they're not long for this earth. Oletha Boatwright knew she was dying."

Phyllis frowned slightly. "Are you saying she didn't have a will until this one was drawn up? This one didn't replace another one?"

"That's right, at least to my knowledge. I suppose some other attorney could have drawn one up sometime in the past, but if so, she didn't say anything to me about it."

Sam said, "You seem to remember the circumstances pretty well, Mr. Kinnison."

"Nothing wrong with my brain," Kinnison snapped. "Besides, I've got good reason to remember the whole business. I got threatened with a thrashing because of it." He shrugged. "Wasn't the first time and wouldn't be the last, but still memorable."

"Someone threatened to attack you over this will?" Phyllis asked.

"That's right. But I won't tell you who. You might go blabbing about it, and then I'd wind up being slapped with a lawsuit for slander."

"You don't have to tell us," Phyllis said. "It had to be Charles Boatwright. Or possibly his brother-in-law, Kent Hughes, because of his wife, Sally. But it was because Charles and Sally were cut out of Mrs. Boatwright's will and Donnie got everything."

Deep creases appeared in Kinnison's leathery old forehead. "Just what are you getting at, Mrs. Newsom?" he demanded. "What business is this of yours?"

Phyllis noticed that he didn't deny what she'd said about Charles Boatwright and Sally Hughes being upset over their mother's will. "Someone murdered Donnie Boatwright," she said. "It seems to me like his brother and sister had a motive."

Kinnison stared at her for a second or two before he said, "That's just loco. I've known Charles and Sally for many years. Neither of them would have killed anybody."

"You just implied that one of them, or Sally's husband, Kent, was angry enough to threaten you over Mrs. Boatwright's will. Are any of them clients of yours, Mr. Kinnison?"

"No, I've never represented any of them," the elderly lawyer snapped. "And just to set the record straight, it was Charles Boatwright who came in here foamin' at the mouth after the will was read. He said Donnie and I were just a couple of cheap crooks and told me he ought to tear me limb from limb."

Phyllis had a hard time imagining the affable car salesman behaving in such a violent manner, but she remembered the flash of old anger she had seen in Charles's eyes and found Kinnison's story more believable.

"But he never struck me," Kinnison went on, "and he calmed down pretty quick after he blew up. I reckon he knew that if he took a swing at me, I'd put him on the ground and then have him arrested to boot."

Sam asked, "Did you call the police?"

Kinnison snorted disdainfully. "No need. I wasn't afraid of Charles Boatwright. Charles knew it, too. That's why he backed down."

The old man seemed to be reveling a little in telling the story. Reliving the days when he had been young, or at least younger, and the prospect of a brawl didn't phase him. Phyllis said, "So there's no record of Charles threatening to attack you?"

"Just my word," Kinnison said. "That ought to be good enough."

"Oh, I believe you, Mr. Kinnison. Mrs. Boatwright still cut her other two children out of her estate, even if this will didn't replace an older one."

"Absolutely," Kinnison agreed. "If Oletha Boatwright had died intestate, things would have been divided up equally between the three children."

"So this will"—Phyllis tapped the copies on the desk—"did cost Charles and Sally some money?"

"Of course. Although Donnie already controlled most of his mother's fortune through the power of attorney she gave him." Kinnison's eyes narrowed shrewdly. "The only reason I'm telling you any of this, Mrs. Newsom, is that I suspect you already know it. And what you don't know, you've guessed at. Now let me make a guess about you."

"Go ahead," Phyllis said calmly.

"You and this tall drink of water, whoever he is, are trying to find out who slipped that poison to Donnie at the peach festival." Kinnison clasped his hands together on the desk. "I won't ask why you're doing it, but I'm here to tell you that you're barking up the wrong tree. Hell, all that business with the will happened nearly forty years ago. Nobody holds a grudge that long."

"You can't be sure about that."

Kinnison snorted again. "I'm sure that neither Charles Boatwright nor Sally Hughes is a murderer. The very idea is preposterous! They're both well-to-do in their own right."

"Money isn't the only motive for murder," Phyllis pointed out. "Maybe one of them finally couldn't stand it any longer that their mother favored Donnie so much over them."

Kinnison shook his head and said, "I just don't believe it."

"It doesn't matter so much whether you believe it . . . as it does whether or not the police do."

"You'd go to the police about this? It's all long forgotten!"

"Maybe it shouldn't be," Phyllis said. "Maybe it's just what they need to know. They're concentrating on someone else, and I'm convinced that person is innocent."

"That's just your opinion. Just like it's my opinion that Charles and Sally are innocent."

"If that's the case, then you shouldn't mind if the police look into this. If you're right, they won't find anything pointing to Charles or Sally as the murderer."

"But it's still a terrible thing to do," Kinnison protested, "setting the cops on them like that."

"You're right," Phyllis agreed, "but it would be even more terrible if an innocent person was arrested, convicted, and sent to prison."

Kinnison's bushy white eyebrows lifted. "You sound mighty convinced that whoever the cops regard as the most likely suspect is innocent."

"I'd stake my life on it," Phyllis said.

Chapter 24

"Let's sum up what we know," Sam said as Phyllis drove back toward the house. "Donnie Boatwright got control of his mother's estate well before she died, and when she did pass away, the will she had made just a week earlier left Donnie everything. This made his brother Charles so mad that Charles went to the office of the lawyer who drew up the will and threatened to go to Fist City with him."

"That's it, all right," Phyllis said.

"Pretty impressive that you found out all of that in only one day of detective work."

Phyllis sort of thought so, too, but she didn't want to say so because it would have been bragging. Although . . . what was it Walter Brennan had said, according to Sam?

No brag, just fact.

"What now?" Sam went on.

"Well, I think this should be brought to the attention of the police. We've got copies of the will, and the fact that Charles threatened Mr. Kinnison—"

"Which Kinnison will probably deny if the cops question him about it. He seemed just as sure that Charles is innocent as you are about Carolyn."

"I don't know. He's an officer of the court, after all. Surely he wouldn't tell the police a bald-faced lie."

"Sometimes legal ethics is a, what do you call it, oxymoron, like jumbo shrimp."

"If Eve was here she'd tell you it's *an* oxymoron."

Sam grinned. "Well, I've got half of it down, anyway." He grew more serious as he went on, "I wouldn't put it past Kinnison to lie to the cops, at least about this. What worries me even more is that he might call Charles Boatwright and tell him that Nancy Drew is on his trail."

"Please! Nancy Drew was a mere slip of a girl."

"I mean it, Phyllis. If Boatwright is a killer, and if he knows you're trying to get the police interested in him . . . well, there's no telling what he might do."

"That's why you talked me into taking on an able-bodied assistant. You're the hired muscle, Sam . . . although I can only pay you in things like meatloaf and mashed potatoes."

"Fine by me. I just hope I don't have to wind up earnin' my wages. I'm a lot better at freeloadin'."

Despite their banter, she could tell that he was actually worried, and to be honest, deep down she was, too. She had gotten caught up in her desire to prove Carolyn's innocence, to the point that she had forgotten it might have been smart to play her cards a little closer to the vest.

But what she was doing was out in the open now, so things would just have to take their course, no matter what that might be.

She found out what that course was when they got home and walked into the living room to find Eve on the phone. She looked a little flustered, which was a warning sign in itself because Eve never got flustered, and as she turned and saw Phyllis and Sam, she said, "Here she is now, Mr. Boatwright. Hold on just a minute." Eve put her hand over the phone and told Phyllis, "It's Charles Boatwright, and he sounds awfully upset about something."

Phyllis exchanged a worried glance with Sam and then sighed in resignation. She held out her hand for the phone. "I might as well talk to him and get it over with."

"I can tell him you can't talk right now," Eve offered.

"No, that would just postpone the unpleasantness."

"Well, all right, dear." Eve handed over the phone.

Phyllis took it. "This is Phyllis Newsom."

"Mrs. Newsom, this is Charles Boatwright," he said unnecessarily. "I just got off the phone with William Kinnison, and I'm very upset about what he told me. I thought when we talked this morning that we got along quite well."

"We did. It was a nice conversation, Mr. Boatwright."

"Conversation!" Charles practically yelped. "From what I understand now, it was more of an interrogation!"

"Not at all. I wasn't there on any official basis—"

"Which makes it even worse," Charles cut in. "You're not a police officer, Mrs. Newsom. You're just a prying old busybody with a morbid curiosity!"

Phyllis stiffened angrily. If Charles had been here, instead of on the phone, she would have been tempted to slap his face for a comment like that.

"You seem to think that I murdered my brother," Charles went on. "Would it do any good if I told you that I had nothing to do with Donnie's death? Would you stop this insane meddling of yours?"

"There's nothing insane about trying to find out the truth."

"You're not after the truth. You're just trying to smear my good name!"

Sam had been watching her end of the conversation with a worried expression on his face, and he had to be able to hear Charles's loud, angry voice, even though he probably couldn't make out the words. He held out a hand and mouthed, *Want me to talk to him?*

Phyllis shook her head and said into the phone, "If you're innocent, Mr. Boatwright, you don't have anything to worry about."

"You know better than that," he said coldly. "Plenty of innocent people have had their lives and reputations ruined by coming under suspicion for a crime like this."

He was right, of course. That was exactly why Phyllis wanted so badly to save Carolyn from that very thing.

"Well, do your worst," Charles went on. "I've retained Kinnison as my lawyer, so he'll be with me if the police come to question me. And he'll be filing a slander suit on my behalf if you start spreading any vicious rumors, too, you old bitch!"

Phyllis gasped at the virulence in his voice. Instinctively, she lowered the phone and pushed the OFF button. She wasn't going to be talked to like that by anybody.

Sam took a quick step toward her. "What is it? What did he say?"

Phyllis took a deep breath and tried to bring her emotions under control again. "He's hired Mr. Kinnison as his lawyer," she said. "I guess the secretary was wrong about him not taking on any new clients."

"That was a smart move on his part. Now Kinnison can claim lawyer-client privilege, and they can both keep their mouths shut about what happened after Mrs. Boatwright died."

"*Mrs.* Boatwright?" Eve repeated. "Dear, what in heaven's name is going on here? What have you been doing to get people so worked up?"

Phyllis hadn't really thought about the fact that Eve had been in the room while she was talking to Charles. Now she had no choice but to say, "I'm looking into Donnie Boatwright's murder."

"Looking into? You mean like investigating? Like a detective?" Eve stared at her. "Dear, why in the world would you want to do that?"

"Yes, Phyllis," Carolyn said from the bottom of the stairs, "why would you want to do that?"

Phyllis turned her head sharply to look toward the stairs. She hadn't known that Carolyn was there, and had no idea how much she had overheard.

"I was just asking some questions—" she began.

"Trying to prove that I'm innocent?"

"Innocent of what?" Eve asked. She looked around sternly. "Something's going on here that I don't know anything about, and I have to tell you, I don't like it!"

Carolyn walked toward them and said wearily, "The police think I killed Donnie Boatwright."

"What? Why, that's ridiculous!"

"I know," Phyllis said. "That's why I'm not going to let this go any farther."

"No one appointed you my protector, Phyllis," Carolyn said. "I don't want you getting into any trouble on my account."

"I'm not going to get into any trouble."

Eve said, "From the sound of that phone call from Charles Boatwright, you already are."

Phyllis waved a hand, dismissing the idea of being worried about Charles Boatwright.

"What about Charles?" Carolyn asked.

Phyllis hesitated but then decided that so much of the story had already been spilled, it didn't make any sense to worry about keeping the rest of it a secret. She let it pour out of her, telling Carolyn and Eve how she'd spent her day and filling them in on the things she and Sam had learned.

"Let me get this straight," Carolyn said when Phyllis finished. She nodded toward Sam and went on, "*He* knew about this and has been helping you?"

"Just part of the day."

Stiffly, Carolyn said to Sam, "Thank you, Mr. Fletcher. But what I said to Phyllis goes for you, too. I don't want my problems getting anyone else into trouble."

"It's no trouble, Carolyn," he told her, his voice gentle. "We want to see justice done, and we know you didn't kill Donnie."

"Then who did?" Eve asked. "His own brother?"

"We have no proof of that," Phyllis said. "None at all. But the police have based their investigation of Carolyn purely on motive and opportunity, and I want them to see that Charles had just as much opportunity and a motive that was just as strong, if not stronger!"

"Well, what you say makes sense, dear," Eve admitted. "Are you going to tell the police about it?"

Phyllis thought briefly about the phone call from Charles. It had had the opposite effect from what he wanted. She was more determined than ever now to share her discoveries with the authorities—especially since they were things the police could have learned themselves, if they had just bothered to look!

"Yes," she said. "I'm going to tell Mike, anyway. He can take the information to the sheriff, and then Royce Haney can tell Chief Whitmire about it. I'm sure they'll take it better coming from Mike than they will from me. I just hope it does some good."

"So do I," Carolyn said, "but I'm not going to count on it. Things have gone too far. It's like there's a runaway train bearing down on me, and there's not a thing I can do to stop it or get out of the way."

For Carolyn's sake, Phyllis hoped that her friend was wrong about that.

"You did *what*?" Mike said as he stared at his mother.

"I talked to Bud Winfield and Charles Boatwright, then Sam and I looked up old Mrs. Boatwright's will at the county clerk's office, and then we went to see Mr. Kinnison. Honestly, Mike, I already told you all this once." Her voice held the tolerant but slightly impatient tone that most parents took when they explained something to their children yet again.

Mike figured he sounded like that sometimes, too, when he talked to Bobby. But that didn't mean he liked it.

"I know," he said. "I'm just having a hard time believing that you could go out and start acting like Nancy Drew."

His mother made an exasperated sound. "Nancy Drew

again," she said. "For goodness sake, do I look like a teenage girl?"

"You remind me more of Miss Marple, dear," Eve put in. "Or that Jessica Fletcher from TV." She looked at Sam. "I never thought of that! You have the same last name."

Sam held up his hands and said, "No relation."

"Well, I should hope not. She's a fictional character, dear."

Mike wondered fleetingly how he'd managed to fall down a rabbit hole in the middle of Weatherford. "Look, Mom," he said, "you can't just go around and start investigating a murder. It's not right."

"Did you know about old Mrs. Boatwright's will, and the fact that Charles Boatwright threatened Mr. Kinnison because of it?"

"No, and I still don't know that, except as hearsay."

Sam held out some sheets of paper. "Here's a copy of the will. You can look it up yourself in the county clerk's office if you want. You'll probably want a certified copy when you show it to the sheriff."

"I haven't said I'm showing anything to the sheriff." Mike looked around at the faces of the people gathered in his mother's living room. They were all here except Mrs. Harris, who was upstairs napping. When he had walked in here, having come by on his way home from work in response to his mother's phone call, he had been able to tell right away that they were worked up about something. But not in his wildest dreams would he have ever expected the things he had heard.

And yet . . . and yet the theory they were pushing made sense, no matter how they had gotten the information it was based on. Carolyn Wilbarger had a motive—something bad Donnie Boatwright had done in the past to her daughter. But Charles Boatwright had a motive based on the past that was just as strong, maybe even stronger because Donnie's alleged underhandedness had affected Charles directly. For that matter, Charles's sister, Sally, had to come in for her share of suspicion, too, since she shared the same motive as her brother. And then there was Sally's husband, who could have acted on her behalf. . . .

Charles was the one who had threatened violence against Kinnison, though. The problem with that was that it had occurred nearly forty years earlier, as had Charles and Sally being cut out of their mother's will. Carolyn's anger toward Donnie was a lot fresher, only a few years old. A jury probably wouldn't be willing to believe that Charles and/or Sally had waited decades to settle the score.

Mike mulled all that over in a matter of a few silent seconds. Finally, his mother demanded, "Well? What *are* you going to do?"

With a sigh, Mike said, "It makes sense to question Charles and Sally again. Any time there's a homicide, the first person you look at is the spouse, and if the victim's not married, then you see if anybody in his family has any reason to want him dead. It's just standard procedure."

"Which wasn't followed in this case," Phyllis pointed out.

"That's because the sheriff and Chief Whitmire thought they had a better suspect." Mike couldn't stop himself from glancing at Mrs. Wilbarger.

"You admit it, then. A full investigation hasn't been carried out."

"Let me talk to the sheriff," Mike said, not admitting anything for the record—and when a fella was talking to his mother, he was always talking on the record. "Chances are, Charles Boatwright and Mr. Kinnison are both going to deny that there was ever any trouble between them, and if we can't shake their story, we're stuck with nothing but the will. And even though it might have been a lousy thing to do, there was absolutely nothing illegal about Mrs. Boatwright leaving everything to Donnie."

Sam said, "Even though he had her power of attorney and

could've used, what do you call it, undue influence to get her to cut out the other two?"

"That's pure speculation," Mike pointed out. "We don't know exactly what went on back then, and with the two people who were involved both dead, we can't ever be sure that we know the whole truth."

His mother looked crestfallen. "Are you saying that I didn't do any good?"

"If we can't prove there was trouble between Charles and Kinnison over the will, which would indicate that by extension Charles was also upset with Donnie about it, then we're left with just a possible motive, and nothing to indicate that it was ever acted on."

"Just like in Carolyn's case," Phyllis pointed out.

Mike shrugged. "Just like that . . . but it's Mrs. Wilbarger who's going to be pulled in for questioning any day now."

Carolyn sighed and looked at the floor.

"I'm sorry," Mike said. "I'm just telling you how it is. It doesn't do any good to sugarcoat things."

"No, of course not," his mother said. "All right, Mike. Take a copy of the will, and do what you can with it. And thank you for listening to us."

"No problem." He got to his feet. "But, Mom, I'd appreciate it if you'd just leave this to us from here on out. I swear, I'll do everything I can to get to the bottom of it."

"I know you will." Phyllis stood up, too, and gave him a hug. So did Eve, and Sam clapped a hand on his shoulder. Carolyn stayed in her chair, looking discouraged. Mike had never seen her that way before. She had always been so loud and hearty and sure of herself. To be honest, he thought, she had always been a little bit pushy. All that self-confidence was gone now, and as he looked at the defeated woman in the chair, Mike realized that he didn't believe she was guilty, either.

The problem was going to be convincing someone in

authority of that—and keeping his mother from getting herself even more involved in the case.

Because if Carolyn *was* innocent, that meant there was an unknown killer still on the loose somewhere.

And probably willing to kill again to remain unknown.

Chapter 25

Mike had reacted pretty much as Phyllis expected him to. He had taken what she had to say seriously, all right, but he hadn't been encouraging about the chances of her information helping Carolyn. And then to top it off, he had told her—politely—to butt out. Expected or not, she was hurt by that.

He was just worried about her, though, she told herself as she prepared supper that night. She couldn't blame him for being concerned about her. She was his mother, after all. And maybe he was right. Whether it was enough to do any good or not, maybe she had done all she could.

But it didn't seem like it. She had already seen plenty of evidence that Donnie Boatwright hadn't always been the fine, upstanding member of the community that he seemed to be at first glance. He had been a lecherous, conniving, unscrupulous bully who evidently stopped at nothing to get what he wanted. If he had treated Sandra Webster the way he had, not to mention his own brother and sister, what *else* had he done that might have been bad enough to get him murdered?

Phyllis couldn't answer that question, but she had the nagging feeling that she had overlooked something important, that she had seen or heard something that might have given her the answer. No matter how hard she thought about it, though, she couldn't come up with that elusive bit of knowledge . . .

And at supper she had yet another worry, as Mattie only picked at her food and didn't seem to feel well. After they had eaten, Phyllis caught a moment alone with Eve in the kitchen and asked her about the older woman. With everything that had been going on lately, Phyllis hadn't spent as much time with Mattie as she used to, and Eve had been around her more than any of the others.

"I'm getting worried about her, the poor dear," Eve admitted. "Of course, her mind has been going for quite a while, and there's nothing we can do about that. But it seems to be getting worse. A lot of the time she's so lost in the past that she doesn't really know where she is. But then at other times her mind is as clear as a bell and she's totally focused on what she's doing. Like when she's tutoring at the high school. Being around the kids seems to really sharpen her thinking."

"What about physically?" Phyllis asked. "She didn't look good tonight."

"No, she didn't," Eve agreed. "And she is getting weaker. Like it or not, Phyllis, the time is coming when she won't be able to live here anymore, even with us to look after her. She'll need more care than that."

Phyllis nodded sadly. Fighting the battle against time was an effort that everyone was doomed to lose in the end, and yet it still came as a blow when you realized that the years were winning. In this case, it was a dear friend who was being overwhelmed by age, not Phyllis herself, but it was still sad to see someone losing that struggle. She hated to think about Mattie having to move into a nursing home, but it was probably inevitable. At least by having her live here, that had been postponed for a good long while.

"To tell you the truth," Eve went on, "I think being part of summer school this year is what's kept Mattie going as long as she has. Helping children with their educations has been her whole life."

Remembering Mattie's volunteer work at the library, the hospital, and other places, Phyllis said, "I'd say helping children in general has been the biggest thing in her life. She never had any of her own."

"No, and I often wondered why she never married. I suppose she thought that marriage and a family of her own wouldn't be as rewarding as what she was already doing."

"You're probably right." Phyllis sighed. "I suppose there's nothing we can do for her except make life as pleasant and comfortable for her as we can. I might talk to Dr. Lee about the situation, too, and see if he has any suggestions."

"Don't forget about taking Mattie to school tomorrow," Eve said on her way out of the kitchen.

"I won't," Phyllis promised. If the one thing that meant anything to Mattie these days was her tutoring, there was no way Phyllis would cause her to miss a session.

Anyway, Phyllis mused, it appeared that her brief stint as a detective was over, so she might as well accomplish what she could in other areas, like helping Mattie.

The next morning, the murder of Donnie Boatwright and the mysterious death of Newt Bishop were still on her mind, of course. She couldn't seem to stop thinking about them, especially Newt. Donnie's murder was so high-profile that everyone seemed to have forgotten what had happened to Newt. The fact that it had never been determined for sure whether his death was deliberate or an accident probably had something to do with the lack of attention to it these days, as well. Mike had talked to Alfred Landers, who had been embroiled in that bitter lawsuit with Newt, and seemed to think that the realtor was a legitimate suspect, but there was no evidence to place him at the scene other than the fact that his car was similar to the one Phyllis had seen at the barn. Just as in the case of Donnie's death, everything went back to motive. Darryl Bishop had had good reason to hate his father, and Landers had cause to want Newt dead, too. As far as Donnie's death was concerned, Carolyn could have wanted to kill him, and Phyllis had to admit as much even though she was convinced that her friend hadn't actually committed the crime. But Donnie's brother and sister had motives that were just as strong.

Motives, motives, motives . . . they all went round and round in Phyllis's head, even while she was fixing breakfast and getting ready to take Mattie to the high school. She kept seeing Newt's face in her mind and then Donnie's, as if there were some sort of link between the men. She wasn't sure why that thought stayed so stubbornly in her head, but it did.

Finally she was able to quiet the clamor in her mind by concentrating on the task at hand, which was getting Mattie to school. During breakfast, Mattie seemed to feel a little better than she had the night before, as if a good night's sleep had revitalized her to a certain extent. Of course, at her age there was only so much that rest could do for her. It couldn't turn back the hands of time.

After everyone had eaten, Sam came up to Phyllis in the kitchen and asked quietly, "What do you have planned for today?"

"Well, I'm going to drop Mattie off at the high school and then probably do some shopping before I go back and pick her up later."

"No detecting?" Sam's face was serious, and there was no hint of mockery in his words. Phyllis was glad he hadn't brought up Nancy Drew again.

"You heard Mike," she said. "I'm supposed to leave the investigation to them."

"You didn't seem too hopeful that the cops would go after Charles Boatwright or his sister instead of Carolyn."

"I'm not," Phyllis admitted, "but I don't know what else I can do. I gave them a perfectly good suspect . . . two of them, in fact . . . all tied up with a bow. If they don't act on that information, it's not my fault."

Sam's forehead creased a little. "No offense, Phyllis, but you don't strike me as the sort of lady who lets go of something once she's got her teeth in it."

"Are you saying I remind you of a bulldog?" she asked with a little laugh that didn't contain much genuine humor.

"Nope, just determined. If you can think of anything else you want to check out, I'll be glad to give you a hand."

"I appreciate that, Sam. I really do. But today I have to help Mattie."

He nodded. "Sure. Just let me know if you change your mind, or if something else comes up that I can help you with."

He was a good man, she thought as she went to get her car keys. Friendly, helpful, and not pushy and full of himself. She liked him and was glad that he had moved in here. But more than that . . . well, more than that just wasn't going to happen. For one thing, she didn't want Eve to get jealous and unsheathe her claws. Phyllis had seen instances in the past when such things had happened, and they weren't pretty.

She found Mattie in the living room, digging through her purse. "What are you looking for?" Phyllis asked.

The older woman glanced up in irritation. "My car keys," she said impatiently. "I can't find them, and I've got to get to school. My class is depending on me to be there."

Phyllis felt a pang of regret, perhaps even sorrow. As gently as possible, she said, "Mattie, you don't drive anymore, remember? But I'm going to take you to school, so don't worry. You're going to tutor the summer school students at the high school."

Mattie frowned at her for a moment, blinking rapidly, and then suddenly her expression cleared. "You're taking me to the high school, aren't you, Phyllis? We'd better get going. Don't want to be late."

She was back to herself again, Phyllis thought with relief. There was no telling how long that state would last, but for now, Mattie was all right.

As they drove toward the high school, which was on the Interstate in the southwest part of town, it occurred to Phyllis that she might take advantage of Mattie's current lucidity. Mattie had been around Weatherford and Parker County longer than anyone else she knew.

"Mattie, I was wondering," she began. "You knew both Newt Bishop and Donnie Boatwright—"

"Sure I did. I dated Donnie once, you know, not long after the war. He was a fine figure of a man, and he took me to Casino Beach—"

"Yes, I remember," Phyllis said quickly, not wanting the reminiscing to drag Mattie too far into the past. "Do you recall whether or not Newt and Donnie ever knew each other?"

"Why, I'm sure they did. Donnie knew just about everybody in the county. There weren't so many people in these parts back in those days. It was easier to get acquainted with folks."

"Do you know if they ever had any business dealings with each other, or anything like that?"

Mattie frowned. "Newt and Donnie? Not that I know of. I suppose Newt could've been a silent partner in one of Donnie's businesses, or something like that. But I doubt it. Newt never seemed all that interested in anything except that orchard of his." Her voice hardened a little. "Loved those peach trees more'n he did his own family, I reckon. I probably shouldn't speak ill of the dead that way, but it's true."

"If they weren't business partners, is it possible they were friends?"

"I don't think so. I don't recall Donnie ever sayin' anything about Newt. Maybe, come to think of it, they didn't know each other. I sure never saw them together."

Phyllis felt her frustration rising. That gnawing sensation

in the back of her mind made her want to draw some sort of link between the two dead men, but it looked like that idea wasn't going anywhere.

She drove under an overpass, and the high school loomed on the left. For years the school had been located on South Main, much closer to downtown, but the student population had outgrown that campus, and this new school had been opened several years earlier. It was a huge, sprawling, red brick complex. While it was under construction it had looked more like a shopping mall being built than a school. As far as Phyllis was concerned, most newer schools lacked the character and personality of the older ones. They had too much steel and glass, sterile edifices that lacked the soul, the special something in the air, that only generations of students could instill in a school.

But that was just her being old-fashioned again, she told herself as she turned the Lincoln into the parking lot, which was about a third full. Years down the road, the kids who had attended this school would probably feel the same way about whatever school replaced it.

She parked close so that Mattie wouldn't have to walk too far. "Would you like me to come in with you?" she asked as she brought the car to a stop.

"No need," Mattie said. "I can make it just fine." She opened the door and got out, seemingly a lot more spry this morning than she had been the night before. "You'll pick me up at lunchtime, about eleven forty-five?"

"I'll be here," Phyllis promised.

Mattie nodded, shut the door, and turned to walk toward the entrance.

Phyllis got on the freeway and drove a couple of miles to what had become Weatherford's main shopping district, with large chain stores on both sides of the highway. She spent a couple of hours there, keeping an eye on the time so she wouldn't take a chance on being late to pick up Mattie. At eleven thirty she headed back toward the high school.

As she pulled up to the stop sign on the frontage road, ready to turn left under the highway toward the school, she heard a siren, and looked to her right to see an ambulance speeding toward the Interstate from the direction of the hospital. Phyllis waited at the stop sign, since the emergency vehicle had the right of way, and then pulled out behind the ambulance after it had gone by.

To her surprise, the ambulance turned into the parking lot of the high school. The thought flashed through Phyllis's mind that something had happened to Mattie. She had no reason to think that, other than Mattie's advanced age and declining health, but worry still gnawed at Phyllis as she pulled quickly into the lot. Mattie could have collapsed or had a heart attack, or something like that. That certainly would have warranted calling an ambulance.

However, the ambulance with its flashing lights didn't go all the way up to the sidewalk in front of the main entrance. Instead, it screeched to a stop part of the way through the lot. Phyllis saw several teachers and students gathered around the spot. She wondered if someone had been struck by a car.

When she had parked the Lincoln and gotten out to hurry toward the ambulance, she saw that her conjecture had been correct. The EMTs—Calvin and Ted, she realized as she came closer—were bending over a figure lying on the concrete pavement. Phyllis felt a shock go through her as she caught a glimpse of blood. The injured person was a woman, young enough so that Phyllis couldn't tell immediately if she was a teacher or a student. Although she couldn't see very well with the EMTs and the rest of the crowd around the woman, Phyllis thought the injury looked like a serious one.

She noticed a midsized car stopped in the middle of the lane, its engine off. There was a dent on the hood, and a spider-webbed place on the windshield where something had struck the safety glass hard. Phyllis felt a little sick as she realized that she was looking at the car that had run into that poor woman. She had probably gone up on the hood, and that impact against the glass had been from her head. . . .

Someone put a hand on Phyllis's arm, and she looked around to see Mattie standing there. "Thank the Lord you're here, Phyllis," Mattie said. "This is awful, just awful. I'm afraid that woman's dead."

Chapter 26

As it turned out, the woman was still alive, which Phyllis realized as she and Mattie watched the EMTs work over her for the next few minutes. Mattie was quite upset anyway. Phyllis asked, "Do you know her?" She didn't have to explain that she meant the woman who had been struck.

"I've seen her around the school," Mattie said. "She's one of the teachers. I think her name's Janie, or something like that."

Calvin and Ted got the woman onto a stretcher and lifted her into the back of the ambulance. Bandages swathed her head, but they didn't completely cover up the bright blond hair now stained with crimson. They had immobilized her head with a brace, too, as if she had a neck injury of some sort.

A couple of police cars, their lights flashing, sped into the parking lot and came to a stop with a squeal of tires. Phyllis didn't know the officers who climbed hurriedly out of the vehicles. They came over to the ambulance, talked briefly to Calvin and Ted, and then one of the officers turned to the people gathered in the parking lot and said in a loud voice, "If y'all would just stay right here for a few minutes until we've had a chance to talk to you, we'd appreciate it."

No one seemed to be in a hurry to leave. The crowd waited patiently, as Ted climbed into the ambulance with the injured woman and Calvin closed the rear doors and got behind the wheel. The siren's wail rose again as the ambulance pulled away and started off toward the hospital.

One of the policemen studied the car with the dented hood and the damaged windshield as the other three spread out and began questioning the crowd. Phyllis overheard enough while she and Mattie were waiting their turn to know that the police were trying to determine if anyone had actually witnessed the accident. From the responses she heard, it appeared that no one had.

She leaned close to Mattie and asked in a low voice, "Did you see what happened?"

Mattie shook her head. "No. We got done a little early, so I came out to wait for you and get a little sun, since it's not too hot yet. I don't know ... I didn't see anybody around. ... I got to thinking about the old days, you know how I am sometimes. My mind sort of drifts. Then I heard some yellin' and saw people runnin' through the parking lot. So I walked over and I saw that woman ..." A shiver went through her. "I thought for sure she was dead. Somebody must've hit her with a car."

That much was obvious. Phyllis waited with Mattie until one of the officers came over to them. He got their names first, then asked if either of them had seen what happened. Mattie went through her story again, her voice halting. She was obviously shaken. The officer looked at Phyllis and asked, "What about you, ma'am?"

"I got here after the ambulance did," Phyllis explained. "I was picking up Mrs. Harris after this morning's tutoring session. The accident had already happened by the time I came up."

The policeman nodded. He seemed sympathetic and friendly enough, so Phyllis ventured a question of her own. "Do you know if that poor woman is going to be all right?"

"I wouldn't have any idea, ma'am. Looked like she was hurt pretty bad, though."

"That's the car that hit her, the one over there with the broken windshield?"

"Yes, ma'am, it appears to be. You know who it belongs to?"

"No, not at all." She had noticed a couple of bumper stickers on the car with odd names on them, which she supposed were the names of currently popular rock bands, but she had never heard of them. "Probably one of the students."

"Well, we'll find out," the officer said.

Phyllis wondered if this qualified as a hit-and-run. Whoever had hit the woman hadn't driven off, because the car was still here, but the driver had definitely left the scene of the accident.

Or *was* it an accident? That sudden thought made Phyllis's breath catch in her throat. After everything else that had happened this summer, she knew she shouldn't jump to any conclusions.

Still, this incident had all the earmarks of a tragic accident. It wasn't unusual for people to be struck by cars in parking lots.

The policeman who had questioned them was about to move on to someone else. Phyllis asked him, "Is it all right for us to leave?"

"Yes, ma'am. We'll be in touch if we have any more questions." He glanced at his notebook, where he had written down their names, and paused. "Say, are you related to Mike Newsom?"

"He's my son," Phyllis said.

"He's a good guy. I played softball against him in the church league. He still a deputy?"

"That's right."

"Tell him Roland says hello, if you would."

Phyllis smiled. "Of course."

She put a hand on Mattie's arm and was about to steer her toward the Lincoln, when she heard a young female voice cry out, "Oh, my God! My car!"

Phyllis turned to see a teenage girl with curly, bright red hair hurrying through the parking lot from the direction of the school. The high school principal and a couple of vice principals trailed after her. She ran up to the car, stared in horror at the dent and the damaged windshield, and said, "What happened to it?"

One of the police officers moved in smoothly and said, "This is your car, miss?"

"Of course it is. Who did this? Did you catch him?"

The officer didn't answer her questions. Instead, he asked, "Are you saying you didn't know that your car had been in an accident?"

"Of course I didn't know! How would I know? I've been in the band hall all morning! I didn't know anything about it until Mr. Hayes came to get me!"

The officer looked over at the principal, who nodded. "I checked with the band director," he said. "Miss Collins was practicing with the band when this happened."

The redhead's eyes got big. "Wait a minute," she said. "You didn't think I ran over somebody, did you?"

"It's your car," the police officer pointed out.

"Yes, but somebody must've tried to steal it! I wouldn't run over anybody." Her voice was shaky as she went on, "There's already a rumor going around. Was it Ms. Garrett, like I heard? Is she dead?"

Again the officer didn't answer. "Was your car locked?"

The girl shook her head. "No, I don't ever bother locking it. I don't keep anything in there that would be worth stealing."

"You took the keys out when you parked it?"

"Of course I did. They're right here." She slid a hand into one of the pockets of her tight jeans. "Oh, crap. I would have sworn—" She checked her other pockets and then looked up with a sick expression on her face. "I was running late this morning. I must've been in such a hurry when I got here that I went off and left 'em in the car."

"You left it unlocked, with the keys in it?"

Tears began to roll down the girl's cheeks. "I didn't mean to," she said miserably. "I was just in a hurry . . . I was running late. . . ."

Phyllis felt sorry for her. She knew the girl hadn't meant any harm. But obviously her carelessness had contributed to the circumstances surrounding the accident.

The principal led the girl away. One of the policemen went with them. Phyllis touched Mattie's arm and said, "Let's go."

"Where? Oh. Home." Mattie shook her head. "Sorry, Phyllis. I'm not quite myself. Reckon all this uproar's gotten to me a little bit."

"I don't blame you. It seems like there's always something bad going on."

Once they were back in the car, Phyllis said, "The girl said that teacher was Ms. Garrett. I think I remember her now. She teaches biology or chemistry."

"Biology," Mattie said. "I remember her now, too. Never had anything to do with her, though. I think this was her first year to teach here."

"I hope she pulls through." Phyllis shook her head. "It looked awfully bad, though."

By the time they got back to the house, Mattie had calmed down quite a bit. Both she and Phyllis still looked upset enough, however, so that when they got out of the car Sam knew right away something was wrong. He was at the workbench, cutting boards for more bookshelves, but after glancing at them, he stopped the saw, took his goggles off, and turned toward them.

"What happened?" he asked.

"There was an accident at the high school," Phyllis said. When Sam looked immediately at her car, she went on, "It didn't involve us. We just saw the results of it. A woman, one of the teachers, was badly hurt."

"Someone you worked with?"

Phyllis shook her head. "No, this was someone young, who started teaching after all of us retired. I knew vaguely who she was, but that's all."

"Whether you knew her or not, that's still bad. What happened to her?"

"She was hit by a car in the parking lot," Phyllis said.

"Run down like a dog," Mattie said.

Sam asked, "You saw it happen, Mattie?"

Mattie suddenly looked confused. "Saw what happen?"

Phyllis knew that look. Mattie's mind had slipped a cog again. She took the older woman's arm and told Sam, "No, she came out afterward, and then I got there a few minutes later. Neither of us actually saw the accident."

"Blood," Mattie murmured. "Blood on the ground."

Phyllis felt worry shoot through her. Mattie hadn't been in good shape to start with. The shock of seeing Ms. Garrett lying there covered with blood might have been too much for her.

"Why don't you go upstairs and lie down?" she suggested. "I'll have lunch ready in a little while."

Mattie nodded slowly. "That's a good idea. I don't feel well."

Phyllis helped her upstairs. Mattie sat down on her bed, took her shoes off, and lay down on her side. She looked so frail and helpless that Phyllis's heart went out to her. Mattie had lived a long, long life, always trying to do good for others, and it was such a shame that she had to endure the hardship of having her mind gradually slip away from her here at the end of it.

Sam was in the kitchen washing his hands when Phyllis got back downstairs. "Mattie looked pretty shaken up," he said as he turned off the water and reached for a towel.

"It was bad," Phyllis admitted. "Seeing that poor woman lying there like that. . . . It got to me, too. It looked like the car hit her so hard she was thrown up over the hood and hit the windshield with her head. I'm not sure how she survived."

"People are pretty tough. Maybe she'll be able to hang on."

"With such a bad head injury, though, even if she lives she'll probably never fully recover."

Sam shook his head solemnly. "Folks never really know what's going to happen from one day to the next. Just goes to show you it's a wise thing to take what joy from life that you can, because you don't know how long you've got left."

"I'd just as soon not think about it . . . but I know you're right."

Lunch was subdued. Mattie didn't want anything and Eve was gone to Dallas for her doctor's appointment, so it was just Phyllis, Sam, and Carolyn around the table. Phyllis explained what had happened at the high school, and Carolyn said, "I know who you're talking about. Her name is Jani, J-A-N-I, with no *e* or *y* on the end. One of those young, really good-looking teachers the boys all ogle."

"She can't help being attractive," Phyllis pointed out.

"No, but the way some of the female teachers dress these days . . . Well, I'm not surprised that the boys get the wrong idea about them, if you know what I mean."

Phyllis knew, all right. Even in junior high, she had seen how some of the boys had gotten crushes on young, pretty teachers. Of course, some of the girls became enamored of the male teachers, too. It was an occupational hazard, and anyone who worked with young people had to learn how to handle problems like that.

Mike surprised her by showing up in the middle of the afternoon. Phyllis greeted him at the door with a smile and a hug and said, "This is unexpected. Nice, but unexpected."

"Roland Wallace called me a while ago," Mike said as he came into the living room holding his Stetson.

"Who?"

"A guy I know on the Weatherford force. We used to play ball against each other."

That jogged Phyllis's memory. "You mean the officer

Mattie and I talked to at the high school this morning, after that awful accident."

"It was no accident," Mike said, his face and voice serious. "Whoever was behind the wheel of that car was doing their best to kill Jani Garrett."

Chapter 27

Phyllis fixed glasses of lemonade for all of them, and they sat in the living room, listening to what Mike had to say.

"The cops checked the tire tracks that car left, and whoever was driving it pulled out of the parking space pretty fast and then gunned it even more. From the looks of the scene, he aimed right at Ms. Garrett and ran her down deliberately."

"Maybe it was just some kid joyriding," Sam suggested. "Somebody walking along who found the car unlocked, with the keys in it, and couldn't resist."

That made sense to Phyllis. She said, "And whoever took the car was driving fast because they wanted to get away. Jani Garrett could have stepped out from between some parked cars, and the driver woud never have seen her."

Phyllis realized that it sounded almost as if she were trying to make excuses for the driver of the stolen car. That wasn't the case at all . . . but somehow she didn't want to think that Jani Garrett had been run down deliberately. That would make the "accident" really attempted murder, and there had been too much of that sort of thing in Weatherford lately. Almost as if the town had its own serial killer. . . .

That was ridiculous, she told herself as she firmly put that thought out of her mind. She hadn't been able to establish any sort of link between Newt Bishop and Donnie Boatwright, and she certainly didn't see any connection between them and

Jani Garrett. The young woman probably hadn't even known either of the older men.

And the idea that there didn't *have* to be a link, that the violence could be completely random, was just too creepy to even think about.

Mike shook his head in response to the comments made by Phyllis and Sam. "The police checked to see where Ms. Garrett would have been coming from. She had left her classroom just a few minutes earlier. Given its location, the most likely scenario is that she was walking straight down that lane of the parking lot toward her car." He paused for a second. "They found her car on that row, farther out past where she was hit."

"That still doesn't mean it was deliberate," Phyllis said.

"No, but the tire tracks sure seem to indicate that, from what I've been told. There are places where the driver swerved back and forth, like Ms. Garrett tried to jump out of the way but the driver kept her right in his sights."

"He might have been having trouble keeping the car under control," Sam said. "Young, inexperienced drivers sometimes do, and it's possible this kid doesn't even have a license yet."

Mike nodded. "That's plausible, I guess. It's not my case, of course, since it happened in the Weatherford PD's jurisdiction, but from what Roland said, they're regarding it as attempted manslaughter. That could be upgraded to attempted homicide, once they find out who was behind the wheel. If the driver had a reason for wanting Jani Garrett dead, that makes it attempted murder."

"If she dies, that makes it murder," Phyllis said heavily.

"Yeah," Mike agreed, "and the last I heard, she was in critical condition at the hospital. She'll be really lucky if she pulls through."

Carolyn hadn't said much so far, but now she said, "I hope she makes it. I hate to see a young person struck down like that, even one like her."

Mike looked curiously at her. "What makes you say

something like that, Miz Wilbarger? What do you mean, 'one like her'?"

Carolyn shrugged and shook her head. "I don't really know. Just an impression I got somewhere that some of the other teachers didn't like her very much."

Mike sat forward in his chair and said, "Didn't like her enough to maybe run over her if the chance presented itself?"

Carolyn's eyes widened. "Mike, that's terrible! A teacher would never do something like that to another teacher."

"Teachers are people, too," Mike pointed out.

"Thanks," Phyllis said dryly.

He gave an exasperated sigh. "You know what I mean, Mom. Any motive for murder you'd find in other people, you'll find in teachers, too."

Sam chuckled. "At least he said *other people* and not *normal people.*"

Phyllis said, "Really, we don't mean to pick on you, Mike. It's just hard for us to believe that a teacher would actually try to murder somebody."

"Yeah, but every murderer must work with somebody who finds it hard to believe that he's a killer."

Phyllis supposed he was right about that, at least in most cases. Nobody liked to think that somebody they knew had taken another human life.

"Anyway," Mike went on as he stood up, "I just thought you'd like to know what's going on. Roland said you were there, Mom, so I knew you'd be interested." He paused, then added, "And since you didn't know the victim and nobody knows yet who was responsible for what happened, I don't suppose there's any reason for you to start investigating this case."

Phyllis felt her face turn warm with anger. "I was just trying to help, Michael, and you know it."

"Sure," he said hastily and started backing toward the

door as if he realized that he had aroused her wrath. "I'll talk to you later."

When Mike was gone and the door was closed, Sam chuckled again. "I'd say you spooked the boy, Phyllis."

"I think for a minute there he forgot who he was talking to," she said stiffly.

"Of course, it's sort of his job to keep folks from pokin' their noses into police business."

"If I recall correctly, your nose did some poking, too, Sam."

"Yeah, it did." She saw him glance toward Carolyn. "I guess just not enough."

Not yet, at least, Phyllis thought.

The thing Carolyn had said about some of the other teachers not liking Jani Garrett nagged at Phyllis the rest of that day. When she got up the next morning, the newspaper story about the accident was on the front page, of course. At press time, the police had no suspects, and the injured woman was still in critical condition at the hospital.

Phyllis withstood the persistent prodding of her curiosity until the middle of the day, when she called Dolly Williamson.

"Dolly, it's Phyllis Newsom," she said when the retired superintendent answered the phone.

Dolly's health didn't allow her to get around much anymore, so it had been quite a while since the two women had seen each other. "Phyllis, how are you?" she asked. "I talk to Mattie occasionally, but it seems like it's been ages since we spoke."

"It's been a long time," Phyllis agreed. "I'm doing fine. How about you?"

The question prompted a couple of minutes of complaints from Dolly, who had never been shy about sharing her problems. Finally, though, she said, "How is everything working out having Sam Fletcher living with you? He's a darling man."

"Well, he's not actually living with me," Phyllis said, "just boarding here."

"Of course, of course."

"But he does seem to be very nice. We've enjoyed having him here."

"I'll bet Carolyn hasn't," Dolly said with a chuckle.

"Carolyn had to go through a period of adjustment, let's say. And I'm not sure it's completely over yet."

"Sam will win her over. He's very charming. I tried for years to get him to come teach down here in Weatherford, but he was stubborn about staying in Poolville. He always said he liked a small school better."

Phyllis tried to steer the conversation around to the reason she had called. "Dolly, have you heard about what happened yesterday at the high school?"

"You mean about Jani Garrett being run over by a car? Lord, yes! I heard about it yesterday afternoon and then saw the story in the paper this morning. A terrible thing, just terrible."

"Did you know her? I don't think she and I ever met."

Phyllis knew that Dolly wouldn't need any more urging than that. Dolly knew everybody connected with education in Parker County, and she still had a network of informants that would rival a European spy ring. And with an old, trusted friend like Phyllis, she would be very open in what she said.

"Of course I'd met Jani, but I wouldn't say that I knew her well. She was so much younger, of course, and today's teachers are just so different from when you and I were there, Phyllis. Last school year was her first in Weatherford, and she'd only taught two or three years before that."

"Where did she come from?"

"One of the suburban districts over around Dallas, I believe. I don't remember which one."

"So she's not from around here?"

"Oh, no, not at all. I think she grew up over there. She'd probably still be there if she hadn't been asked to leave."

That caught Phyllis's interest, and despite feeling a little too much like a gossip, she asked, "What happened? Was there a problem where she taught?"

"Well, from what I understand," Dolly said, "some of her male students were a little too fond of her, if you know what I mean. And the real problem was that she returned the feeling."

"You mean she got romantically involved with some of her students?"

"I don't think there was any *romance* involved. Just good old-fashioned lust. Jani couldn't resist those big handsome football players. That was probably true when she was in school herself, and it didn't change when she got on the other side of the teacher's desk."

That was Dolly for you—always plainspoken.

"Evidently she started carrying on a little too openly with some of the boys, and even though there were never any charges brought against her, she was told that her contract wouldn't be renewed and was advised that she ought to seek employment in some other district, preferably a good long distance away." Dolly paused for a second, then mused, "You know, it might not have been so bad if she had confined her attentions to one student. Still completely improper, of course, but we both know such things happen. It was her habit of flitting from boy to boy like she was still a teenager herself that caused the problem. She left too many broken hearts in her wake. And no one's heart breaks quite as violently as that of a teenage boy."

Phyllis felt a chill go through her. As she had expected, Dolly had had a lot to say, and it gave Phyllis a lot to think about. She said, "The police think whoever it was who ran over Jani Garrett did it on purpose. Could she have been involved with some boy here in Weatherford, like she was back where she came from?"

"And then had him get angry enough when she dropped

him that he wanted to kill her?" Dolly speculated. "I suppose it could have happened that way, all right. What a terrible, tragic thing."

Phyllis had to agree with that. And everything Dolly had told her backed up the feeling Carolyn had about some of the teachers not liking Jani Garrett. If Jani had been a little too friendly with some of her male students, and if she had been a bit too indiscreet about the relationships, the word would have gotten around and most, if not all, of the other teachers would have disapproved. Everything pointed to a jilted young lover being the culprit in the hit-and-run.

But even if that theory was right, what business was it of hers, Phyllis asked herself. She hadn't known Jani, and chances were she didn't know the driver who had run down the young teacher. This wasn't like the cases of Newt Bishop and Donnie Boatwright. She hadn't been there when it happened, and she had no stake in it herself. She could feel sorry about the tragic aspects of the incident, but that was as far as it went.

So why, as she thanked Dolly and hung up, did she feel something pulling at her, something that told her she knew more about the attempt on Jani Garrett's life than she thought she did? Had her brief taste of being a detective been so intriguing that she wanted more of it?

She tried to put the whole thing out of her head, but it was difficult. More than difficult, she was finally forced to admit.

It was impossible.

Chapter 28

Somewhat to her surprise, Phyllis found herself sitting the next day outside the office of George Hayes, the principal of Weatherford High School. She had known George since he was a PE teacher and coach at the junior high, before he had gone on to be the head football coach at the high school, then vice principal, and ultimately principal. For a while there, the trend in education had been not to promote from within, so that every time an administrative position opened up, an outsider had been brought in to fill it. Phyllis had never agreed with that stance and was glad that it was less prevalent than it once had been. Promoting from within kept good people like George Hayes in the district instead of forcing them to seek advancement elsewhere.

Phyllis wasn't quite sure why she was here. She kept telling herself that it was none of her business. But it was for her own peace of mind, she supposed, that she wanted to know if the rumors about Jani Garrett were true. Two days after being run down in the parking lot, the young teacher was still alive but in critical condition, although the doctors were beginning to be guardedly optimistic about her chances for survival.

Unlike a doctor's office, there were no old magazines in the little waiting room outside the principal's office. The receptionist and the secretary were both gone at the moment, running errands elsewhere in the school, so Phyllis was alone. She passed the time by looking around. She hadn't spent much time in this school—hardly any, in fact. Even though it had been open for a few years, everything still had the gloss of newness on it. Eventually the thousands of students who would pass through here over the years would give the place a life of its own, perhaps, but right now Phyllis didn't care much for it. It just didn't feel *lived-in*.

Which was silly, of course, because people didn't live at school, she thought. This was just a place where they came for a period of time each day during certain seasons of year.

And yet it was more than that, although she knew that anyone who hadn't devoted their life to education would never understand all the nuances of it. A good school really was like a home away from home for the people who worked there.

A bad school, of course, was more like hell on earth.

The sound of loud, angry voices startled her out of her reverie. She sat forward in her chair and looked along the hall toward the door of George's office. It was closed, but it wasn't soundproof enough to keep the sound of outrage in.

Phyllis couldn't make out most of the words, but she heard "that woman" and "shameful" and "lawsuit." A few minutes later, the door opened and a man and a woman came out of the office. Both of them looked angry, the woman more so than the man. In fact, she looked mad enough to chew nails. The way the man had hold of her arm told Phyllis they were probably husband and wife. With their faces set in taut lines, they stalked past Phyllis and left the school office.

George Hayes stepped out into the hall, lines of strain etched on his beefy face. He still wore his hair in the same crew cut that he had sported for as long as Phyllis had known him, only it was gray now instead of brown. He looked exactly like what he was: a football coach turned administrator.

"Phyllis," he said as he saw her sitting there. He smiled,

but that didn't completely relieve the tense look on his face. "What are you doing here?"

"I was wondering if you could give me a few minutes, George." Back in the old days, she had occasionally called him Gabby, since he had the same name as the old cowboy movie sidekick Gabby Hayes, but she didn't think this was really the time or place for that.

"Sure, I can always make a little time for an old friend," he said. He held out a hand to usher her in.

When they were both sitting down, George grimaced and said, "I guess you heard the uproar going on in here before."

"Upset parents?" If he wanted to talk about it, that was fine with Phyllis, because she had a feeling from what little she had overheard that the argument had something to do with the same thing that had brought her here.

"Yeah. Ever since Jani Garrett got hurt in the parking lot the other day, certain things have come out that have people blowing their tops. By the way, I saw you out there in the parking lot that day, but with all the confusion going on, I didn't get a chance to say hello."

Phyllis smiled. "Don't worry about that. I know you had your plate full."

"Yeah, and it's getting fuller all the time," he said with a sigh. "That was Mr. and Mrs. Dietrich who just left. Parents of Shawn Dietrich, who'll probably be the starting quarterback on the football team this fall . . . if I don't wind up having to expel him."

Phyllis raised her eyebrows. "Expel him? For what?"

"Having an inappropriate relationship with a teacher."

"Jani Garrett?"

George nodded. "Yeah. And the Dietrichs aren't the only parents who've come in here to see me about the same thing. That gal . . . sorry, that woman . . . whatever you call her, she cut a pretty wide swath through the male students. Their parents are just finding out about it, and they're plenty mad, especially the mamas."

"You can't blame them for not wanting their innocent little boys corrupted."

George grunted scornfully. "Innocent, my hind foot. I tell you, Phyllis, if you knew what went on in the schools these days . . . well, you should just be glad that you retired when you did, that's all I've got to say. Another couple of years and I'll be out of here." He sighed, shook his head, and then sat up a little straighter in his chair. "Sorry, I didn't mean to go off on a tangent like that. I guess I just needed to blow off a little steam. Those parents don't realize that if they can't control their kids, I sure can't!" He held up his hands. "Wait a minute. There I go again. Tell me, Phyllis, before I rant some more . . . what can I do for you?"

"I wanted to let you know that Mattie Harris won't be able to do any more tutoring for the summer school students. She's upset about what happened to Ms. Garrett, and to tell you the truth, George, her health just isn't very good these days."

The principal frowned in concern. "I'm sorry to hear that. Mattie's always been one of my favorite people. And for somebody as, ah, old as she is, the kids really respond to her pretty well."

Phyllis smiled and said, "That's because Mattie is still young at heart."

"Yeah, I suppose so. Well, I'm sorry that she won't be helping us out anymore, but the summer session has less than a week to go. It really shouldn't make any difference." He paused. "Was that the only reason you stopped by, to tell me about Mattie?"

"And to say hello to an old friend."

George leaned back in his chair and grinned. "I don't suppose I could interest you in taking over and being acting principal of the high school for a while?"

"George," Phyllis said honestly, "there's not enough money in the world to get me to do that."

* * *

She felt a little uneasy about the whole thing. It was true that Mattie had asked her that morning to let George Hayes know she wasn't coming back, but Phyllis could have called the school and told George about that.

Instead she had driven out to the school to talk to him in person . . . and, she might as well admit it, to confirm what Dolly Williamson had told her about the injured teacher, Jani Garrett. As luck would have it, she had seen firsthand some of the results of Jani's poor judgment. The Dietrichs had been angry and upset when they left George's office.

As Phyllis drove home, she wondered if either of them had been angry enough to get behind the wheel of a convenient car and race it straight at the woman they thought had seduced their son.

That was a crazy idea, she told herself. No one would go to such lengths just because they were upset about an illicit affair between teacher and student. At least, no one who was sane.

But she didn't know all the parents of all the students Jani Garrett had carried on with, Phyllis reminded herself. Maybe one of them was just unbalanced enough to do such a thing. Maybe someone—like Mrs. Dietrich, say—had discovered that her son was involved with a teacher and had gone to the school to complain to the principal, or even to have a showdown with Jani herself. That parent, upon seeing Jani walking toward her, might have seized the moment, jumped into that little redheaded student's car, started it up, and gunned it right at the object of her ire. Then, having struck Jani down, it would have been simple enough for the driver to get back into her own car and drive away.

Or his car. Phyllis couldn't assume that it had been a woman who had run into Jani. But she agreed with George that it was more likely to be the mothers who were really upset about what was going on. Some fathers, no matter how they might bluster and carry on, deep down were probably a little proud of their sons for getting involved with a beautiful older woman, whether they would ever admit to such feelings or not.

By the time she got home, she hadn't reached any conclusions about what had happened to Jani Garrett, but she knew the whole situation was going to bother her until it was resolved. She wasn't sure *why* it was so important to her that the driver of the car be found, but it was. She supposed that everything that had happened over the summer had sharpened her appetite for justice. If Newt Bishop had indeed been murdered—and Phyllis was convinced he had—it appeared the murderer had gotten away with his crime. And since the police still had no fresh ideas about Donnie Boatwright's killer, that murder might well go unsolved, too, unless it was pinned on someone innocent, like Carolyn. Now there was the near-fatal attempt on Jani Garrett's life, and again, the suspects were numerous, and as far as Phyllis knew, the authorities weren't any closer to finding out who had done it than they had been two days earlier when the hit-and-run took place.

All of that rankled Phyllis. She knew that life wasn't fair, but she liked to think that the universe was an orderly place, at least at times. Cause and effect, that was what history was. If you knew the effect, you could trace it back and discover the cause, and once you knew the cause, you knew who was responsible for the events in question. But could you ever know for sure, the skeptic in her asked, while the part of her that still had faith said that the reason was there, if you just looked hard enough. There always had to be a reason. . . .

Her head was full of those thoughts—too full, all stuffed up like a person having an allergy attack—as she parked the Lincoln in the garage and went into the house through the kitchen. Sam wasn't at his workbench—odd how she thought of it as *his* workbench these days—and she didn't know where he was. Eve, whose checkup at the doctor's in Dallas the day before had gone just fine, was back out at the high school, finishing up her own tutoring sessions. Carolyn and Mattie were probably upstairs, since the house was quiet. The ringing of the phone suddenly shattered that quiet and seemed unnaturally loud to Phyllis. She grabbed the receiver off the phone that was hanging on the wall in the kitchen. "Hello?"

"Hello, Phyllis, this is Walt Lee," the voice on the other end said in a pleasant twang. Although both of Dr. Lee's parents had been born in Taiwan, he had been born and raised in Texas and sounded like the native of the Lone Star State that he was.

"Oh, hello, Dr. Lee. Did you want to talk to me, Mattie, or Eve?"

"Actually, I want to talk to you, Phyllis . . . but it's about Mattie."

Phyllis stiffened in alarm. She had assumed that Mattie was here when she came in, but she didn't know that. It was possible that while she was gone something could have happened to Mattie; she could have gotten sick or had an accident or—

"Is she all right?" Phyllis asked anxiously.

"Right now, you mean? You'd know that better than I would, since I assume she's there at your house."

"Oh. I thought something had happened. . . ."

"Something *has* happened," Dr. Lee said. "Nothing dramatic, but nothing good, either. Could you come to my office, so that we can talk about this in person?"

"This afternoon, you mean?"

"As soon as possible."

Phyllis glanced at the clock. It wasn't quite three yet. She could get to Dr. Lee's office, find out what he had to say, and still get back in plenty of time to fix supper.

"I'll come right over."

"Thank you. And I'd appreciate it if you wouldn't say anything about this to Mattie."

Phyllis hesitated. "I'm not sure I'm comfortable keeping secrets like that."

"I know *I'm* not. That's why I want to talk to you. Just trust me and reserve judgment for now, if you would."

If you couldn't trust your doctor, who could you trust? Phyllis said, "All right. I'll be there in a little while."

She said good-bye and hung up, wondering what this was all about.

Whatever it was, she had a strong feeling that it wouldn't be anything good.

Chapter 29

Phyllis was in the garage, going around the back of the Lincoln to get in, when she heard a car stop at the curb in front of the house. She looked over and saw a vehicle she didn't recognize, a black SUV. Annoyed that she was going to have to wait and deal with whoever this was instead of going straight to Dr. Lee's office, she walked a few feet out onto the driveway.

Somewhere she had seen the woman who got out of the SUV and came toward her, but for a moment Phyllis couldn't remember just where. The woman was large—big-boned, as people used to say—and handsome, rather than pretty. She had short, curly brown hair, but when she came closer Phyllis decided that it was dyed, and that the woman was older than she appeared on first glance, at least seventy. That was when she realized that she had seen the woman at Donnie Boatwright's funeral, sitting up front in the pews reserved for family, next to Charles Boatwright. She was Sally Hughes, Donnie's and Charles's sister.

"Mrs. Newsom?" she said curtly.

"That's right," Phyllis replied. "What can I do for you?"

"My name is Sally Boatwright Hughes," the woman said, telling Phyllis what she had already figured out. She lifted her chin defiantly. "I was Donnie Boatwright's sister."

"Of course, Mrs. Hughes. What can I do for you?" Phyllis asked again.

"You can stop going around town spreading lies about me and my brother Charles."

Sally Hughes was close now, close enough to make Phyllis uncomfortable. Phyllis took a step back and held up the hand that wasn't holding her purse. "Wait just a minute, Mrs. Hughes," she began. "I haven't been spreading any lies."

"No? Then why have Charles and I had to hire a lawyer to protect ourselves from being harassed by the police?"

"You hired Mr. Kinnison, too?" The question was startled out of Phyllis before she could stop it.

Sally Hughes's eyes widened angrily. "So you admit it!"

"I'm not admitting anything," Phyllis shot back. "And I certainly haven't spread any lies about you."

"You said that one of us killed our brother!" Sally's voice went up into a half shout. "You've been telling people that we hated poor Donnie and wanted him dead! The police have been asking us all sorts of questions about Donnie and our mother and that old will!"

Phyllis was torn between apprehension—she didn't like confrontation, and Sally Hughes was really angry—and excitement. Clearly, the police *had* taken her information seriously and interrogated Sally and Charles. That meant they were no longer focusing on Carolyn as their only suspect in Donnie's murder. Maybe Phyllis had done some good after all.

"Look, Mrs. Hughes," she said. "I'm sorry you're upset, but I didn't tell anyone about your mother's will except the authorities, and they had every right to know. Besides, what happened with your brother and your mother's estate is all public record. Anyone could have found out about it."

"No one else cared anymore. Not even Charles and I cared. Everyone had forgotten about it. And then you came along and made it sound like we . . . like we *murdered* our own brother because of it!"

"Does your husband know you're here, Mrs. Hughes?" Phyllis asked cautiously.

"Leave Kent out of this! The next thing you know, you'll be accusing *him* of killing Donnie! Well, I won't allow it, do you hear me?" She shook a finger at Phyllis. "I won't allow it!"

And with that, she drew back her other arm and swung the heavy black purse in that hand straight at Phyllis's head.

Phyllis let out a gasp and jumped back. The purse zipped past her face, just a few inches in front of her nose. "Mrs. Hughes!" she cried. "Stop that!"

"I'll shut you up!" Sally Hughes shouted as she bore down on Phyllis, forcing her back toward the garage. "I'll teach you to lie about my family!"

She drew back the purse for another mighty swing.

Before she could strike again, though, someone came up behind her, and fingers clamped around the wrist of the hand holding the purse. She spat out an expletive that Phyllis, having taught school for all those years, had heard before, of course, but not lately, and never from the mouth of a well-to-do woman who had to be at least seventy years old.

Sally Hughes twisted around and used her other hand to slap at the man holding her, whom Phyllis had recognized by now as Sam Fletcher. She didn't know where Sam had come from, but she was greatly relieved that he was here.

Sam might have bitten off more than he could chew, though, because Sally either outweighed him or came close to it, and she was still spitting mad. "Let go of me!" she shrieked. "Let go of me, or I'll have you arrested! Oh!"

Sam was able to fend off the blows and catch hold of her other wrist. "Settle down!" he told her. "Dang it, ma'am, stop tryin' to hit me!"

"You . . . you terrible man!" Sally panted. She was almost hysterical by now.

But after a minute she abruptly stopped struggling, and her face collapsed in tears. She dropped her purse. It popped open and spilled some of its contents as it hit the driveway. Sam released her wrists and stepped back quickly in case she threw a punch at him, but all the violence in her seemed to have burned itself out. She put her hands over her face instead and stood there sobbing.

Sam looked at Phyllis with a slightly walleyed stare and said, "What in blue blazes is goin' on here?"

Phyllis moved around Sally Hughes, keeping as much distance as she could between her and the woman, and came to Sam's side. "This is Mrs. Hughes," she said quietly, nodding toward the distraught woman. "Donnie Boatwright's sister. She's upset with me."

"No kiddin'," Sam muttered.

"She thinks I've been telling people that she and her brother Charles murdered Donnie. I think the police have tried to question them."

Understanding dawned on Sam's face. "You think we'd better call the cops? She tried to attack you, after all."

Sally Hughes lowered her hands. Her face was red and puffy and wet from crying. "You might as well call the police," she said miserably. "My reputation is already ruined. All my friends will think that I killed Donnie."

"You know," Phyllis said slowly to Sam, "I don't think she did it, or she wouldn't be this upset."

"Of course I didn't do it! I loved Donnie. I wouldn't have hurt him." Sally waved a hand. "Oh, of course I got infuriated at him sometimes! He could be a real pain in the ass! But he was my brother and I loved him, and Charles and I forgave him a long time ago for what he did about Mother's estate."

"You forgave him," Sam said, "but he didn't give you your share of the money, now did he?"

"Well . . . no. But we never asked him to. It wasn't worth tearing the family apart over it. Charles felt the same way. It wasn't like either of us really needed the money."

It looked like being a detective had some drawbacks, Phyllis thought. Investigating a crime meant that sooner or later, some innocent people were going to be under suspicion, and that might well be hurtful to them.

But there was no other way to find out the truth. She said, "Don't you want your brother's murderer caught, Mrs. Hughes?"

"Of course I do! But that's not Charles or me."

"And once you're eliminated as suspects, it'll be that much easier to find the killer."

Sally sniffed and said acidly, "Finding killers isn't your job, Mrs. Newsom. It's a police matter."

Phyllis couldn't argue with that statement. But neither could she stand by and let Carolyn be blamed for something she hadn't done. Sally Hughes wouldn't be interested in that explanation, though.

Sam picked up Sally Hughes's purse and the things that had fallen out of it. "I'm a little leery about doing this, but here." He held them out to her.

Sally took them with another sniff. "Are you going to turn me in for attacking you?" she asked, with a defiant glare at Phyllis.

"No," Phyllis said. "Just go home and leave me alone."

"*You* leave *me* alone," Sally snapped. She stalked toward her SUV parked at the curb. Phyllis saw now that Sam's pickup was pulled in behind the SUV. He must have driven up, seen Sally coming after Phyllis, and charged across the lawn to stop her.

The two of them stood there in the driveway and watched silently as Sally Hughes got into her vehicle and drove off with an angry screech of tires.

Phyllis turned to Sam. "Thank goodness you got here when you did. She went completely crazy."

"Crazy enough that maybe she *did* slip that poison to Donnie?" he asked.

"I don't think so," Phyllis said slowly as she shook her head. "I don't think she's that good an actress. She was really offended and upset."

"That still doesn't rule her out."

"No, not entirely. But I don't believe she did it."

From inside the garage, Carolyn asked, "What in the world happened out here? We heard all sorts of commotion. Who was that yelling?"

Mattie peered curiously out from behind the larger Carolyn. The sight of the older woman's wrinkled face sent a pang of guilt through Phyllis. If Sally Hughes hadn't shown up when she had, by now Phyllis would be at Dr. Lee's office, listening to whatever it was the doctor wanted to tell her about Mattie. The idea of going behind Mattie's back like that nagged at Phyllis's conscience.

But Dr. Lee had made it sound very important, and in the long run, Mattie's welfare came first. Phyllis just hoped that the doctor hadn't decided she wasn't coming.

"It was nothing to worry about," she said in reply to Carolyn's questions. "Sally Hughes stopped by. She was upset about something."

"What?" Carolyn asked bluntly.

Phyllis took a deep breath. She didn't want to give Carolyn any false hope, but she deserved an honest answer.

"Evidently the police are taking an interest in her and her brother as possible suspects in Donnie's murder. That lawyer, Mr. Kinnison, must have told her that I was to blame for that, because of the questions I've been asking."

Carolyn's eyes widened with shock and relief. "Then . . . they don't think I did it anymore?"

"I wouldn't go so far as to say that," Phyllis cautioned. "You're probably still a suspect. But at least you're not the *only* suspect anymore."

Mattie shook her head. "All this fuss over a fella like Donnie. I've never seen the likes of it."

"Fuss is right," Sam said with a smile. "She came after Phyllis swinging her purse like a club."

"My God," Carolyn said as she started forward. "Are you all right, Phyllis?"

"I'm fine," Phyllis assured her. "She never laid a finger on me, thanks to Sam."

"Yeah, I'm glad I got back from the lumberyard when I did." He glanced at Phyllis's purse. "Were you on your way somewhere when she came up and stopped you?"

"As a matter of fact, I do have an errand to run. I'll be back in plenty of time to get supper ready, though."

"Are you sure you're all right?" Carolyn asked.

"I'm fine," Phyllis said.

But she wasn't sure she really would be until she heard what Dr. Walt Lee had to say . . . and even then, if the news was as bad as she expected, she wouldn't be fine at all.

Chapter 30

As she drove toward Dr. Lee's office, which was located near the hospital, Phyllis thought about the confrontation with Sally Hughes. While there was little doubt in her mind that Sally was not guilty of Donnie's murder, she had to admit that Sally—and her brother Charles—had strong motives. A double motive, so to speak, because Donnie's death not only avenged the wrong that he had done to them so many years earlier, but it put money in their pockets as well. She assumed Donnie's estate had gone to Charles and Sally, but she realized she didn't know for sure. That might be worth checking into.

Carolyn, on the other hand, didn't profit financially from Donnie's death. If she had killed him, the only thing she got out of it was vengeance.

That started Phyllis thinking about the other tragedies that had occurred. Like Sally and Charles, Darryl Bishop would have had a double motive in killing a relative, in his case his father, Newt. Although again she couldn't be sure of it, Phyllis assumed that Darryl had inherited his father's farm. That would make him a lot better off financially than he had been, and he also would have had the satisfaction of striking back at the man who had mistreated him as a child. Alfred Landers would have had no reason to kill Newt except for pure spite over losing that lawsuit.

Jani Garrett was the wild card here. Phyllis had no idea what the young teacher's life was like other than her predilection for messing around with male students. As a schoolteacher, though, it was highly likely that she didn't have much money. The attempt on Jani's life had to have been a crime of passion, carried out by a parent of one of the young men she had seduced, or by one of the students themselves. As Dolly Williamson had said, a young man with a broken heart was liable to be so upset that he would do almost anything. . . .

Once again an insistent feeling nudged at the back of Phyllis's brain, a not-so-gentle reminder that she was overlooking something. She thought about Newt Bishop, Donnie Boatwright, and Jani Garrett and asked herself again what the three of them could have had in common.

By the time she reached the doctor's office, she still hadn't come up with an answer. With a sigh, she put the matter out of her mind as she parked the car. The past was dead and gone and couldn't be changed. Now she had to deal with the present.

She went into the office and told the receptionist that Dr. Lee was expecting her. "I got delayed a little," she said apologetically. "I hope I haven't caused a problem."

The receptionist smiled at her. "I'll let the nurse know you're here."

A few minutes later, the door into the hallway where the examining rooms were located opened and a nurse stuck her head out. "Mrs. Newsom?" she said. "Come on back."

This felt like she was visiting the doctor for a checkup of her own, Phyllis thought, as she followed the nurse into the hall. Instead of stopping at one of the little exam rooms, however, they went all the way to the end of the corridor, where the nurse opened the door into Dr. Lee's private office.

"Go on in and have a seat," she said with a pleasant smile. "The doctor will be with you in just a minute."

Phyllis knew good and well that "just a minute" to a doctor could mean forty-five minutes to an hour or more, but

Walt Lee surprised her by coming into the office less than five minutes later. "Hello, Phyllis," he said as he went behind the desk and set down the large manila file folder he was carrying. "Thanks for coming."

"I'm sorry it took me so long. I got delayed," Phyllis said again, without offering an explanation of what had happened. She didn't want to admit that she had almost been clobbered by a large, angry, purse-swinging murder suspect.

As Dr. Lee settled into his comfortable swivel chair, he asked, "First of all, how are you doing these days? It's been a while since I've seen you."

"Oh, I'm fine," Phyllis said without hesitation. "No complaints. I haven't missed a checkup, have I?"

"No, I don't think so." Lee reached forward and opened the file folder. "Actually, as I mentioned on the phone, it's Mattie that I want to talk to you about. I got some test results today . . ."

"Are you sure you shouldn't be talking to Mattie herself about this?" Phyllis broke in.

"I would . . . but Mattie told me some months ago, when she realized that she was starting to have more and more trouble with her thinking, that I ought to talk to you if anything serious came up."

Phyllis blinked in surprise. "I didn't know that."

Lee nodded solemnly. "Mattie knew the day might come when she wouldn't be able to make her own decisions. As you and I have discussed before, she has a mild case of Alzheimer's, and it's slowly progressing."

Phyllis had the sense that he was working his way around to something else. "This isn't about the Alzheimer's, is it?"

"No, I'm afraid not. When Mattie was here about six weeks ago, I noticed some things that disturbed me about her behavior, and that's why I had an MRI done on her."

Phyllis remembered that quite well. She had taken Mattie for the procedure back in early June.

"I found something then," Lee went on, "but I thought it

would be best to get a second or even a third or fourth opinion, so I sent the films off to a geriatric specialist and an oncologist I know, as well as a neurosurgeon, for consultation. I've heard back from all of them now, and they all agree with my initial findings."

Phyllis wanted to grab him and shake him and tell him to spit it out, for God's sake. Instead she forced herself to remain calm. "What were your findings, Doctor?"

Lee took a deep breath and then said, "Mattie has a tumor in her brain. Given all the considerations—her age, the tumor's location and state of advancement—surgery isn't an option, and neither is radiation or chemotherapy."

Even though Phyllis had been expecting that answer or one similar to it, the news still hit her hard. "You're saying there's nothing you can do?"

"I'm sorry," Dr. Lee said.

Phyllis sat there stunned for a long moment. She looked down at her hands, listened to the silence in the office. It wasn't often that you heard a death sentence pronounced on a good friend. Her mind went back to her own early days as a teacher. Even though they had taught at different schools, Mattie Harris had been a mentor of sorts to her. A lot of what she knew about teaching, about caring for the kids and putting their needs first, she had learned from Mattie.

Finally, she swallowed hard and looked up again. "How long?"

"Two or three weeks, maybe a month," Dr. Lee said quietly. "For what it's worth, there shouldn't be a great deal of pain until near the end."

"And Mattie . . . Mattie has no idea about this?"

Dr. Lee hesitated. "Actually, she does. I was rather upset when I realized what we might be dealing with, and I said too much. Mattie knows there's a good chance she might not have much time left."

"She never said anything to me. . . ."

"I'm not surprised." Dr. Lee smiled. "She wouldn't have

wanted to worry you. You know Mattie, always putting other people first. Now that it's certain, and we have a better idea of the time frame we're looking at, I thought it might be easier if she heard the news from you."

Easier on whom, Phyllis wanted to ask, Mattie or you? Because it's sure not going to be easy on me.

Still, some things had to be done, no matter how hard they were. Phyllis nodded. "I'll talk to her."

"Thank you."

Some stubborn part of her prompted her to ask, "Are you sure there's nothing that can be done?"

"Well, when I talked to Mattie before, we discussed alternative treatments. There are various drugs that haven't been approved by the FDA, and herbal and vitamin supplements, and the sort of off-the-wall things that some people swear can cure cancer even though there's no medical or scientific evidence for their claims. As far as I'm concerned, though, those are all just false hopes, and usually very expensive ones, at that. Some of them are even dangerous and can make the situation worse. I explained all of that to her and warned her not to try anything without talking to me about it first."

"She should have told me what was going on," Phyllis said, as much to herself as to Dr. Lee.

He shook his head. "It wouldn't have done any good. She said she wasn't going to bother you with it right then because you were about to start getting ready for the peach festival and the cooking contest. She didn't want to distract you from that."

Phyllis laughed hollowly. "As if any cooking contest could be more important to me than an old friend."

"That's Mattie for you," Dr. Lee said with a shrug.

Yes, it certainly was, Phyllis thought. Mattie was the ultimate volunteer, the person who just wanted to do good for the community and everyone in it, even if that meant not making a fuss about her own impending death.

"All right," she said, clutching her purse tightly. She stood up. "Thank you, Doctor. I'll tell Mattie that your diagnosis has been confirmed."

Lee got to his feet as well. "If there's anything I can do, just let me know."

Phyllis smiled sadly. "It doesn't seem like there's anything anybody can do."

"All things have to come to an end. As doctors, we don't like that, but it's inevitable."

"Yes. And I don't like it, either."

She left the office, still a little stunned by the news she had heard. She had known that Mattie's health was failing, of course. Mattie was in the December of her years, as the old saying went. But Phyllis had expected that they still had more time together than a few weeks. It wasn't that she was unacquainted with the death of someone close to her—she had endured the loss of her husband, after all—but to lose a good friend was a shock and always would be. The idea of a world without Mattie Harris in it just seemed so wrong somehow. Mattie had always been there, a part of Phyllis's life.

Death had a habit of snatching people away, and the old gentleman had been busier than usual this summer, it seemed to Phyllis. First Newt and then Donnie and then—almost—Jani Garrett, although Jani had slipped out of that bony grip, at least for now. Somehow, through coincidence, she supposed, Phyllis had been close at hand for both of those deaths and the near miss. And now, she would soon have to face the loss of Mattie. . . .

Those thoughts were running through her head as she drove, and suddenly it was all too much for her. She had to pull over into the parking lot of a convenience store and bring the Lincoln to a stop. Tears burned hotly in her eyes, and there was a pounding in her head so strong that she feared for a moment she was about to have a stroke. She gasped as all the events of the past weeks came together, all the things she had seen and heard and read: Like a flower blooming in her mind, the truth opened up to her. She grasped the steering wheel tightly and shook her head, but it didn't do any good. The pounding didn't go away. It was a drumbeat of mortality and inevitability, the marching cadence of death.

And just as she had thought before, there *was* a reason for everything that had happened, an answer for all the questions. The lessons of history were true again, as they always were. Cause and effect, one following the other as ceaselessly as the tides, as eternal as the stars.

The tears still rolled down her face, but the pounding in her head gradually slowed and faded away. She took a deep breath, then another and another and stopped only when she realized she was about to hyperventilate. With the back of her hand she wiped away the wet streaks on her face. When she felt that she was calm enough to handle the car safely again, she put the Lincoln in gear. She hadn't ever turned off the motor.

There was nothing left to do now but go home.

Chapter 31

Eve was there by the time Phyllis got back to the house. The four friends were together again, only now there were five because Sam was there, too. Even though he had only been living in the house for a relatively short time, Phyllis already felt like he was one of the group.

"You've been busy as a bee lately, dear," Eve said as Phyllis set the table. "It seems like you're always running around somewhere and are never here."

Phyllis smiled. "That's about to come to an end. I won't have any more running around to do."

"No more detecting?" Eve asked.

"No. No more detecting."

While they were eating, Carolyn talked about Phyllis's run-in with Sally Hughes. Phyllis would have just as soon kept the whole thing quiet, but Carolyn was more animated tonight than Phyllis had seen her in quite a while and wanted to talk. She supposed that was because—while Carolyn wasn't in the clear yet—the specter of Donnie Boatwright's murder wasn't looming quite so menacingly over her as it had been.

Sam took up the story from the point where he'd arrived. "Just as I pulled up, I saw this big ol' woman tryin' to clout Phyllis over the head with her purse. I thought my eyes were playing tricks on me at first. I didn't figure such a thing could really be happening. But it sure was."

Eve laughed. "I wish I could have seen it." She turned and gave Phyllis an apologetic look. "I'm sorry. I know it must have been terrifying at the time. But it really does sound like it might have been amusing to watch."

"I'm sure it was," Phyllis said politely, keeping her real thoughts to herself.

"I don't mind tellin' you, I was more than a little scared myself," Sam went on. "That lady was really mad, and when I stopped her from goin' after Phyllis, I was afraid she might turn on *me*."

Eve reached over and took hold of his hand. "And of course you're too much of a gentleman to ever lay a hand on a lady."

"Well, I wouldn't go so far as to say that. I just figured that if she got in a lucky punch, she'd deck me."

"I don't know what to think," Carolyn put in. "Sally Hughes doesn't seem like the sort of person who would murder anybody, especially not her own brother. And yet she got so mad she was basically out of control when she came after Phyllis. If she got mad enough at Donnie . . . well, who knows what she might have done."

Phyllis said, "I'm sure the police will continue investigating both her and Charles."

"Yeah, but they're lawyered up now," Sam said. "It'll be hard to get anything out of 'em."

"Lawyered up," Eve repeated with a laugh. "Dear, you've been watching cop shows on TV again."

Sam just grinned and shrugged.

Phyllis looked around the table and was glad to see that they seemed to be enjoying themselves, even if a little of it was at her expense. After the summer they'd had, they all needed a bit of lightheartedness.

Unfortunately, things were going to get worse before they got better.

Mattie was quiet during supper, not taking part in the gentle joshing that went on between Sam and Eve and, to a lesser extent, Carolyn. She didn't eat much, either, Phyllis noted. Her appetite was fading these days. She had always been birdlike, but now she was thinner than ever.

When the meal was over and Phyllis was clearing the table, she said, "Mattie, would you be willing to give me a hand with the dishes tonight?"

"What?" Mattie seemed a little surprised by the question, as if she hadn't been quite aware of what was going on around her.

"I can help you," Carolyn offered.

"No, no, I'll do it," Mattie said, as Phyllis had known she would. "I'm fine, I'm fine."

Carolyn frowned. "Are you sure, Mattie? It wouldn't be any trouble for me to—"

"I said I was fine, didn't I?" Mattie asked a little testily. "The day comes when I can't wash or dry a few dishes, you can just send me to the rest home."

"Nobody's going to do that," Carolyn said.

That was true, Phyllis thought. Mattie wouldn't be going to a rest home.

Carolyn went upstairs, while Sam and Eve drifted off into the living room, Eve holding on to Sam's arm while she told him that she wanted him to explain to her some of the finer points of the baseball game that was on TV that night. Phyllis happened to know that Eve had played on several championship-winning softball teams when she was a girl, and she didn't need anything about the game explained to her. Sam cast a sidelong glance in Phyllis's direction as Eve led him out of the room, as if hoping that she would come to his rescue as he had to hers that afternoon, but Phyllis had to disappoint him. He would just have to defend himself from Eve. She had confidence in his ability to do so.

Phyllis had something else she had to do.

"I'll wash, you dry," she said to Mattie when the two of them were alone in the big kitchen.

"All right. I thought you usually used the dishwasher, though."

"Oh, sometimes I just like to do things the old-fashioned way," Phyllis said as she got dishpans from under the sink and began filling one of them with hot, soapy water.

"Lord, I know the feelin'," Mattie said. "Sometimes it seems like so much has changed that I feel like old Rip Van Winkle, like I went to sleep for years and years and missed a lot of things." She took a dish towel off a hook and toyed with it in her gnarled hands. "Sometimes I even forget that the war's not goin' on anymore, or the Depression. I was just a little girl then, but I sure do remember it. The bread lines, and the way so many men didn't have a job, and President Roosevelt and the way he'd come on the radio and talk. . . . We had an old Sylvania, the biggest, prettiest radio you ever did see, and I'd always listen to Little Orphan Annie on it, and the Great Gildersleeve, and, oh my, Fibber McGee and Molly, they were so funny. 'Don't you open that closet, McGee! Don't you open . . .'"

Mattie's voice trailed off and she looked down at the dish towel in her hands for a long moment without saying anything.

"It's all right, Mattie," Phyllis said gently. "It's all right to remember things."

"But it seems like that's *all* I do lately. Seems like I'm always back there in the past somewhere. I don't mean to be. There's lots of things I don't *want* to remember. But I can't seem to stop."

"You were all right while you were helping the kids at the high school, the ones in summer school you were tutoring."

"I could always teach," Mattie said with conviction. "Kids listened to me. For some reason I was able to get through to 'em. To tell you the truth, Phyllis, I usually felt better bein' around the kids than I did around grown folks. A kid'll be honest with you, at least most of the time. Some of 'em have some meanness in 'em, no doubt about that, but not any real evil. They won't hurt you bad for no good reason like a grown person will. That's why I hate worse'n anything to see a kid bein' hurt. They didn't do anything to have it comin'."

"Like Darryl Bishop," Phyllis said, her voice quiet now, as if she and Mattie were the only ones in the house. The noise of the TV from the living room had faded so that she no longer heard it.

Or maybe it was just that the beating of her heart was so loud it drowned out everything else except her voice, and Mattie's.

"Poor Darryl. Too little to fight back, and too proud to ask for help. I know how kids think. He probably believed it was his fault that Newt was beatin' him. Figured if he could just be a good enough boy, the hittin' would stop. But it didn't. It just went on and on, until that little boy looked like a dog that's been whaled on with a stick. If you lifted a hand or raised your voice or even looked at him wrong, he'd just cringe so that your heart went out to him. I tell you, Phyllis, there was more than one night I cried myself to sleep over what happened to Darryl Bishop."

"I'm sure you did. I know you were upset about that boy who killed himself, too."

Mattie's hands knotted on the dish towel. "Billy Moser. He wasn't little, like Darryl. No, he was a big, strappin' boy. But he was hurt, too. Couldn't stand what she did to him. That tramp. She had no right. She's a *teacher,* for heaven's sake. She shouldn't have been leadin' Billy and those other boys on. What was wrong with her?"

"I don't know," Phyllis answered honestly. "I guess she was . . . broken somehow, inside."

Mattie snorted contemptuously. "She just didn't give a damn about anybody but herself. She had her fun, and if it hurt somebody else, that was just too bad. Why, Billy told me . . . he told me that she *laughed* at him when she told him it was over between them. Said he was old enough to know better and that what did he expect, she was going to marry him or something? She *laughed* at him. Wasn't a week went by before he was dead. A kid doesn't understand that just because something hurts now, it won't always be that way. He thinks his pain's the biggest thing in the world—so big he can't ever get past it. But Billy could have. He could have gone on and had a good life, if it hadn't been for her."

A sudden wave of weariness seemed to wash over Mattie. She pulled out one of the kitchen chairs and sank down into it. She had been talking a lot, more than Phyllis had heard her say in a long time, and it had to be taking a toll on her, emotionally as well as physically.

But it wasn't over yet. No matter how badly Phyllis wanted it to be, it wasn't over.

Mattie looked up and said, "I thought we were going to wash dishes."

"In a minute," Phyllis said. "Do you really think Billy could have gotten over a broken heart?"

"Of course he could. Everybody's heart gets broken sometimes. Folks get over it."

"Even when someone they trust hurts them really badly? Like Donnie Boatwright hurt you?"

Mattie gazed off into the years rolling back through her memory. "Donnie was so handsome and such a good dancer," she said in a husky half whisper. "We went to Casino Beach one time, you know, that place over on Lake Worth where you could dance right out over the water. Fred Waring was there that night. Fred Waring and His Pennsylvanians. Lord, I never saw anybody so famous. I'd heard them on the radio, and there they were, in person, and I was dancing to their music. Oh, I know Baptists aren't supposed to dance, but Donnie said it would be all right that one time, because it was *Fred Waring,* and we just couldn't pass up the opportunity.

"My, Donnie could dance! He was so light on his feet for a big man. You'd never know he had a bad knee that kept him out of the service. We danced until my heart was poundin' and I couldn't get my breath, and we laughed and walked out on the boardwalk over the water and drank punch and it was just the best night . . . until finally we had to come back to Weatherford . . . until . . . Donnie stopped the car, somewhere out there in the middle of nowhere on the old Weatherford road. . . . He had . . . he had a '36 Ford, and it was just as shiny as could be and ran like a top—nothing but the best for Donnie Boatwright, that was what he always said, nothing but the best for him. . . . And then he went to smoochin' on me and tellin' me how pretty I was, and I tell you, I didn't really mind all that much because he was such a handsome fella and he'd shown me such a good time, and I figured that since I'd already sinned a little by dancin' to Fred Waring and His Pennsylvanians I might as well sin a little more by kissing Donnie Boatwright.

"But he didn't want to stop with smoochin', and I didn't want to do any more than that, because dancin' or no dancin', I was a good girl. You know I was a good girl."

Phyllis nodded, hot tears in her eyes, and whispered, "I know you were, Mattie."

"Donnie said I was so sweet and pretty that he just couldn't stand it, and he claimed he had something comin' because he'd taken me out and shown me such a good time, and there weren't all that many young men around at the time, you know, because of the war and all. He said I needed to stick with him because he'd take me places and show me things. He was going to be a big man in Parker County, he said, and I could go right along with him . . . if I went along with him that night. I told him I didn't want to go anywhere with him if he was going to act like that and for him to take me home. But he wouldn't do it. He just kept on and kept on. . . . He made me do what he wanted. . . . He forced me to . . . to . . ."

She twisted the dish towel in her hands until it was as tight as it would go.

"And then after that . . . after he *did* that . . . he had the gall to call me a week later and ask me out on a date again, as if nothing had ever happened. I told him I'd never go out with him again, and do you know? *He* got mad at *me*, like I was the one who'd done something wrong! Can you beat that? He sure had his nerve, Donnie Boatwright did, and from what I saw of him after that, he never changed. He fooled a lot of folks, but not me. He never fooled me again."

Mattie sighed, long and deep, as if all the memories were running out of her. Phyllis moved over to the table and sat down in the chair beside her. She reached over and took one of Mattie's hands in both of hers.

"It sounds to me like the world is better off without people like Newt and Donnie and Jani," Phyllis said quietly. "Like getting rid of them is almost . . . a public service. Something that a volunteer would do."

Mattie looked up, and her eyes were clear as they met Phyllis's gaze. "You know, don't you?"

"Yes," Phyllis said. She wished she didn't, but she knew.

And like history, that knowledge could never be changed.

Chapter 32

Phyllis called Mike, and it seemed like he was there immediately. Eve and Sam wondered why he was in such a hurry when he came in, but when Phyllis asked them for some privacy, Sam seemed to understand that something had happened. Eve was more curious and wasn't quite as cooperative, but when Sam mentioned that they could watch the rest of the baseball game on the TV in his room, Eve went with him. "I want to see all those bookshelves you've been building, dear," she said as the two of them started up the stairs. "I don't believe I've ever been in your room."

Fleetingly, Phyllis hoped that Sam had the sense to leave his door open.

Mattie was still sitting at the kitchen table. Phyllis and Mike joined her, and Mike said, "Evening, Miz Harris. How are you?"

"Feeling better now," Mattie said. "Feeling a mite better."

Mike looked curiously at his mother. "All right, Mom, you said this was important. What's it all about?"

Murder, Phyllis thought, or perhaps, in a way, justice.

But she said, "Mattie has some things she wants to tell you, Mike."

"All right," he said with a nod. He smiled at Mattie. "Go ahead, Miz Harris."

"It's about what happened that day, out at Newt Bishop's farm," Mattie began.

That caught Mike's interest. He leaned forward slightly and asked, "You've remembered something?"

"You could say that. I remembered something that day, all right. I remembered how badly Newt treated his little boy and how miserable poor Darryl was because of it. I saw Justin, Darryl's boy and Newt's grandson, out there at the orchard, and it took me back. Lord, it took me back. I thought Justin *was* Darryl at first. When it got through to me that he wasn't, I knew I'd been given another chance. I had to make sure Newt never mistreated Justin like he did Darryl. So when I came out of the house after usin' the facilities, I stopped in at the barn to give Newt Bishop a piece o' my mind, like I should've done years ago."

"And you saw what happened to him?"

Mike had jumped to that conclusion, and Phyllis didn't blame him. She said quietly, "Let her tell it her own way, Mike."

"Sure. Sorry, Miz Harris. You go right ahead and tell me what you saw."

"You don't understand, Mike," Mattie said. "I didn't *see* what happened to Newt. I *did* it."

Mike could only sit there and stare, obviously unable to fully comprehend what he was hearing. Phyllis knew just how he felt. She had been so stunned that afternoon when she realized the truth that she had almost passed out.

"Newt was under that old car of his, workin' on it, and I saw that old bumper jack was all that was holdin' it up. He didn't have it blocked up or anything. So I said to him that he never should've mistreated Darryl and I'd see to it he never hurt Justin, and while he was askin' me what I was talkin' about, I grabbed that tire iron and hauled off and gave the lever on that jack a good wallop, and it came right down, right on top of Newt. Then I wiped off the tire iron—I've seen enough mystery shows on TV to know to do that—and tossed it down and went back to the orchard. I could hear Newt gruntin' a little, but I didn't pay it no mind."

Mike stared at her, wide-eyed with disbelief. His mouth opened and closed, but no words came out. Phyllis wondered if this was the first murder confession he had ever heard.

Mattie fell silent, and Phyllis had to say, "That's not all. Tell him about Donnie."

Mike's gaze switched to Phyllis for a second, growing even more astounded. He looked back at Mattie as she began to talk again.

"Well, Donnie was different, you see. With Newt, I didn't really think all that much about what I was doing. I just made sure he wouldn't ever beat on Justin. But once I'd taken care of Newt, I figured that Donnie had it comin' to him, too. What happened with him was because of what he did all those years ago, and I had to think about it for a while before I decided what to do."

Mike couldn't contain himself. He said, "You killed Donnie Boatwright?"

"He had it comin'," Mattie repeated snappishly. "He raped me. Date rape, they call it now, but that doesn't make it any better. He hurt me . . . inside, you know . . . so I couldn't have any kids of my own. Not ever."

"Oh, Mattie," Phyllis said softly. The older woman hadn't told her about that part of it earlier.

Mattie's spine stiffened and her chin lifted. "I know he did a lot of good for Weatherford and for Parker County. I'm not disputin' that. But it didn't change what he did to me. Nothing could ever change that. So I got to thinkin' about what Dr. Lee told me a while back, when we were talking about cancer treatments. He told me all about that laetrile stuff and how they made it from apricot pits, but peach pits had the same chemical, and if you were taking the stuff you shouldn't eat peaches because it might kill you. He said it wouldn't do any good for cancer anyway and that I didn't need to take it."

Mike glanced at Phyllis. "Cancer?"

"I'll explain later. Go on, Mattie."

"Well, like I said, I got to thinkin'. I took a bunch of peach pits out of the trash after Phyllis was through with 'em, and I got me a hammer and mashed 'em up and put them in water and boiled 'em, and then I took the water and saved it and later got some more peach pits and did the whole thing again, oh, two or three times I guess, until I figured that water was just full of that chemical that turned into poison. Then, come the day of the peach festival, I had it in my purse and when I got my chance I poured it into Donnie's water bottle. Wasn't too hard, because Donnie was always talkin' to people and he'd put that bottle down and not pay any attention to it while he was carryin' on and makin' jokes and such."

"So you admit that you killed him?" Mike asked.

"Just did, didn't I?"

"I don't understand," Mike said, and the strain in his voice made it clear he was telling the truth. "You knew that the police suspected your friend Miz Wilbarger of murdering him, but you didn't speak up?"

Mattie grimaced. "And I feel mighty bad about that. I never would've let Carolyn go to jail. I figured she wouldn't, though, because I knew she didn't do it. Half the time, too, I didn't really know what was goin' on. I'd forget that Donnie was even dead, let alone that I had anything to do with it. Seemed to me like he ought to still be alive."

"This is . . . incredible," Mike muttered.

"Oh, you haven't even heard all of it," Mattie told him. "I haven't said anything yet about how I tried to kill that young teacher out at the high school."

Mike looked like it was all he could do to stay in his chair and not bounce up in amazement. "You're talking about Jani Garrett?" he asked, after a moment of struggle to control himself.

Mattie nodded solemnly. "Now that was like it was with Newt Bishop again. I didn't plan it out or anything. I was

mad as a hornet at her because of what she'd done to poor
Billy Moser—"

"Who's Billy Moser?" Mike interrupted.

Phyllis said, "He was a student at the high school who
committed suicide because he was having an affair with Jani
Garrett and she broke it off."

"Good Lord," Mike murmured. He let out a long sigh.
"Well, go on, Miz Harris, if you want to."

"Oh, I want to. It feels mighty good to be telling you
about all this, Mike. I never was good at keepin' secrets. . . .
Anyway, I got done with tutoring a little early and walked
outside to wait for your mama to pick me up. I was out in
the parking lot with nobody else around, and I saw that
woman come out of the building and start toward me, and
there was a car right there with the keys in it. . . . I could see
'em in the ignition . . . so I tried the door and it was unlocked. I got in and started it up and pulled out. It'd been a
while since I drove a car . . . I don't see too good anymore,
you know, and I guess my reflexes are slower'n they used to
be . . . but they were fast enough to aim that car at her while
I tromped on the footfeed. She tried to get out of the way,
but I was able to hit her. Then I just turned the car off and
got out and went back up to the sidewalk in front of the
school, and it wasn't long before some other folks came
along and found her lyin' out there where she fell." Mattie
shook her head. "I remembered later that I didn't think to
wipe off the steerin' wheel. I've been expecting you to get
my fingerprints off it and come to arrest me."

"The police got some unidentified fingerprints off the
wheel, all right, but all anybody knew was that they didn't
match the girl who owned the car or anybody in her family.
Miz Harris, your fingerprints must not be on file anywhere.
We didn't get any matches from the unidentified ones found
on Mr. Boatwright's water bottle, either."

Mattie frowned in thought for a moment and then said,

"You know, I suppose you're right. I've never been arrested before, or anything like that."

Phyllis patted her hand. "You're not under arrest now." She glanced at her son. "Is she, Mike?"

"No, not yet," he said with a shake of his head. "This is all unofficial. I didn't advise Miz Harris of her rights or anything like that. But I'll have to tell Sheriff Haney and Chief Whitmire what happened, and I'm sure they'll want to come talk to you, Miz Harris."

"Let 'em come," Mattie said calmly. "I'll tell them the same thing. No good can come of keepin' secrets. I can see that now."

The three of them sat there quietly for a moment, and then Mike asked, "Is there anything else?" He sounded like he was a little afraid of what the answer might be.

"No," Mattie said. "No, that's all of it."

"Why don't you sit right there for a few minutes while I talk to my mother?"

"All right."

Phyllis and Mike got up and went into the living room. Mike glanced toward the kitchen and said quietly, "I don't suppose there's any chance she'll try to get away."

"She's not going anywhere, Mike," Phyllis said. "In fact, there's a chance that in another five or ten minutes, she won't even remember the conversation she just had with you."

"Wait a minute." He looked alarmed. "You mean you think she'll recant her confession?"

"I mean she won't remember it. She has Alzheimer's. Really, she held it together in there a lot better than I've seen her do in a long time."

"But . . . but if her mental state is that bad, how are we going to arrest her and put her on trial and . . ." He trailed off helplessly.

"You may have to arrest her," Phyllis said, "but there shouldn't be any need for a trial. I talked to Walt Lee this afternoon. Mattie has a tumor in her brain, and there's nothing that can be done about it. She has two or three weeks to live, maybe a month. A trial would just be a waste of time."

"Oh, Lord. I'm sorry, Mom. I know how close the two of you have always been."

Phyllis smiled sadly. "I think that's why I never saw until today what had happened. My instincts told me there was *something* linking all three incidents, but I never saw what it was, other than the fact that I was close by every time. But so was Mattie. It just never occurred to me to think that she might've had anything to do with them."

"What made you realize that she might be involved?"

"Walt Lee told me he let it slip to Mattie that she might not have very long left. I think that's what set her off. You know how she's always been, always putting other people first and doing everything she could for the community. That's what she was doing here, ridding it of people it would be better off without. She had seen with her own eyes the harm that Newt Bishop and Donnie Boatwright and Jani Garrett had done. It was more personal vengeance with Donnie, of course, but I suppose she figured that if he would do such a thing to her, he must have hurt other people, too. And sure enough, it turned out that he had."

Wearily, Mike rubbed his hands over his face. "Nobody's ever going to believe this," he said. "Just the fact that all three crimes turned out to be connected is incredible enough, but to think that they were carried out by somebody like Miz Harris . . ."

"You'll keep it as quiet as you can, won't you? There won't have to be a spectacle, will there, at least not until after she's gone? She has so little time left."

"I can't promise anything," he said, "but Sheriff Haney and Chief Whitmire are both good men. I'm sure they'll do what they can to make it easier for her."

"I hope so," Phyllis said.

A footstep at the bottom of the stairs made her turn. Sam

stood there, a frown on his face. "What's going on?" he asked. "You two look like you just lost a good friend."

"I think that's exactly what happened," Phyllis said. She moved over to Sam and clutched his arm. "Can you get Eve and Carolyn and come back down here in a few minutes? I need to talk to all of you."

Sam nodded. "Sure." He started up the stairs but paused to look back at her. "Are you all right, Phyllis?"

"I will be," she told him. "After a while, I will be."

Then she went back into the kitchen. Mattie still sat at the table, with her eyes closed now, moving her head a little as if in time to a tune only she heard. When Phyllis touched her arm, Mattie opened her eyes and looked up and said, "That's Fred Waring, you know. Fred Waring and His Pennsylvanians. The music's so pretty, and it's just a beautiful night. . . ."

Chapter 33

The six of them walked away from the gravesite. It was September now, but still warm. Fall wouldn't even begin to arrive for another few weeks. Despite that, there was a sense of finality in the air, a feeling of something coming to an end. How could it be otherwise in a cemetery, Phyllis thought, where a dear old friend had just been laid to rest?

Sam, Mike, and Sarah were slightly in front, with Phyllis, Eve, and Carolyn behind them. The service had been very well attended. Over half the current teachers in the district and many former teachers had been there. A crying Dolly Williamson had hugged all of them. Most of the mourners were aware, at least to a certain extent, of what had happened, but of course nothing was said about that. They were there to honor a woman who had done good all her life.

"I hope this is the last funeral I have to go to for a long time," Carolyn said fervently.

"I couldn't agree more, dear," Eve put in. "I'd much rather attend a wedding than a funeral. Not that I intend to ever get married again." She looked pointedly at Sam. "Although plans can always change, of course."

Skillfully, Sam pretended not to have heard that comment, even though Phyllis could tell that he was well aware of what Eve had said. He sort of confirmed that by changing the subject.

"You know, I was readin' in the paper the other day that there's a fair or a festival or an expo or something like that somewhere in Texas nearly every week out of the year. And most of them have cooking contests that go along with 'em."

Carolyn perked up at that. "Really? I've heard of such things, but I didn't know there were so many of them."

"It's the gospel truth," Sam said. "I'll show you the article in the paper. It even had a list of some of the contests."

"You know, I've always said that a good cook ought to be able to come up with a recipe for any situation. I'll bet I could enter almost any of those contests and stand a good chance of winning."

"You think so, do you?" Phyllis said.

"I don't see why not. Of course, with some cooks, it's better if they stick to the one thing they do well . . . or even not so well, as the case may be."

Phyllis looked over at her with narrowed eyes. "Is that a challenge?"

"Certainly not. I just understand why you wouldn't be interested in anything like that, Phyllis."

Sam said, "What's that line from that old Dirty Harry movie? 'A man's got to know his limitations.' I guess a cook does, too."

Phyllis stopped short, forcing the others to come to a halt, as well. "I know what you're trying to do," she said. It was little short of amazing that Sam and Carolyn would cooperate on anything, even something like snapping her out of the funk that had gripped her these past few weeks. But it was obvious to her that was what was going on. . . .

And she loved them all for it.

Carolyn sniffed. "I'm sure I don't know what you're talking about."

"Uh-huh," Phyllis said. "What kind of cooking contests are we talking about?"

"Oh, all kinds," Sam said blithely. "Chili cook-offs and pie contests and the best recipe for goat stew and barbecue and strawberries and, oh, yeah, the peanut festival, can't forget the goobers. . . ."

They walked on toward the cars, through the late summer sunshine and the dappled patches of shade from the post oaks, past flower beds and granite markers, out of death into life, and by the time they left the cemetery the challenge had indeed been laid down. As Sam had said, there were contests and cook-offs and bake-offs all over Texas. A person could stay busy entering just half of them, and could see a lot of interesting sights at the same time.

Too busy, Phyllis hoped, to ever run across another murder.

Phyllis's Spicy Peach Cobbler

1 Tbsp. cornstarch	⅓ cup water
1½ Tbsp. minced candied ginger	4 cups sliced peaches
⅓ cup brown sugar	

Preheat oven to 375 degrees. Combine cornstarch, minced candied ginger, brown sugar, and water in saucepan. Cook until thickened and then add peaches. Cook until peaches are hot, about 5 minutes. Pour into buttered 9-inch pan, making sure the ginger is evenly distributed.

Basic Pie Crust
for 1 (9-inch) pie crust.

1⅓ cup all-purpose flour	3 Tbsp. ice water
½ cup shortening	1 tsp. granulated or
½ teaspoon salt	turbinado (raw) sugar

Mix flour and salt in chilled bowl, then cut shortening into the flour with a pastry cutter, until mixture resembles the texture of tiny split peas. When the mixture is the right texture, add the ice water and combine with a fork. Quickly gather the dough into a ball and flatten into a 4-inch-wide disk. Wrap in plastic, and refrigerate at least 30 minutes.

Remove dough disk from refrigerator. If stiff and very cold, let stand until dough is cool but malleable. Using a floured rolling pin, roll dough disk on a lightly floured surface until it's bigger than the pan. Transfer dough by carefully rolling it around the rolling pin, then lift and unroll dough, centering it over the fruit. Vent crust, and sprinkle granulated or turbinado (raw) sugar on top to give a delightful sparkling appearance.

Bake cobbler for 50 minutes or until golden brown.

The candied ginger gives this dessert a warm, zesty taste.

Carolyn's Peaches-and-
Cream Cheesecake

8 oz. cream cheese
    softened
½ cup sugar
2 eggs
1½ tsp. vanilla

2 cups fresh sliced peaches
1 cup sour cream
3 Tbsp. sugar
½ tsp. vanilla

Mix cream cheese and ½ cup sugar together. Beat in eggs and add 1½ tsp. vanilla. After well blended pour cream cheese mixture into a deep-dish, baked nutty graham cracker crust. Bake in 350 degree oven for 20 minutes. Cool for 5 minutes. Arrange a layer of sliced peaches on top of the baked cheesecake. Mix sour cream, 3 Tbsp. sugar and ½ tsp. vanilla until blended. Spread on top of peaches and bake 5 minutes. Cool. Refrigerate.

Nutty Graham Cracker Crust

1 cup finely ground graham
    cracker crumbs
2 Tbsp. white sugar

3 Tbsp. butter, melted
2 Tbsp. finely chopped pecans

Mix graham cracker crumbs, sugar, melted butter or margarine, and pecans until well blended. Press mixture into a deep-dish 9-inch pie plate. Bake at 375 degrees for 5 minutes. Cool.

Mama's Roast Beef Supreme (Coke Roast)

5–6 lb. beef roast   8 oz. cola
flour   salt
oil   pepper

Season meat to taste with salt and pepper. Dredge roast in flour. Brown roast on all sides in a small amount of oil. Place roast in a baking dish and cover. Bake at 375 degrees for about 3 hours. Uncover during the last 30 minutes and pour the cola over the roast. Baste often. When done, drain off the liquid to use in the gravy.

Supreme Roast Gravy

3 Tbsp. butter or margarine   1 Tbsp. vinegar
½ tsp. powdered mustard   3 cups broth

Melt butter in pan, add flour and lightly brown. Add powdered mustard, vinegar, and broth from roast. (Can use bouillon cubes and water with liquid from roast to make 3 cups.) Cook until thickened.

Author's Note

Parker County peaches are known for being some of the best in Texas, and each summer the Parker County Peach Festival is held in Weatherford, Texas. For dramatic purposes, I've taken a few liberties with the facts of the peach festival, such as adding a cooking contest.

Most of the settings in this novel are real and are described as accurately as possible. However, the characters and their actions are completely fictitious products of the author's imagination, and are not based on any real persons, living or dead.

Read on for an excerpt from the next
Fresh-Baked Mystery

MURDER BY THE SLICE

Coming from Signet in October 2007

The sun blazed down on the sidewalk in front of the Wal-Mart located in Weatherford, Texas. Phyllis Newsom was glad she had worn a hat to shade her head. That didn't help the part of her that was sitting on the uncomfortable metal folding chair, though.

According to the calendar, autumn had started, but that didn't mean the weather had begun to cool off. That was still a month off, maybe even longer. For now, it was still hot—Texas hot.

On the chair beside Phyllis's, Eve Turner waved at someone she knew and called, "Hello there, dear. Would you like to buy a cake or some cookies and help out the Retired Teachers' Association Scholarship Fund?"

The man she had spoken to looked a little uncomfortable, as well he might since his wife was with him. Eve had probably had one or more of their children in her English class when she was still teaching, and knowing Eve, she had flirted shamelessly with the man at every school function the parents attended. As she smiled brightly at the man, he said, "Ah, maybe when we come out."

His wife just tightened her grip on his arm and kept walking.

Phyllis wasn't surprised by Eve's failure to sell anything. She had been out here for nearly an hour with Eve, Carolyn Wilbarger, and Sam Fletcher, the four of them sitting behind a folding table filled with cakes and plates of cookies, and they'd sold very little. The cookies were holding up just fine, but the icing on the cakes was starting to melt against the clear plastic wrap that covered each of them.

Phyllis glanced up at the sun. It would move on around the building so that they would be in the shade in another hour or so, but it was going to be a long hour until then.

She was as enthusiastic a member of the Retired Teachers' Association as anyone—she had spent almost her entire adult life teaching, after all—but she wished she hadn't let herself be talked into helping man this bake sale table.

But it was awfully difficult to say no to Dolly Williamson, the retired superintendent of the school district and the head of the RTA. Besides, the scholarship fund needed to be built up again. Each year the association awarded college scholarships to two deserving students. The amount of those scholarships depended entirely on how much money the association could raise during the year.

The fall bake sale was the first major fund-raiser each year. Dolly had persuaded Carolyn to help with it, and from there it was inevitable that Phyllis, Eve, and Sam would be drawn in, as well. The four of them shared the big house that Phyllis and her late husband, Kenny, had lived in for years, and they were good friends.

One thing you could say about Wal-Mart: The place didn't lack for customers, especially on a sunny Saturday afternoon. A steady stream of people had gone in and out of the store ever since Phyllis and the others had set up their table, chairs, and the signs Phyllis had printed on the computer announcing the bake sale. A few people stopped and bought cookies on their way back to their cars. Phyllis didn't think they had sold a single cake.

In a way, she could understand why. It cost so much to live these days that most folks had to watch what they spent. But it was for a good cause, and the price wasn't really that bad.

A pickup drove by with country music blasting through

its open windows. It was followed a few minutes later by another pickup with loud rap music coming from it. Phyllis was always a little amused by the sight of young white men in snap-button shirts and cowboy hats listening to rap, but it was becoming more common.

She saw an attractive woman in her thirties emerge from the store and start toward the bake sale table with a couple of elementary-age children in tow, a boy and a girl. She had shoulder-length light brown hair and wore blue jeans and a T-shirt with LOVING ELEMENTARY printed on it. Phyllis knew that wasn't a declaration of affection but rather a reference to Oliver Loving Elementary School, one of several elementary schools in the Weatherford School District. It was named for the famous rancher and cattleman who had been the inspiration for one of the characters in *Lonesome Dove,* either Gus or Call; Phyllis never could remember which. Loving was buried here in Weatherford.

The woman had a somewhat harried look about her—going to Wal-Mart with a couple of kids would do that—but she smiled pleasantly as she came up to the table and said, "Hello, Carolyn."

"Marie, it's good to see you," Carolyn said. "How's Russ?"

"Oh, all right, I guess."

Carolyn turned to Phyllis and asked, "Do you know Marie Tyler?"

"I don't believe so," Phyllis said.

Carolyn performed the introductions quickly, adding, "And that's Amber and Aaron. Marie and her husband, Russ, go to the same church I do."

"It's nice to meet you, Marie," Phyllis said.

"You, too." Marie turned back to Carolyn and went on, "You know I'm on the PTO board at the school."

"No, I didn't know that, but I'm not surprised."

"Yeah, I'm the fund-raising chairman. You know what that means at this time of year."

"The carnival," Phyllis, Caroyln, and Eve all said at the same time.

Marie nodded. "That's right."

Sam leaned back in his chair, propped a foot on the other leg's somewhat knobby knee, and said with a smile, "Coachin' at the high school, I never had much to do with the elementary carnivals, except one year when they decided to put on a donkey basketball game in conjunction with it." He shook his head. "Before that was over, I sure wished I'd never agreed to let those donkeys in my gym."

"Well, we're not going to have any donkey basketball games," Marie said, "although we may have a pony ride. But it'll be outside on the playground."

Phyllis had taught junior high history, but she had been involved in several elementary school carnivals when her son, Mike, was that age. She had been a member of what was then called the PTA—the Parent-Teacher Association— at the scool he'd attended. These days it was called the Parent-Teacher Organization, but pretty much only the name had changed. The group was still composed mostly of parents and run by a board of a dozen or so volunteers, almost all women. It was very rare to find a man willing to be on a PTO board. Finding enough volunteer moms to take care of everything was a big enough chore.

The PTO spent most of the year raising funds. The money was spent on things the school needed that weren't included in the budget, such as copy machines, extra books for the library, and playground equipment. One of the major fund-raisers was the school carnival, usually held sometime during October. In the old days, they had often been tied in with Halloween, but of course such things were forbidden now. They had to be called fall carnivals or harvest festivals or something noncontroversial like that.

The classic school carnival was set up on the playground, with open booths around the edges formed by bales of hay or sketchy wooden frameworks. Each homeroom in the school was responsible for one of the booths, where games designed to appeal to young children were played, such as ring toss, throwing a baseball at stacks of milk bottles, and "fishing" in wading pools filled with sand and little prizes. Other games that required more room were conducted out in the middle of the playground. There were also face painting and temporary tattoo booths and sometimes dunking booths, pony rides, miniature trains, "bounce houses," and anything else the PTO board could scrounge up to make a little money. There was no charge to attend the carnival, but to take part in any of the games required a ticket at each booth, and the tickets cost fifty cents each. Kids raced from booth to booth, clutching strings of tickets and the prizes they had won. Inside the school, in the gymnasium and the cafeteria, other activities would take place, such as entertainment by local musicians and dancers, and there was a snack bar selling cold drinks, hot dogs, nachos, and candy.

And there was usually a bake sale, too, Phyllis suddenly remembered, which was why it came as no surprise to her when Marie Tyler said, "I could really use some help, Carolyn, and from the looks of this, you and your friends have a lot of experience with bake sales."

"Oh, I don't know . . ." Carolyn said, as Phyllis was silently pleading, *Don't get us involved in this. Please, Carolyn.*

Marie leaned closer to the table and lowered her voice to a conspiratorial tone. "It would mean a lot to me if I could find somebody willing to take over the bake sale. There's just so much involved in putting on one of these carnivals, and to tell you the truth, Shannon's really been on my ass lately about getting it all done."

Phyllis tried not to let her lips tighten in disapproval at Marie's crude language. She didn't like to be judgmental, and she knew perfectly well that this was a different day and age from the one in which she had grown up. But it still bothered her to hear a lady talk like that, especially in front of little ones.

Carolyn looked over at her and asked, "What do you think, Phyllis?"

I think you're trying to pass the buck and make me be the bad guy, Phyllis thought. But she said, "We pretty much have our plates full with the Retired Teachers' Association—"

Before she could actually say no, another woman walked up to the table. She was older and heavyset, and the brightly colored dress she wore made her look even bigger. Her hair was dyed a startling shade of black. She said in a booming voice, "Hello, ladies. And you, too, of course, Sam."

"Howdy, Dolly," he said with a nod. "Good to see you again."

"Marie, how are you?" Dolly Williamson said as she put her arms around Marie and gave her a hug. Phyllis wasn't surprised that Dolly knew who Marie was. The former superintendent was still so plugged in to the school district that she probably knew all the PTO board members from every campus.

"I'm fine, Mrs. Williamson," Marie said. "I was just trying to recruit Carolyn and her friends to run the bake sale for the carnival at Loving."

"Why, I think that's a wonderful idea!" Dolly beamed at the four people behind the table. "I know you'll all do a fine job."

"Wait a minute," Phyllis began, but she had a sinking feeling that it was already too late. Once Dolly got an idea in her head, she was the original unstoppable force.

"After all," Dolly went on as if she hadn't heard Phyllis, "you're doing so well here."

"Haven't sold much," Sam said.

"You will, you will. Everything looks so good." Dolly turned back to Marie. "This was lucky for you, my dear. Now you can concentrate on the rest of your job."

"I know," Marie said. She gave Phyllis and the others a smile and added, "Thank you guys so much."

Phyllis felt like pointing out that she wasn't a "guy," and neither were Carolyn and Eve. But there was no point in worrying about such things now, she told herself. What mattered was that she, along with her friends, had been roped into helping with the carnival bake sale. They might have been able to withstand the pressure from Marie, but once Dolly had walked up and found out what was going on, they were lost.

Dolly gave Marie another hug and waved a pudgy hand at the others, then went on into the store. Marie said, "I'll give you a call, Carolyn, and let you know all the details you'll need to know. Thanks again."

Carolyn nodded and smiled weakly. "You're welcome."

"This'll help keep Shannon from giving me so much shi—I mean, trouble." Marie waved and added, "Bye, guys," as she led her kids into the parking lot and headed for the family SUV.

Carolyn turned to the others and said, "I'm sorry. I don't know what happened."

"Dolly happened," Sam said. He chuckled. "Sort of like a force of nature, isn't she? Doesn't have to stay around very long, but when she rolls through, she brings changes."

"Well, maybe it'll be fun," Carolyn said. "It might be, you never know. And we *do* have experience at putting on a bake sale."

Eve said, "Perhaps you do, dear. I was never really the domestic type." She smiled at Sam, with whom she had been flirting ever since he had rented a room from Phyllis and moved into the big old house on the tree-shaded street. "Which isn't to say that I couldn't still learn if I needed to. If the right man came along and asked the right question . . ."

Sam called to a family going into the store, "You folks want to buy some cookies?"

Phyllis leaned over to Carolyn and asked, "Who's this Shannon that Marie was talking about?"

"Shannon Dunston," Carolyn replied. "She's the president of the PTO board at Loving. And from what I hear, she runs things with an iron first, as the old saying goes."

"That's odd. Usually you try to get people to do things by being nice to them, especially when you're relying on volunteers."

"That's not the way Shannon looks at it. Although I shouldn't say that, since I don't really know her. I'm just going by what I've heard."

"Well, maybe with our help, she'll get off Marie's, uh, posterior." Phyllis looked at the other three. "Right . . . guys?"

Now Available in Paperback
from New American Library

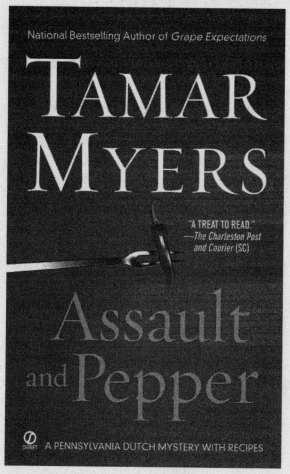

National Bestselling Author of *Grape Expectations*

TAMAR MYERS

"A TREAT TO READ."
—*The Charleston Post
and Courier* (SC)

Assault
and Pepper

SIGNET · A PENNSYLVANIA DUTCH MYSTERY WITH RECIPES

Available wherever books are sold or
at penguin.com
0-451-21567-2